SHADOWS

S. Edward Aanes

Order this book online at www.trafford.com
or email orders@trafford.com

Most Trafford titles are also available at major online book retailers.

Printed in the United States of America.

ISBN: 978-1-4251-8258-8 (sc)
ISBN: 978-1-4251-8259-5 (e)

Trafford rev. 10/31/2013

 www.trafford.com

North America & international
toll-free: 1 888 232 4444 (USA & Canada)
fax: 812 355 4082

for Rebecca Lee

1

APRIL 1663

Colonial Virginia

THE BEING GLANCED about in panic, seized by an apprehension he had only been told of by a select few others of The Kind. They had warned him it could happen, and now it was his turn to experience it. Alone and descending to the surface of an uncharted world, his discoidal ship was spinning out of control, its exterior glowing with a bright crimson in response to the progressively thickening atmosphere of oxygen and nitrogen. The Being knew he had to act fast and unerringly if he was to continue his mission... and for The Kind, mission success was the prime reason for existing.

His strong, slender arms glistened with oil-based synthetic speed additives as his triple-digited hands tightly gripped the craft's twin stabilizer sticks. From under each wiry limb, a pair of cybernetic tentacles busily snaked about a plethora of knobs, buttons, and levers at a dizzying pace. The pilot's single luminous oblong green eye flashed from side to side. Should he abandon ship?

In that microsecond of doubt, the smoldering ship lurched wildly, then suddenly straightened, losing its spin. The Being had succeeded in reestablishing orientation but the craft was still losing altitude and was now less than two miles above a vast, thickly forested, and menacingly unknown landscape.

He activated a front display screen and hurriedly scanned the rugged terrain. The badly overheated exterior-based sensors could not give him any vital data such as wind speed, temperature, or elevation. In the distance, under a dark cloud mass, the Being spied the telltale parallelogram of a spring thunderstorm in progress. He knew that if he could cool the ship, he might be able to climb and later put down when and where he chose.

The streaking ship punched headlong into the torrent, leaving a rapidly dissipating steam trail in its wake. It continued its descent at a lesser angle and slower rate. Vainly, the Being struggled to turn the saucer's nose up in a desperate bid to increase wind resistance.

Light in the ultraviolet range flashed dire warning of an imminent crash. A tentacle whipped backwards and snapped a switch rearward. Immediately, a hatch door over the Being's head exploded away.

The Being felt the pelting raindrops and heard the rushing wind and hissing steam for less than a minute when the initial impact nearly bounced him out of the craft. A second, third, then a fourth crippling jolt stunned his artificial body. Musty earth clods and leaf shards flew into the cockpit and there was a constant crunch of metal on ground.

Gathering his wits as much as he could, the pilot raised his head out into the storm. The ship was sliding sideways, cutting a swath through a dense carpet of soggy, composted leaves and rotting pine needles. Ahead was a bend in the trail and a massive earth bank atop which stood a towering and unavoidable oak tree.

The smashing stop was merciless, the terror of it accentuated by a blinding lightning flash and a deafening thunderclap. The saucer was hopelessly jammed between oak roots. The Being carefully lifted himself and sat on the hull, his backside protected by his seat pad.

Unexpectedly, his head slammed into the hatchway rim. A heavy mass of dark brown mud had collapsed from above and pushed him suddenly and rudely back into his ship. He fought to get back out of the craft, but the surprise avalanche of saturated dirt was too much. The oppressive weight of it pinned him fast.

Over the topmost oak root a larger and mountainous heap of rain-weakened earth wavered, threatening to permanently imprison the Being and engulf the crippled saucer.

From the Being's eye streamed a fluorescent green gas that jetted into the outside environment beyond the mud's grip. Raindrops brutally punctured the escaping verdant aurora again and again, but it continually reformed like melting Swiss cheese in defiance of the watery barrage.

The dirt mound collapsed in an unspoken groan, leaving no clue as to what lay beneath it. The storm quickly slackened and the clouds moved aside to let the sun shine through.

A small viscous mist lazily wafted around an oak limb, frightening an emerging blue jay into flight. For a few seconds the apparition formed a shiny green ring around the limb, only to instantly dissolve into the outer layer of bark.

Late September 1785

HOW THICK THE sweetness in the air! Quanah thought, smiling broadly. A luxuriant growth of Queen Anne's lace lined both sides of the well-traveled path and the great oak's shade cooled the sitting Cherokee. It was so good to rest after running all day! From his aquiline nose fell a bead of sweat as he proceeded to unroll his woven grass sleeping mat.

Almost dark, he mused, glancing at his leather bag. He ran his fingers through his long black hair and thought of the adventurous past week and of what he had bought with his beaver pelts. He ate an apple for supper, afterwards taking a strange blonde porcelain doll from the leather bag in which it had traveled the past ten miles. He smiled again, wondering how his daughter would react to it. He knew she would never believe him. *She would have to see for herself these yellow-haired people, some of whom have eyes the color of grass, others that of the sky. Maybe one day, one or two of them might visit the village. She will see for herself. No*, he decided. *They will never come this far west.*

Quanah broke his train of thought and briefly considered making a campfire. *It might get awfully cool tonight... but no, no, too tired*, he decided, lying back and momentarily eyeing his daughter's present. He shifted his gaze to the stars beginning to glint warmly beyond the darkening boughs. *No rain tonight. Good.* A hovering ribbon of green caught his attention. *What is this? A hummingbird?* he asked himself idly before lapsing into a deep slumber.

Quanah saw daylight washing the night away, but the stars were still there. Moreover, they all shone a bright red. Confused but captivated, Quanah watched them and listened to their mournful whistling. The volume and tempo became a chaotic cacophony as the approaching stars changed into barrel-sized flat discs. They surrounded him, and from the discs' opening underbellies emerged small, stocky, slit-eyed men who floated to the ground. Quanah pressed his hands over his ears, trying to block the mental message he refused to believe.

You... Need you...

Stunned, choking on his own spit, Quanah struggled to his bare feet, hoping the bough shadows were playing tricks on him. The sudden rush of blood out of his head dizzied him. Quanah clapped his hands and jumped up and down, trying to completely wake up. Perhaps he was still dreaming. At least the red stars and tiny men were gone.

Or were they?

You... you...

The doll staggered, haltingly outstretching an arm. It began walking with a tortured, shaking gait toward him, its eyes flashing an unnaturally brilliant green. The silent message came again:

You... why do you not answer?

Screaming, Quanah grasped the figurine, snapped off its arms, and gripping its stubby legs, struck the oak with its body. The head careened into a thick clump of *Smilax*-covered thorn bushes ten yards away. He hurled what was left of the doll with every ounce of strength he had. To Quanah's greater horror, it bounced, minus the legs, off of the oak tree's trunk to fall squarely between his naked feet. The Cherokee wasted no time in spinning about and kicking up a whirlwind of trail dust.

Quanah's hurried footsteps receded into the distance, his pack and mat forgotten. The smashed porcelain torso vibrated for a few seconds and the drama ended, a solitary passing imperial moth, following the track of the moon, its uncaring and only witness.

3

Autumn 1902

"Bobby Lee Jacobs!"

"Yes ma'am?"

"When you and your daddy get back home, I want you to clean up that mess you made. Ain't no excuse now, son, you're old enough to fix up your own messes!"

"Yes ma'am!" the skinny tow-headed boy in overalls responded, pleased with his mother's recognition of his status as a child growing older and more capable of doing things than he had been in younger days.

"Get on up here with me, Bobby Lee!" the eight year old's lean, sun-bronzed and stockily muscled father directed, patting the buckboard seat with a powerful right hand.

"We got important men's work to do in town, woman!" he called to his raven-tressed beauty of a young wife standing on the tiny porch of the modest log cabin. "Don't be aggravating this young fellow! It's time he learned all about selling tobacco!"

The mother rubbed her hands in frustration along the length of her dingy cotton apron and countered,

"That stuff stinks to high heaven, Conner! You two make sure you sell every bit of it and get rid of it all!" She twisted her face in a mock grimace, adding, "And don't you let him smoke any of it, neither! He ain't but a boy still, and you remember that!"

The husband laughed heartily at his wife's admonition while young Bobby Lee clambered over the pleasantly aromatic pile of yellowed tobacco leaves. The boy slid beside his approving and obviously proud father, urging him,

"Let's get, Daddy!"

"Yeah, boy, we'd better and before she thinks of something else to get on to us about!"

Two ebony and dun-blotched mules strained at their sweat-soaked leather collars, pulling the heavily laden buckboard out from under the comforting shade of the ancient oak and onto the hot, dusty road. An old bird dog charged ahead of the wagon.

"See, boy, old Goober head's clearing out our way ahead for us!" Bobby Lee's father said. The young farmers pretended not to hear the lady of the house add, with a considerably raised voice,

"And don't you smoke any of that nasty stuff and then expect to kiss me! And if you have any reeking and stinking smell of beer on your breath when you come in - - "

"'Bye, Linda Mae!"

"'Bye, Mama! See you tonight!"

The frail woman halfway managed a smile while she watched the dust settle in the distance. "Well, I guess you are old enough to go to market with your daddy now. Sure wish I could have another baby. I get so lonesome during the day..."

She turned, sighing at the state of affairs in the cabin. "Durn men," she muttered, eyeing the hunting rifle on the floor and the bottle of cleaning oil beside it. "Well, Conner Jacobs, you can pick that thing up. I'm not touching it.... Goober head! Get your mangy tail on out of here! You know you're not supposed to come in the house."

The chocolate hunting hound spun about in the doorway and without breaking stride cleared the slightly elevated porch with a single leap. He halted in the front yard, perked his floppy ears as much as he could and, whining, glanced about in apparent confusion. Unexpectedly, the big dog darted across the road and vanished with a noisy parting of briars into the brush.

"You crazy dog, what's got into you?" Linda Mae asked aloud before refocusing her attention on the chaos. "Durn lead soldiers! Bobby Lee, what am I going to do with you! How many times have I told you... put your lead soldiers in your box with the other toys!" She gathered several gray figures and corrected herself. "No... Conner bought him expensive pewter soldiers. He likes to play with them as much as Bobby Lee does. Well, Mama told me all men was, was just big boys. The big boys can pick them up, then..."

Linda Mae entered Bobby Lee's tiny, stuffy room and breathed deeply. "It's so hot in here! When is Conner going to get around to cutting out a window? All they do is talk... dadburn men! Well, at least he put a good tight door on Bobby Lee's room." She blushed, recalling her husband's urgent and not totally unselfish reason for placing the door in their son's room's entrance. She giggled and took a phosphorous match from her apron pocket, setting it alight with a fingernail before touching it to the wick of a partially melted white candle set into a cheap copper stand on a tiny end table.

You...

"Who is that? Who's here in my house? You get on out of here and knock on that door like a decent gentleman, whoever - - "

You... Need you...

Linda Mae tensed up suddenly, thinking of the rifle as she shook out and dropped the match, reflexively stepping on it hard with a sandal heel to crush any ember remaining in it. Just what did this unseen intruder mean by "need"? Her calves hidden under her calico pleats tingled and her throat tightened.

"You, ah, you just hang on a minute! Don't you move! I'm coming. You just stay where you're at!" Her throat hurt from the exertion of speaking when abruptly she realized....

Whoa! She hadn't actually heard a voice!

"Am I going crazy like Goober head? Naaaah, it's just too hot in this room. Yeah, that's what it is, it's the heat making me think - - "

Linda Mae screamed shrilly. Two, then three of the pewter soldiers materialized in the doorway.

"What devil stuff is this? This can't be!"

A total of six little soldiers marched single-file into the room. The one in front dropped his tiny metal rifle, his eyes eerily iridescent as he neared Linda Mae. The terrified young mother sat with a vertical fall onto Bobby Lee's hay-stuffed bed, trying to force her back through the solid timber wall.

"No! You can't be real! You're a pack of demons! Get out of my house and get out right now!" Nearly in tears from fright, she jabbed a finger toward the front of the clapboard cabin.

No... Not you... Unfit...

Several figures worked their way up to the stupefied woman's exposed feet. The apparent leader remained still, watching her, his eyes still glowing with an odd and bright shade of green.

Without warning, five tiny bayonets slashed simultaneously into Linda Mae's legs.

"Stop it! Stop it, you little demons, you're killing me! Stop!"

Linda Mae attempted to leap for the doorway, but her bare toes hung on several loose mattress cover thread loops. She fell heavily on her stomach, pinning the leader under her. Her wounded, flailing legs toppled the lit candlestick and her left arm struck the door, unintentionally slamming it hard.

Two metal arms shoved brutally from below into her thoracic cavity. Bobby Lee's dry straw mattress exploded in flames and Linda Mae's lungs were instantly gorged with cruelly superheated black smoke.

"Lord Jesus, please don't let them get...." she choked out weakly, unable to finish her plea as her dress followed the flaming example of the mattress. Less than a minute later, her dying, baking lips parted to allow a curl of green wisp to escape through the gaps between her teeth. The iridescent swirl vertically undulated toward the hairline crack under the door, melding as it moved into the increasingly billowing death cloud to become lost in a shapeless mass of grimly growing dark brown anonymity.

2

OCTOBER 8, 1967

BILLY BEAUDET HESITANTLY extended his shaking right hand and unlocked the bathroom door. What had he done to get his stepfather so mad this time? *Oh well*, Billy reasoned, *what will he do to me on Sunday morning? Anyway, I'm on the commode. He won't pull me off of it to whip me. Besides, I'm almost fifteen - -*

"Boy, when your mommer tells you to do something, you do it! You hear me?" The brutish Jack Capler strapped Billy's pale bared legs twice with the fly swatter before the boy could resume his sitting position.

"Ow! What're you talking about?"

"Don't you try to lay a con job on me, boy!" Capler spat. "Why didn't you clean up your mess in the basement like your mommer told you last night?"

"I - - I was going to do it this - - this - - " Billy stammered, remembering his unsuccessful foray into papier maché sculpting and bracing himself for the inevitable flurry of additional hits.

Capler delivered three and stormed off, running his tough hands through a head full of dark, greasy curls as he vanished into the gloomy hallway's recesses.

For a minute Billy could only stare at his crimsoned, stinging upper legs.

"You could have at least closed the door," he whispered, fearing another attack should Capler hear him. Billy wiped and pulled his pants up, an admixture of conflicting emotions besetting his soul. He looked disapprovingly at his reflection in the mirror. *Why are you such a reject?* he silently asked. *You don't look bad... you're not stupid... what a shitty world.*

Billy broke his reverie and followed his stepfather's path a few feet before entering his own room. *Sunday morning*, he thought again. *Only good thing about it is going to Grammaw's...*

■ ▪ ▪ ▪ ■

"Ah, how about that? A nickel on the floor!"

Despite the flowing traffic, Jack Capler effortlessly swung his long arm backward, striking Billy across the forehead and knocking him against the sedan's rear door handle. The nickel disappeared between Capler's fingers. It happened so quickly that Billy wasn't sure what to think.

The ache on the bridge of his nose from the impact of his horned-rims affirmed that indeed he had been hit, as well as his mother's terse remark to Capler,

"Be careful, Jack, you'll break the child's glasses. They're... expensive."

"You should have picked that nickel up first, boy," Capler advised matter-of-factly. "When you opened your mouth, you set yourself up to get faked out."

"Why'd you hit me?"

"Didn't mean to, but you were in the way."

Billy was always confused about his stepfather's actions. There was neither hostility in his tone, nor the least hint of parental concern. The boy glanced at his mother. She drew deeply on her ever-present menthol cigarette and stated flatly,

"Next time, get the money and then talk about it, William."

"Yeah," Capler added.

Billy tried to relax. The car halted for a red light, and the lack of incoming air exacerbated the teenager's nausea brought on by the smoke concentration.

"Can you roll your window down some more, Momma?"

"It's too cool, William," Mrs. Capler replied coldly without looking at him.

"It's hard to breathe!"

"Um-humm," Mr. Capler agreed, managing a weak grin. An unlikely ally, Billy knew, but he's got to breathe, too. But, why won't he roll down his own window?

"I'm going to roll down mine."

"No, you won't, William!"

Damn, how Billy hated the way she said his name! *What's the use?*

Mrs. Capler grunted, inhaling another deep drag before muttering, her words spraying a toxic cloud,

"Don't be ridiculous."

■   ■   ■

Lunch tasted awful. But it was worth it, Billy felt. *Grammaw can't cook but I enjoy being here.* He prodded his partially prepared meat gingerly, half expecting it to scream in pain. Usually at this time of the year he would dump his unwanted meal, minus any bones, into the heater beside him. He wasn't able to do that today. It wasn't lit. Not cold enough outside.

He eyed the television screen warily. An evangelist was loudly haranguing his captivated audience with a no-holds-barred scriptural assault. Billy silently asked: *And Grammaw wants me to do that kind of bullshit?* Billy scowled as the camera panned in on the worshippers dutifully reaching into their pockets and parting with their hard won, factory earned dollars. He could not help but notice how different they appeared from the antiseptic, meticulously coiffed preacher and his well-clad, beefy assistants.

Billy shifted his attention to the adults' conversation in the kitchen dining area. His mother, true to form, was trying her best to solicit gossip from her hostess.

"Well, don't you think he's... odd, Mom?"

"I'm not fit to judge, Betty. I do know he's done some fine things."

"Well... did you know... "

Billy tried to hear his mother's words. *Who is she knocking down now? For once,* he figured, *it's not me. Or is it?*

"Betty, that's just hearsay!"

Good for you, Grammaw! Make her choke on it! Billy smiled, raking his uneaten spinach into a pile, wondering if he could sneak into the bathroom and flush the stuff. The evangelist's pleas to "give 'til it hurts" and "love offerings to the unfortunates" totally gutted what was left of Billy's appetite. *To hell with it,* he decided, picking up his plate. *I can't eat any of this shit, or listen to his.*

The verbal jousting ended with Billy's entrance. Three pairs of eyes made the boy very aware of the mélange on his plate.

"Billy, I swear, you don't eat enough to keep a bird alive!"

"That's okay, Grammaw. I won't be able to fly away then, you know?"

The two smiled at each other. Although she was his stepfather's mother, there was a genuine familial type of chemistry between them. The much-appreciated pleasantry died with Betty Capler's unwelcome barb,

"Well, you're gonna have to fly on your own. You're not going to sponge off of me like so many durn young 'uns do to their parents these days." Her eyes met those of the elderly lady and Betty's aggressive demeanor instantly weakened. "When they get grown they ought to move on," she added and asked her husband, "Young 'uns these days think their parents owe them a living, don't they?"

Jack Capler snorted lowly and continued feeding his stocky, powerful body a mixture of spinach and black-eyed peas. It wasn't quite the sound of bemused agreement it would have been had the elder Mrs. Capler not been present. Billy knew from experience what was about to be said.

Returning to the living room, he heard Grammaw's gentle defense of him and his mother's accusative "Well, he is," response, followed by the inevitable snap-click-snap of a well-used cigarette lighter.

■ ■ ■

"Now!" Billy whispered, reading the command of the Greek adventurer Ulysses. "Uhh!" Billy groaned, imagining how the giant Cyclops Polyphemus, his single eye blinded by a fiery lance, must have awakened in pain and anger. "My favorite story," he quietly told himself. "I love it when the men escape by hanging on to the sheeps' tummies. Boy, did they fuck old Polly up!"

The boy caught his expletive too late. In the next room, the grownups kept talking. With relief, Billy realized that no one had heard him say the "f" word.

Billy quickly thumbed through the rest of the book. Grammaw had given him a recent version of *The Odyssey,* but he preferred this turn-of-the-century edition with its dark, sinister Gothic woodcuts. Briefly, he imagined himself as Telemachus, side by side with his father Ulysses, slashing down their enemies in the great hall of the Ithaca palace...

"Bullshit," Billy softly mumbled, closing the yellowed book and indulging in a bit of self-pity. "Must be nice to have a damn father." He broke from the depressing knowledge that his natural dad would not return from war as Ulysses had and resolved to again tell the tale of Polyphemus to Franco and Donald. The brothers Campbell might be on Billy's mother's shit list but they were his friends and they listened to him. They accepted him and he accepted them. They even liked to hear about other stories that Billy had read, even though they themselves didn't care to read much except for comic books and Franco could never quite get the characters' names straight.

■ ■ ■

Jack Capler's rude snoring resounded powerfully, shaking the walls. *It should cover up the sound of my getting out of bed*, Billy reasoned. He knew that his mother was still awake. She always coughed for a long while after going to bed. Sometimes she would get up, barge into his room, and try to catch him masturbating. She had never caught him, but she claimed to have plenty of times. Jack Capler would jokingly attempt to defend Billy, and she would then transfer her anger to the stepfather.

Got to hand it to him, Billy ceded. *He does try to help sometimes. But then, Momma, any excuse to call me odd… well, as long as she coughs, she isn't up…*

Billy's room was at the end of the hallway. Mr. Capler's room was on the front side of the house and Mrs. Capler's was on the rear. They rarely slept together. When they did, Capler's snoring aided Billy's movements all the more. Tonight, however, Billy would have to time his motions to coincide with the snoring.

Within a minute, Billy's feet were on the floor and he was almost to the bookcase. The moonlight danced eerily about the outside boughs and their shadows pranced merrily across the back yard. A patchwork ballet of blacks and grays performed in Billy's room, enhancing his desire to make it to his goal.

The boy reached behind a section of small paperbacks and gingerly felt the plastic figures sequestered behind them. *Got to have Rémy*, Billy resolutely decided.

"Ah," the adolescent accidentally whispered, his fingers grasping the four inch high French Legionnaire's buff yellow form. *You'll always be my favorite*, Billy reflected. *Had you since I was real little.* Billy stood Rémy on the window sill and groped in the bookcase hideaway again, producing two smaller figures.

"Blue boy and Rubberbuster… okay… three's enough," the teen cautiously breathed. He placed an azure alien holding ray pistols and a kneeling soldier poised to shoot a nonexistent rifle with the larger manikin on the window sill.

Billy backed away and began to squat, again pacing himself to his stepfather's snoring. Delightfully for Billy, the small dolls appeared to stir, to move, an illusion created by the interplay of moonlight, the shadows of tree limbs dancing with the wind, and an unhappy young man's fertile imagination.

What a natural high this is! Billy thought. *How could anyone want to smoke dope when they could do this? God, if You're real, then make them come alive! Alive! And do anything I say! Come on, God, please! If You never do a thing for me again, do this! Come on! Grammaw says You can do anything!*

To get a clearer view, the boy picked up his hated, heavy horned-rim glasses from the desk fronting the window. How he'd give anything to have perfect sight, no astigmatism, to be free of having to wear these unattractive things! He could do without, as his mother put it, "looking sophisticated."

A plank underfoot creaked loudly.

Damn! Billy, alarmed, listened with bated breath. His stepfather continued to snore and his mother kept hacking weakly. *Did she hear that?* the teen wondered, agonizing over whether to put his styrene men back or observe them a while longer. He could not resist the latter option.

The incoming moon rays brightly reflected off the corner of a battered Corona cigar box set underneath the shelf where Billy kept his troops. Distracted, the boy thought of its contents and again wished he could have known the original owner. He had tried so often to understand how the yellowing off-white and black imitation ivory chess pieces within the box were moved during a game, but perhaps, he sadly considered, he never would.

In Billy's deepest heart he was longing for his father just to be there for him. First Lieutenant Jacques "Jock" Beaudet had often played chess with his fellow Marine officers. Billy felt life would have been immeasurably better had his father not died on the other side of the world. Surely he wouldn't have given me excuses like:

"I don't know nothing about chess, boy," Jack Capler had said to Billy more than once, usually adding a "shit" for effect meaning: *Go away.*

"Mnn," his mother would grunt. "I couldn't learn it, William. Jock offered several times to show me, but I didn't care for it. I wasn't… interested."

Maybe you were too damn dumb, Momma, Billy angrily thought, *and maybe I am, too.* The boy shifted his gaze back to his soldiers, trying to push back the wounding hole in his soul, the bottomless void which deep down, somewhere at a level he could not yet grasp, he knew defined him.

After a few more minutes of wistful watching, he replaced the figures and his despised glasses and stealthily returned to bed. The Caplers were, as far as he could tell, blissfully unaware of anything. From underneath the muffling security of his bedcovers, Billy Beaudet astringently spoke,

"Momma would throw them away. All twelve of them. I used to have more than two hundred little guys. All kinds of them. She threw them away. She and Stepdad called them little dollies for first graders. I could only save a few, and I can't let her know I still have these. She'll call me 'Oddball' again and these will end up in the trash like all the others. I'll never get them back.

"See, God, I'm kind of like their Ulysses. Rémy's kind of like my first mate, my right-hand man. So if you could, God, like I said… I… ah, shit," the boy abruptly spat, suddenly stung by the absurdity of his childish fantasy, thinking further but not daring to whisper, just in case He was listening, and with a twinge of shame,

Maybe You're not even there, God. What difference would it make to me, anyway?

3

OCTOBER 9

"SO YOU SEE, folks, the Roman method was innovative. It at least gave the conquered peoples a large say in how they were ruled. And guess what? It worked. For hundreds of years it worked. That's quite a track record."

"But I don't, like, understand," the leggy, red-lipped young ash blonde complained, interrupting her world history teacher's lecture. "I mean, if they... still were gonna... rule themselves, why'd the Romans come in and, you know, take them over in the first place?"

"Good question, Dena," the burly fortyish man replied, noticeably distracted by the girl's purposeful twisting of her nylon-covered, perfectly formed foot. Several of the heftier boys tuned in on the action and smiled at one another. Dena was teasing the man who was also the school's head football coach and the jocks thought this quite funny.

"Well, but, if they were just gonna leave them alone... why, you know..."

"They did allow the people they conquered, to a large degree, to keep on governing themselves." Mr. Hale forced his mind out of the gutter and gazed absently at the worn map hanging on the board. "But they didn't actually, as you said, 'leave them alone.' They tended to put their own flunkies, some call them puppets, in charge, and the Romans watched what they did real close.

"You all take a look on page, uh, sixty-three. There's a Gaul chief surrendering to the Romans. This guy tried to get all the Gaul tribes together to kick out the Romans. Like Pontiac and later, Sitting Bull did in this country about a hundred years ago, trying to stop all the white settlers from coming in."

"Didn't do the Indians any dadburn good, neither," someone opined. No one argued the statement.

Mr. Hale scrawled a lengthy name on the blackboard, repeatedly referring to his text for guidance.

"Who can pronounce this fifty dollar moniker?"

Heads shook in bewilderment. In the back, a rather disheveled boy whispered, "Shee-yit," eliciting laughter. The coach suspected but had not heard the vulgarity, choosing to press the question,

"How about it? Beaudet, where are you?"

"Sir?" Billy, in the third row, a bit unwillingly responded.

"Surely, the only boy at Gilmore High, and probably in the whole county, who knows the Greek alphabet and can put Greek names and words together can pronounce this old French name in Roman letters."

"Vercingetorix," Billy flawlessly stated, not looking at his satisfactorily smiling teacher whom he knew was about to put him on an unbearably temporary pedestal.

"Fine, very fine. I want the rest of y'all to say it together. Ver – Vercin - - Billy, say it again. Y'all listen to him."

There was a momentary burst of adolescent laughter. Everyone knew Coach Hale could not pronounce the name any better than he could write it.

The young star of the moment, conscious that every eye was on him, began to form the long-dead Gallic chief's name with his lips.

His mouth immediately spread into a broad smile. Billy was determined to revel in this rare few seconds of glory.

■　　■　　■

The surrounding constant clatter of cheap utensils shoved about with their plastic flatware accentuated the lunchroom clamor. Billy spoke loudly,

"He always calls on me, Franco. It is kind of nice to get called on something you know. It's the only course I got a B in so far. Everything else is Cs and math is a D. Low D, too."

"Hell, I ain't got no class with nothing over a damn D," the denim-jacketed boy beside Billy volunteered, taking a sip of milk and continuing. "Foque eet," Franco Campbell self-amusedly mumbled in his unique way. "I don't give a day-um, neither." His peroxide-induced red streak traversing his otherwise brown head of hair seemed to symbolize his apathy. "Race car driver or surfer don't need none of this bool sheet. Right?"

Billy didn't answer. He combined his meat loaf and mashed potatoes while his best friend bemoaned being only fifteen. Franco blamed his problems on his father, a successful contractor and a political crony of Mr. Capler. Billy's stepdad was a job appointee of the governor himself. Their elders' association allowed the boys to hang out together, along with Franco's nine year old brother Donald, despite Mrs. Capler's domineering disapproval.

"You want to meet at the pipe sometime today?"

"Yeah. Me and Doo-nell'll meet you about when? About four?"

"Okay. Sounds good." Billy felt excitement tingle up his legs. How he looked forward to these after-school meetings in the big drainage pipe under the road! But sadly, Billy knew that, "I got to get my homework done first. Boy, it's piling up today. Always does on Monday."

"Don't do your god-day-um sheety homework. I don't."

"I don't want to flunk tenth grade, Franco."

"I wish I was - - hey, take off your damn glasses, Billy. Here comes your girlfriend!"

The horned-rims were cased in Billy's shirt pocket before Sharee Post, tray in hand, ambled by. She was pretty, but not made up. There was a raw, open honesty in her that Billy found refreshingly different.

"How did you know how to say that name, Billy? I heard all about it." she asked, smiling alluringly, her coiffed curls partially obscuring her right eye.

"Oh, uh, I just, uh, I tend to know stuff like that." Billy's face blushed scarlet. To his relief, several of Sharee's friends caught up with her and the group moved on to an adjacent table. Billy was handsome but shy, and content for now to settle for flirtatious passings-by.

"You should have asked her to sit with us, Billy. She likes you. I bet she would give you some poo-sy."

"Nah. She's too nice," Billy countered, shamefully remembering the snobby way his mother had spoken regarding Sharee's parents. Billy, because he'd verbally defended the Posts, had received for his gallantry a guilt-laced tongue-lashing about social status. *Who the hell was Momma to put down factory workers? The Posts are good, honest people, well thought of at church... so what if they don't live in a split-level house in a new subdivision like Garden Pines?* "Ah, I'd probably get her pregnant, anyway."

"Use a rubber, bro'. Go get you one at old man Hoffman's gas station. In the damn bathroom's a damn rubber machine. Nobody will see you. Quarter apiece, get it? Quarter for a piece... so you can get you some poo-sy. Feel good," Franco added, losing a pea from his grinning mouth.

■ ■ ■

"And the answer, Mr. Beaudet, is... ?"

"Stra - - " Billy shot unthinkingly before catching his error. Mr. Kline wanted the correct response to the math problem, and it was not the word strabismus.

"I know it's almost the end of another one of your vigorous, trying school days, Mr. Beaudet, but do try your best to keep your mind on the equations and out of the girls' locker room."

"Yes sir," Billy uttered to his stern, unmerciful sixth period algebra teacher.

"Miss Stewart? What would you say? Number sixteen."

Billy's eyes darted around. No one knew he had almost said the medical term which described one of several conditions disabling the left eye of Jimmy Cass. Jimmy was the class bully and had been aggravating Billy for a fight since the beginning of the past month. Billy guessed that he was trying to prove himself to Big Red Pinson, the nineteen year old tenth grader. *Yeah*, Billy's mind drifted, *what a bunch of shitheads in that crowd.*

Something hot and wet bounced off the nape of Billy's neck. *Oh, nuts, a spitwad!*

Billy turned and, as expected, spotted a smirking Jimmy Cass and his own little retinue. The hollow pen Jimmy dangled from his fingers presented mocking evidence of his guilt. Jimmy's freckle-bordered lips formed the mute but familiar words:

Nigger lover.

Billy resumed looking at the problem materializing under the noisily whipping chalk in Mr. Kline's fingers. At the desk to his left John Marston, Billy's black algebra partner, was soaking up the calculations. Billy bitterly reflected,

Thanks to you, John, I might pass this class. As for you, Jimmy, fuck you, you stupid redneck, one-eyed dumbass! Fuck you to goddamn hell!

"Clear yet, Mr. Beaudet? Mr. Beaudet, would you please return to earth?"

Billy pleadingly peeped at his partner, who nodded affirmatively to Kline. The teacher's face twisted and he sarcastically told John,

"Thank you, Mr. Beaudet. So... What does y equal?"

"Uh, see, uh... y equal six, see..." responded Marston, stuttering with embarrassment.

"Good, Mr. Beaudet, good," Kline pressed, to the amusement of the other kids, especially Cass and his straphangers.

■　　■　　■

Billy halted, recognizing his friends' silhouettes at the far end of the five foot wide concrete drainpipe. Franco was telling Donald something, but the rumble of the car passing overhead coupled with the loudness of the watery cascade beyond and below the brothers Campbell masked the words.

"Tu say?" Billy called.

"Hey yay!" Franco answered instantly, flipping a cigarette into the drainage pool.

"Hey-ull, yeah," his little brother cheerfully added.

Billy stepped into the pipe and straddled the creek bisecting it.

"Whoa, guys, I almost forgot."

"Where you going, sheety bro'?"

"Just right here beside me, Franco." Billy swung to the outside rim of the pipe to bend over a twisted chunk of rotten oak tree root. It was still connected to the massive trunk jutting horizontally forty feet out of the embankment. Billy, ever impressed by the slowly decomposing relic, stared for a few seconds. "Big and solid as a Doric column in a Greek palace. I'll bet that tree could tell some wild stories. It probably sprouted before Columbus came."

"Say hey, bro'?"

Billy pivoted, breaking the grip of his impromptu daydream. Franco had come over to him with Donald at his heels.

"I gotcha something, Franco. I forgot to tell you about it at lunch."

"Aw, man, you got me some weeds!" Franco's face beamed with pleasure as he gratefully accepted the twelve foil-wrapped Alpine brand cigarettes Billy had spent the past week stealing, one or two per pack, from his mother.

"These are menthols, but I knew you wouldn't care what kind they were."

"Naw, hey-ull, naw. Thanks, Billy! You're my best friend! Really, sheety bro'!"

"Weeds! Can I have one, too?" Donald begged.

"Let's all have one," Franco suggested, extracting from his jeans' right pocket an unused book of matches.

Oh, nuts. Well, I can fake it as usual, Billy figured, resolving anew never to inhale the smoke.

"Ah, shit!" a prepubescent voice squealed.

"God durn, Doo-nell, don't step in the damn mud! Step higher on the sides of the goddamn pipe!" Franco's jestful advice resounded down the length of the concrete corridor. The boys soon sat, their feet on opposite sides of the pipe's inner surface with the creek flowing under their legs.

They always felt safely hidden there. Indeed, the world did seem so different at the swamp between the lakes, and even more so within the pipe. Billy stared blankly again, this time into the water's muddy bronze translucence, permitting himself for a moment the luxury of speculating about the origin of the mysterious wall of large rectangular stones defining the far limit of the exit pool. Several of them lay on the moss-covered bank above the wall where Billy and Franco had put them two summers earlier. The stones were blackened, charred as if by an intense heat. His remembrance was interrupted by Franco's loud chiding of Donald,

"Goddamnit, Doo-nell, don't chuckasuck it! You done wasted a whole damn weed! Billy didn't steal them weeds just to see 'em get wasted."

Donald gave a little laugh. Near his lips perched an inch and a half long brightly glowing vermilion ash.

"Hey, fellas!"

Billy spotted motion beyond the thick thorn bushes girdling the pool's borders. A well-known but unwelcome voice repeated,

"Hey, fellas! Hey! Look! It's me!"

"Oh, god-day-um," Franco sputtered disgustedly. "It's that day-um boy who lives across the street from you, Billy. What's his name?"

"Al. Al Gates."

"Yeah. I see him around school sometimes. Isn't he that kid I…"

"I'm surprised he wants to come in here with us after you beat the shit out of his arms last summer."

"That was funny as hell," Donald opined. "He looks just like a little old titty baby when he cries."

They could hear thirteen year old Al sliding down the embankment on the other side. Billy had correctly figured that Al would go across the road and not come through the bushes and pool. Al was terrified of snakes and would not come near the pool since he had seen one four feet long swimming in it that past July.

Franco recalled that day. Al had had to relieve himself after having seen the harmless water snake. To regain some lost masculinity he had asked Franco for a cigarette.

"Hell, he told me he wanted a weed, so I gave one to him. I thought he might be pretty cool until he stuck it in his damn turd. Took one fucking god-day-um puff and stuck a brand new weed in a damn turd. Day-um right I beat his ass."

"He is a pest," Billy agreed, forcing his voice to a whisper as Al's skinny form darkened the pipe's entrance. "Tell him there's a snake in the pipe, but don't y'all be mean to him. Okay?"

"He's fucked up!" Donald said loudly.

"And I ain't gonna give him no more damn weeds!"

■　■　■

Jack Capler's dark glasses could not obscure his glaring eyes. Assaulted on one side by his stepfather's intimidation and by his mother's acrid cigarette smoke on the other, Billy could only hope for refuge in his room.

"Can I please be excused?"

"You may, William," she answered emotionlessly, staring blankly at the contents of her still-filled plate.

"Thank you, ma'am."

"Very good supper," Capler injected into the stilted, ritualized exchange with equally mechanical indifference. He crushed his napkin after wiping his cruel slit of a mouth and, all too predictably, tossed it onto Billy's plate.

At least he put off his napkin bullshit until I was finished this time, Billy silently, bitterly, said to himself. The boy went straight to his room and sat at his plain little desk, relieved to be there. He removed his glasses, closed his eyes, breathed slowly and deeply, trying to relax, and placing his hands palms down on the desk, waited.

In several minutes the repetitive sound of footsteps riding the air currents up through the heating vent entered Billy's ears. Assured that the grownups were settling into their routine of basement television watching, Billy fetched several of his men: a standing soldier, a red robot-like fellow named Max, and a yellow man carrying a bazooka and wearing something resembling a World War I era gas mask.

"Got to have you, Rém." Billy instead pulled out a big blue caped legionnaire. "You can stay too, Louie." The teenager found his favorite and resumed his seat. An idea sprouted in Billy's brain.

"Say, I wonder… "

Putting his five men on the window sill, Billy as quietly as he could moved his chair back ten feet and clicked off the overhead circular fluorescent light. The boy waited impatiently for his eyes to adjust to the altered light level, his ears tightly tuned in to detect any movement at the bottom of the air vent.

"Daaamn!" Billy murmured, transfixed by the enrapturing mirage on the sill. "This is better than waiting! Much better! Just look at Max and Little Yeller!" he exclaimed lowly, trembling with excitement. "And you, Rém…" Billy felt an unexpected calm come over him as he addressed the buff legionnaire. "I'll have you until the day I die, Rém. I mean it. It may be stupid, Rém, but I'd like to be buried with you one day… but not even Franco would understand. I can't tell nobody. Never."

A shiny sliver of green broke the cover of the waltzing shadows. It gave Billy the impression that it undulated, eel-like, through the window screen, but it made no sound. The apparition hovered around Rémy's head for about three seconds and vanished.

Did Rémy's eyes flash?

"What the hell?" Billy, shocked, wondered aloud, restoring the light and inspecting his troops. "Golleee-damn!"

Heavy wingtips pounded the stairs, warning the boy of his stepfather's approach. Billy hastily laid a dog-eared book atop Rémy and dropped the rest of the figurines into the top desk drawer.

Cold wind touching Billy's face reminded him to be sure to shut the window or get another speech concerning his inability to appreciate the heating bill. *Nahhh... Later. It feels so good...*

Capler stopped at the hallway bathroom, unloaded his bladder, and returned to the basement. He said something which evoked gurgling laughter from his wife's tar-coated respiratory tubes.

The Odyssey, Billy read. "Yeah!" The youth lifted the book off of Rémy. "I must have been seeing things, Rém'. You look okay."

Billy scanned his favorite chapter, smiling as he thought about how much Polyphemus the giant cyclops reminded him of Jimmy Cass! *Ah, hell,* Billy angrily thought, *he'll probably start on me as soon as he gets on the damn bus! And now, Lou Jones, Jimmy's idiot retard of a sidekick, is picking on Franco. Well, Franco won't back off...*

"Shit, Rém', I guess me and Franco will both end up getting our asses beat. But why me? I played football with him and his buddies last summer. He just lives up there at the top of the hill... in the big house on the left. And Lou lives in the yellow wood house up from him. I mean, how can someone get to be such an asshole in just two or three months?"

"Ah, hell, I know. Who am I trying to kid? He's trying to be cool in front of Big Red. He wants to show Big Red how tough he is. What am I telling you for, anyway? You don't even hear me. Do you?"

Nagging concern for his personal safety brushed away all other priorities. Rémy momentarily forgotten, Billy found a long, thin-bladed pocket knife in his desk's middle drawer and carefully concealed it under a partially unwound ball of string.

"I'll not let the bastard hurt me," Billy promised himself.

■ ■ ■

"Billy's the only one who never made fun of you," pretty, long-haired Sara Cass pointed out to her fraternal twin brother. "Why him?"

"Why not?" Jimmy evasively retorted, adding, "Look, it's not that he's a weirdo or anything, it's just that after I do this I'll be a full-fledged member of Big Red's bunch."

"You and Lou Jones, too."

"Right." Jimmy turned off the little black and white TV set on its flimsy wooden stand and flopped backwards carelessly onto the thick navy blue quilt covering his bed. "What's all this to you, anyway?"

"You could have picked on someone else besides Billy."

"Do you like him or something?" Jimmy's sneer turned upwards into a grin. His functioning right eye focused bemusedly on Sara, his unseeing left one rotating wildly as usual.

Ignoring the unwelcome verbal probe, Sara warned,

"You're really going to get in trouble for this tomorrow. It's not going to be worth it."

"Nah," the boy shot back. "Key Chain and the boys will make sure there's no witnesses. Me and Lou will whip them both so fast it will all be over with before you know it."

"'Both of them'? Who else gets unlucky tomorrow?"

"That retard Campbell. You know, dumb ass Franco."

"And this is all about joining Big Red's crowd."

"Sure is," Jimmy concurred. "Look, I'll make it up to Billy later on somehow. Billy's okay, I suppose, even if he is a damn nigger lover. Besides that, hell, I don't hate him. I'll do my best not to hurt him... too much, anyway."

"He's just a way for you to get something you want."

"You got it, Sis," Jimmy agreed, pausing to let his blunt admission have its full effect, surprised when he no longer saw his sister standing there.

Jimmy turned off his end table lamp and lay back on the bed. In the darkness of his room he could barely make out the duality of his own feet, their toes jutting upward past his gray cotton sweat pants.

For a while he lay there considering what might happen before first period class. What could go wrong? He resolved again to do the job fast and be done with it. As for what Lou Jones was going to do with the school idiot, who cared? That was Lou's business.

The moonlight splitting the night clouds over the Cass home created a waltzing monotone pattern of grays on the boy and his quilt. It reminded him of the kaleidoscope he had been given as a small child, and he recalled how his mother had told him that nothing ever stayed the same.

■ ■ ■

Jimmy slowly came to, the dull ache in his bladder protesting the quantity of its contents. He still lay on his back, and he wondered what time it was. The clock was behind him to his left, and to see it with his good eye, he lazily rolled over onto his stomach.

2:52, the boy read, noting how pleasingly crisp the outline of the radium coating the clock hands was. *At least*, he reminded himself, *my one good eye is perfect.*

The clock's glow momentarily blackened, then returned. Something moved close to Jimmy's face, and whatever it was, was coming still closer. There was a soft shuffling sound with it, like that of tiny feet.

Must be a cat, he thought, still not fully awake. *Did anyone let a cat in the house?*

Jimmy smiled and began to reach for what he hoped was a new fuzzy friend. Instead, his fingers contacted something hard and slick, like plastic.

"What the fuck?" He pulled his hand back. For a split second he saw three, no, four tiny human-like shapes carrying a thin sliver of what looked to be shiny metal. A momentary ray of moonlight showed that one of the intruders, the one in the rear, was nearly twice the height of the others.

The taller one appeared to be aiming the metallic object at Jimmy's face.

"Shit, this is a damn dream," he blurted, beginning to chuckle.

The small group lunged, their steel lancet finding its target and digging in deeply. There was a twisting motion, a second or two of numbness, and then came the hellishly searing pain.

Jimmy Cass's scream shook the window panes in every room of the house.

4

OCTOBER 10

THE INTRUDING BRISK wind washed away Billy's grogginess. He shut the window and speedily put the men in their cubby hole behind the books. Pulling his trousers up, Billy eyed the disheveled mass of string on his desk. *It didn't look that jumbled up last night,* he casually recalled.

Nervously, his fingers dipped into the pile and pulled out the red-handled pocket knife. Reluctantly, he dropped it into his pants and prayed that he wouldn't be compelled to use it.

"You're running late, William!" a voice from the kitchen warned.

"I'm coming, Momma! I'm coming!"

Through the blue haze filling the kitchen, Billy saw his breakfast sandwich of peanut butter and concord jelly lying on its usual single ply, plain paper napkin.

"Take your sandwich with you, William!"

"Nah, Momma. Ain't got time," Billy told her, moving past his ignored meal and opening the aluminum screen door that connected the kitchen with the carport.

"Mnnhh," she groaned. Billy felt a twinge of pity for her. She was only forty-two years of age, but she looked over a hundred this and many other mornings. She would sit and smoke all day, pining for her younger days, the days when she was a stunning auburn-haired beauty. Mr. Capler was already up and out by the time she awakened Billy, and often the man was gone for days on end due to state business. He was a hard worker, that much was certain. Sometimes, though, Billy wanted and needed something more than benign neglect... that need was something he had in common with his mother.

The screen door shut slowly, emitting a harsh metallic whisper which blended with the braking whine of the approaching school bus. Billy trailed the small group of boarders, Al Gates among them, mentally bracing for an impending verbal barrage. *Back seats empty,* Billy saw. *Good. If I'm there, Jimmy won't be able to thump my ears.*

"Come on, bro'!" he said to Franco, seated about midway down the length of the bus. "Where's Doo-nell?"

"Aw, he said he was sick. He ain't. He just don't want to go to school," Franco explained, rising to follow his best friend and adding, "Hell, I don't neither, but I got to 'til I turn sixteen. I'm going to quit then. Ain't you, too?"

Billy didn't answer his friend's oft-repeated query. The bus grudgingly stopped with a harsh jolt, and his attention focused sharply on the vehicle's front door.

The tow-headed first grader mounting the triplet of steps smiled at her brother, the bus driver. The senior returned the smile and watched the Cass house. After a few seconds the driver, satisfied that no one else was coming, shoved the gearshift forward and the bus resumed its journey.

"None of the Casses got on," Billy informed Franco. "Not Jimmy nor neither one of his sisters."

"Ain't neither car there."

"Maybe they went off," Billy longingly speculated. "Maybe they won't be back for a week or two."

"We both ought to whip his ass, bro! Then we'll get Lou. I see that mo-la-foquer up there now."

Once more, the dull yellow beast ground to a tedious halt. Lanky, greasily flat-topped Lou Jones, displaying his constant grin, pushed an elementary grade child out of line, then laughingly pulled him back.

"Sumbitch has always got to be fucking with somebody," Franco observed. "I'm tired of his smart-ass mouth. He was calling me a nigger lover yesterday, too. I know why. Don't get mad, Billy…"

"I know, Franco. He called you that because of me."

Lou's body slammed into Al Gates, knocking the smaller boy sideways. For a fraction of a second, Al's face contorted in pain at the impact and Billy hopefully thought the boy might dare to protest this rough treatment.

Instead, Al offered the taller, older, and stronger boy a weakly unconvincing grin of appeasement. Lou sneered at Al as he sat heavily, his head from which grew an immaculately tended top-chopped bush of light brown hair swiveled, and his eyes burned at Franco for an unbearable moment as if to say: *Look at what I can do! You're next!*

"He won't say nothing without Jimmy being with him. He's a coward without Jimmy. Like I said, Billy, I can't stand niggers and it's - - well, them ones at school - - you act like they're real people like us and - - "

"Look, bro," Billy quickly interrupted. "I don't let anyone tell me who my friends are and you shouldn't, either. There's a difference between a black person and a nigger and there's a difference between a white person and a redneck. And that," Billy emphasized with a finger jabbed toward Lou's narrow head, "is a redneck."

"But I don't like them damn nee – gars."

"You're only cheating yourself, bro."

Franco went into his predictable sulk and Billy realized his friend did not even want to try to understand what he was attempting to tell him. In that sense, Billy knew that Franco was unfortunately like nearly everyone else in his grim, untidy, and maddeningly confusing little world. *Maybe,* Billy silently wondered, *some people just aren't capable of even wanting to understand...*

■ ■ ■

The booming clamor just inside the school building was deafening. Dozens of voices purposely raised above the next ones, each competing to be heard. Billy told Franco,

"Watch him go up to Big Red and then turn and say something to you. Watch him. Maybe you'd better just go on first."

"Naw. I'll fight him right here. I don't care."

"Take this," Billy advised, pressing the knife handle against the thigh of a gratefully accepting Franco.

"I'll cut his guts out."

"Hey, Campbell!" Lou called at the top of his lungs. "You're a queer!" Several boys in the group laughed. Big Red Pinson, however, appeared indifferent, even bored. "You're a queer, Franco!" Lou repeated.

"Come on, mullafucker!" Franco fired back. "I'll fight you right now. Let's fight right now!"

The crowd parted as if on cue, clearing a lane for the feuding pair.

"Fight!" someone bellowed over the considerably lessening hubbub of voices. "Fight!"

"I'll cut your goddamn guts out right in front of everybody!"

"No, Franco! Not here!" Billy grabbed Franco by his arms. "Give me the knife. I see Bull Broward coming!"

The huge form of the vice principal stepped out of the mass of adolescents and into the cleared lane. Instantly he spotted the posturing Franco, who wisely slipped the knife back to Billy.

"Campbell, you come with me. I won't have this filthy language," Bull commanded. The heavy set, dark suited man, never known for humor, scowled harshly, his cruelly curled lips set solidly into a seemingly permanent five o'clock shadow. From under a Neanderthal-like shelf of bone, the vice-principal's gaze darted left and right. Unable to determine the object of Campbell's ire, Broward added loudly, "Anyone else feeling stupid this morning?"

Franco, looking at the floor tiles, complied. Billy cast a final glance at Lou Jones's grinning face and drifted into the enclosing human crush. With frustration he realized that Franco would say nothing in his own defense.

■ ■ ■

"Hey, Billy! Get your day-um butt over here! I heard something about Jimmy Cass! Come on!"

"What is it, bro'?" Billy queried Franco, his curiosity flaming high. Young Beaudet sat and invited Arty Johnson, a huge black junior and star guard of Gilmore's gridiron line, to join them at the lunch table.

"Damn, bro," Franco muttered in complaint. Happily, Arty sat. Within seconds the table was filled with other black students. An almond-complexioned girl coming to sit beside Franco only heightened the boy's self-conscious embarrassment. Her unusually bright and wide eyes scanned him as if he were a mouse and she the cat ready to play. Franco appeared as if he might jump up and leave.

Billy knew he had to placate his friend and do so fast.

"It's okay, bro'. What is it? What did you hear about Jimmy?"

"Jimmy Cass..."

"Louder, bro', I can't hear you with everybody sitting here around us talking. What about Jimmy Cass?"

"His sister came into Latin class late," Franco loudly spoke over the new arrivals at the table. "All of them damn Casses was at the hospital this morning."

"Hospital?"

"Last night, dumb ass Jimmy somehow rolled over in his sleep and stuck a fucking pencil in his goddamn eye." Franco laughed heartily at the thought of it happening.

"His good eye?"

"Yeah. The fucker's blind as a damn bat now! Shit! I wish something like that would happen to Lou."

"Who? Somebody got stuck? Who did? Who stuck who?" The pretty almond ninth grader asked. "You done stuck somebody, boy?"

"No... it was Jimmy - - Jimmy," Franco stammered, his discomfort with her presence all too detectable. "Jimmy Cass. You know him?"

"Naw, boy. I don't know no white boys. What your name is?" she squealed, amid thunderous laughter from her friends.

Franco silently answered with a leer that screamed of intense irritation.

"I'm Billy. You're Dorothy, right?" Billy stepped in to try and allay Franco's embarrassment. Dorothy answered,

"Yeah, honey, I know who you is. You a cutie pie, boy. I seen you around here lots of times."

"And so are you," Billy with a smile and a cocked right eyebrow told her. Her pretty face beamed with pleasure at this unexpected attention, and Franco wondered why his friend was so brave with her but not with white girls. To Franco, it was unfathomable, but then, to Franco, most things were.

"I know him," Arty spoke up. "What did he do? Stuck his eye out? He only got one eye anyway, only one good one, that is, don't he?"

"Not no more, he don't," Franco rapidly returned, looking at Billy who sat stunned and awash with mixed feelings. He felt happy because his adversary was no longer a physical threat, yet that same person who had in the past been a good playmate if not a friend was now horribly handicapped and in all probability, permanently.

"I don't believe it!" Billy wheezed, unable to keep from being on the glad side of the emotional fence but not wanting to openly show it.

"Yeah, bro'!" Franco continued with relish. "He put out his good eye his god-day-um self. Stupid mo-la-foquer! Foque heem! He deserved it!"

"Shut your mouth, boy!" the girl ordered. "You hush up that nasty talk! You too cute to be talking like that! Why don't you be like handsome little old Billy there? Bet Billy know how to make that sweet sugar talk I want to hear, um-hum."

Arty's grin spread from ear to ear as he watched Franco's blush deepening. Most of the black students knew what Franco's attitude toward them was, but hoped that in time, Billy's influence would bring him around. Arty in particular liked Franco's fuck-the-world outlook.

The boiling ambiguities of Billy's clashing feelings subsided as he realized aloud,

"It's going to be a real dull algebra class now."

■ ■ ■

Billy made his way from the crowd in the main hallway to the side path which led to the library, irritated by the thought that he had no clue as to what he was going to say when he arrived there. The real reason he was going for just a moment was to say hello to Sharee Post working behind the desk.

He paused at the doorway and looked in. No Sharee. He let out a bit of a sigh of relief, aware of the fact that had he seen her, he might be expected to do this every day.

Two students roughly brushed past him, their fur-lined parkas sneezing with a Dacron hiss on his cheap jacket's polyester single layer. The impact turned him partially back the way he had come, and he noticed a hand-lettered sign beside the typing classroom:

Chess Club Meets After Sixth Period.

THERE WAS BOB Grizzle at the table just inside the doorway, squared off in serious cerebral combat with Chet Baldwin. Billy had known them both since third grade, and actually he had known Bob a little longer. They had both been Cub Scouts in the same troop before then, but Billy had never advanced. Bob was a full-fledged Boy Scout now and he wore the olive uniform with white numbers sewn on that displayed the only indication of convention about him.

Bob was very nerdy, with oversized braces on his likewise sized teeth which matched his equally outsized black glasses. Seeing Bob's glasses made Billy feel a lot less self-conscious, and he thought he would go in and say hello to him.

Across from Bob, Chet Baldwin sat scanning his field of battle. Chet was the typical American mother's dream son, handsome and smart, but unspeakably arrogant to all around him who might make the mistake of getting close to him personally, especially as regarded the game of chess. Young Baldwin fancied himself an up-and-coming Grand Master of the game and let everyone know it.

Realizing his bus wouldn't leave for about fifteen minutes yet, Billy wandered in. The air of competition inside felt electric as the various pairs of players concentrated on their moves. Billy envied them and wanted to be one of them. He had tried and tried to read the rules but never could understand them. Maybe if he could visit with Bob, he might explain it a little...

"Say, Chet?" Billy greeted the taller boy first.

Baldwin slightly nodded his brown-carpeted curly head, his manner connoting disdain at Billy's effort of cordiality.

"Hi, Bob."

"Hi, Billy!" young Grizzle immediately answered, still eyeing the board of conflict intently, invitingly adding without taking a breath, "You ever going to get around to joining us here for all these wars on sixty-four squares?"

"Maybe. Hey, how come you're playing against Chet?"

"He's the best there is here at Gilmore," Bob unhesitatingly replied. "If I can ever beat the Chetster here, I shall have climbed the highest hill in all of Virginia."

"Don't call me that, Grizzle. You're really going to piss me off."

"Sorry, Chet. I forgot," Bob apologized to his icily staring opponent.

"And not just 'the highest hill in all of Virginia,' Baldwin continued, picking up a white rook. "Beat me and you'll be on the mountain top of Mount Everest.... but that'll never happen... of course."

"Why's that?" Billy dared to query, noting that the club's advisor, who was also his algebra teacher, had neared the trio and was listening in on their banter.

"I own that mountain," Chet smugly declared, adding, "and come this December, I'll clean the clock of the whole tri-county division, maybe even take the Virginia state title."

"We wholeheartedly hope so," Mr. Kline interjected. "If anyone from Gilmore can accomplish such an epic feat, Mr. Baldwin here can."

"How do the horses move?" Billy asked Bob, ignoring the praise Kline was heaping on Baldwin.

Before Bob, who had smiled at the question, could respond, Baldwin broke in,

"Beaudet, please go away. Why don't you go find a barn somewhere with some old farmers playing checkers in front of it? That's a game you might be able to understand... by the way, Grizzle... look and you'll see you're in check."

Bob leaned forward and squinted at the rook that Baldwin had just moved laterally across three open spaces. The smaller boy shook his head and grinned from the corners of his mouth, stating,

"He got me again. Still, it's no bad thing to get beat by Chet. Took you a little longer this time, though," he added with a widening metallic smile.

"Only because we were rudely interrupted. Same number of moves as usual," Baldwin countered, insulting both Billy and taunting his condescending adversary.

Billy wanted to toss the expressionless Baldwin out of his seat, stomp his sneering face, urinate in his mouth in front of everyone present, but thought the better of it, especially with

Mr. Kline still standing there as an accomplice, even abettor, by his silence in helping Chet to maintain his attitude of superiority.

This just ain't right, Billy thought to himself as he turned to go to his waiting bus, hearing the advisor and algebra teacher say after him, his tone utterly devoid of any hint of sympathy,

"As with all endeavors, one must first learn the rules, Mr. Beaudet."

■   ■   ■

"Goddang, I still can't believe it! I mean… I know I'm supposed to feel bad about it, but I don't. Telling you the truth, the more I think about it, the more glad I am it happened."

"Hey-ull, yeah," Franco smugly concurred, dragging deeply on his Winston before shunting the hot stub out into the drainage pool. "Don't worry about it, Bee-ly, hey-ull, it's natural to feel good about it. All we need's something to happen to Lou now."

"Let's burn his damn house down so they'll have to move!" Donald proposed, his eager excitement heightening still more the prepubescent pitch of his voice.

Franco guffawed. He expected Billy to be in the same humor. When he saw that Billy wasn't, he said,

"Goddamn, Doo-nell, so they'll have to move! Don't you know you'll go to jail for doing sheet like that?"

"We won't tell nobody," Donald offered, trying to change his brother's mocking attitude.

"We'll think of something," Billy broke in. "For right now, though, we need to celebrate." Franco was quick to suggest,

"Let's go see if Pammy will give us some poo-sy."

"Hey-ull, yeah!" Donald squealed.

"Day-um! You don't even shoot off yet, you little turd head! You don't even make no spaaarm in your nutsack yet, you leetle sheet hey-ud!"

"That's okay. I can't get her pregnant then, Franco."

"You might finally get you some, bro."

Franco's words lay like lead in Billy's ears. *What if she does let me? I hear she has let a few others.* Billy's concern echoed Donald's point,

"But what if she does get pregnant?"

"Who keers? We'll all say we foqued her. Nobody will be able to tell whose damn baby it is."

"Yeah, Franco, but what if we get some kind of VD disease? You know, like syphilis?"

"We'll go to the damn doctor. Give him five dollars and he'll give you a shot. Doctor won't tell nobody. Some kind of code or something them doctors got, not to tell nobody."

"What's sy - - syphma - -syphmalus? What is it?"

"Day-um, Donald!" Franco again laughed. "Syphilis. It's a disease you get from some girls. You know, the ones who 'do it' a lot. You know you got syphilis when you feel something going 'round and 'round in your stomach. Damn doctor gives you a shot, all that 'round and 'round stuff stops. Then you got to drink a lot of water and hold your pee all day. When you can't hold it no more, you pee and all of this black sheet comes out in the pee. That's the syphilis."

Now it was Billy's turn to chuckle. *Where had he heard that pile of crap? Certainly not in Coach Hale's health class...*

The boys had been clambering up the embankment during Franco's impromptu medical lesson. At the roadside, two hundred yards uphill, the paper boy wrestled a string-bound bundle of Tuesday afternoon's local edition into his bicycle basket.

"Aw, shit," Franco blurted, seeing him first. "It's Stanley Marx. I swear this neighborhood's getting to be full of queers."

"I don't think Stanley's a queer, bro'. He's just scared to do stuff like regular boys do. And he does have a job. You got to say that for him."

"He won't even rassle me," Donald boasted. "I can beat his skinny butt. And he's a lot taller and older than me! And he's a ninth grader, supposed to be tenth, and - -"

"He's so day-um skinny, you probably outweigh him!"

Donald nodded, ceding that point to his brother.

The boys zipped over the narrow blacktop and moved into the mixed forest, their feet treading on a rotting mat of pine needles and hardwood leaves. Billy entered last, but not before he saw Marx wave to him. Without telling his friends they'd been spotted, Billy reluctantly returned the gesture.

Ten minutes of walking on the beaten path brought the trio to a discarded oil tanker trailer, its struts deeply, permanently, violating the earth, and its fifty-three foot long hull plentifully pitted by rust. The boys had often wondered how it had come to an end stop there in one of the few remaining patches of woods in Garden Pines subdivision. Maybe a road had once been there long ago...

But it did not matter now. They were at their destination, and Franco told the others,

"Ain't nobody home but Pammy. Come on, let's take off our clothes and she might come out. Foque us. Feel good!"

"How come you know, ain't nobody home but her?"

"Ain't no car there, Doo-nell! Stupid ass! Look!"

Donald scrutinized the brick house ten yards away on the other side of a mass of tangle foot vines. A sudden thought prompted the question,

"What if her sister's there? She'll tell!"

"Naw, she won't. Shit on her, we'll fuck her, too. Who gives a day-um if she ain't but twelve? Still feel good."

Some assurance! Billy knew, as they all stripped to their shoes and socks. The air was chilly despite the late afternoon sun's welcome warming rays.

Better keep these hateful glasses on, Billy reasoned. *If I lose them, I'll never hear the end of it. Oh, nuts... do I really want to do this? What if - -*

"What if we get in trouble?"

"Ain't nobody going to see us but Pammy. Come on, you chicken-shits!"

Hesitantly, Billy and Donald brought up the rear. They'd barely arrived at Pammy's bedroom window when her face popped up. She laughed.

"Hold it a minute, y'all. Wait…"

She disappeared for a few seconds. Upon her return, the glint of light over her nose meant she'd put on her own teardrop-style glasses. Billy managed a smile, feeling a bit of empathy that for the space of a single heartbeat's time doused his awareness of his being, except for his shoes and socks, quite naked.

"Come on out to the tank with us, Pammy! We can go naked in the woods!"

"Y'all all got to dance for me first, Franco."

"Like this?" Franco responded, performing a jerking, spasmodic dance of sorts that suspiciously resembled jumping jacks.

"Hey! What are you boys doing?" boomed a disembodied, threatening, and very close by adult male voice.

"Goddamn!" the two older boys cried simultaneously, wheeling about and bounding, gazelle-like, over the thick, tough tangle foot. Billy and Donald snatched their clothes from beside the old tanker. Franco sped on.

"Franco! Get your clothes!" Billy commanded.

"God-day-um!" Franco again swore, retracing his hurried steps. Somebody big was crashing toward them through the bushes.

The panicked trio's flight was interrupted only when they came to an unexpected clearing. The older boys helped Donald, crying and numb with fright, step into his underwear. It was another half a mile of running before, out of breath and cut by an endless army of thorns and bristles, Franco called for them to stop and, gasping, confessed,

"Damn, I didn't think no one was around. Next time, we'll go inside her house before we take off our clothes."

"I hope whoever that was after us don't know our parents."

"Ah, who cares, Billy? Foque heem!"

"Shit!" Donald panted. "I lost my damn belt! The one with my name on it! They'll know who we was!"

"Real good, Doo-nell, you little shitter!"

"I didn't mean to drop it, Franco!"

"We'll find it tomorrow." Again, Billy played the mediator, the peacemaker. At school, he was a nobody, but with the Campbells, he was part of the team. He counted. He mattered.

5

OCTOBER 11

"LOU DIDN'T SAY nothing at all to me all day-um day. Maybe he's gotten to be all right. I still don't like him, though. He still is a sheet hey-ud."

"I think he'll act all right now. Without Jimmy he's nothing. I think he'll leave you alone."

"Oh, Billy... Sara, you know, Jimmy's big sister, was talking to some of her friends. I heard her say Jimmy's eye was gouged out. Plumb fucking out! He really did fuck himself up! Hey, is that Doo-nell I hear coming?" Billy lifted his strawberry blond head out of the Campbells' hillside bomb shelter corridor. Al Gates was sliding down the muddy, thorn-laced pathway with something metallic, apparently chromed, in his hands.

"What's that, Al?" Billy asked.

"Aw, shit," Franco groaned.

"A damn gun! I stole it yesterday!"

"That's a nail gun," Franco explained, a rare expression conveying knowledge evident on his tanned young face. "Daddy's got one a lot like that one. He uses it building houses. You stick a blank in that end, put a nail in the other end, push that flat part on a board, and boom! You don't have to do any hammering. Damn thing costs 'bout two hundred dollars. You better put it back where you got it."

"Y'all ain't going to tell on me for stealing it? I did steal it, you know! I really did! I stole it from that new house they're building down on Westgate."

"Naw, hell, naw," Franco and Billy replied together.

"Look, I can fire real bullets in it! I hold this end against my feet, and then I - - "

"Shit!" Franco spat, watching Al pull a fistful of .22 caliber shorts from his shirt pocket. "You ain't going to fire them damn things around here!"

"Nah, I figured we'll go 'way over yonder way somewheres and we'll shoot some of these bullets Joe gave me."

"Your big brother Joe gave you those?" Franco demanded.

"Sure. Just to get me out of his hair. So I decided to come see y'all. Y'all won't tell me to go on, will you?"

"Uh, Al..." Billy began.

"I'll let you shoot all the bullets! Just don't beat me up or get rid of me!" Al pleaded, his pale blue eyes quivering in their sockets. "Let me be part of the club! Please!"

Billy observed Franco's face turning purple. He knew Al was a few seconds at best from receiving another severe arm pummeling. He proposed,

"Tell you what, Al..."

"Aw, hell," Franco objected.

"We'll go over to the old Meyer place. You can shoot all you want over there."

Al breathed a grateful sigh, again offering the bullets to the pair, who refused. Franco made a half-hearted slap at Al's outstretched hand holding the bullets and pointed out,

"That damn thing's dangerous."

Al led the way, brandishing the loaded, segmented device. He pretended to be a soldier, insisting, over his shoulder,

"Hey, y'all! Look at this! This is like we're on patrol! You know, like in Vietnam! Ain't this cool?"

Franco tugged at Billy's shirt sleeve, wanting to fade back into the bushes and abandon Al. Billy had a sudden mischievous inspiration and whispered to him,

"I got an idea, bro'. Just act like you like him and - - "

"Aw, Billy, he - - look at him! He's a - - what a fuck head!"

"Ba-ba-ba-ba-bow! Bow! Bow!" Al cried, delighting in his fantasy of mowing down battalions of Viet Cong.

"String along with me, Franco. You know that lake at the Meyers' farm?"

"What about it?"

"The boat."

Franco smirked, aware of what his friend had in mind.

■   ■   ■

"See, Al, get in the boat, shoot a hole in the bottom of it, we'll push the boat out, it'll sink, and you'll be in the club. Okay? It's your initiation."

"Hey-ull, yeah," Franco concurred.

"But why do I have to get inside the boat? I can hold the gun between my feet and shoot holes in it," Al wondered, barely able to see the Meyer house through the woods lining the hundred yard wide pond. The boys resumed their cautious walk to the end of the rotted, creaking pier. Billy jerked the aluminum boat's tether taut, stretched out an arm to help Al get aboard, and answered, feigning concern,

"Because you might shoot your foot off."

Al smiled and unsteadily seated his wiry frame in the fourteen foot long craft which was in actuality not much more than a wide, flat-bottomed canoe.

"Y'all don't want me to get hurt!"

Billy cringed with a momentary stab of remorse owing to the betrayal he and Franco were about to commit. Franco was busily untying the dock rope as Al pressed the gun muzzle against the bottom of the boat's hull.

Cr – rack!

Al straightened. His self-pleased smile vanishing when he saw what Franco was up to. "Whatcha doing?"

"It's okay. Shoot another hole in it."

"Franco's right, Al. Shoot it again. We can pull you in faster this way."

As water spurted onto his feet from the hole he had made, Al reloaded and again came the staccato sound echoing through the autumn woods,

Cr – rack!

"Sucker!" Franco teased, kicking the side of the hull so hard that the occupant tottered and quickly sat, nearly falling out.

"No!" Al begged as the boat, maneuvered solely by the kick's directive kinetics, rocked toward the pond's center. "Don't leave me!" He gazed, shocked, at the mooring rope dangling uselessly in the water where Franco had dropped it. Al's feet became cold and soaked. He repeated, "Don't leave me! It's sinking!"

Roaring with hilarity, Billy and Franco melted into the opposite wood line. Their legs found renewed strength when they heard a door slam nearby at the Meyer house.

■ ■ ■

The next day was a Thursday, and it brought cheerlessly dull monotone gray skies which, as dusk settled over Garden Pines subdivision, deepened into a chilly blackness. The boys didn't care. They were extremely impatient. Donald leaned back, the cold metal of the old tank gnawing at his skin through his brother's ragged denim jacket.

"She ain't going to do it, Franco!"

"Shut up, Doo-nell!" the elder Campbell barked, his fingers dancing with agitated anticipation on his father's binoculars. Billy sat cross-legged nearby on a sylvan rug of mulched brown leaves. He took off his sock cap and, with more than a touch of disdain, donned his cumbrous horned-rims.

"You should have called her right before we left the house. She might have forgot."

"I know it," Franco admitted. "What time is it getting to be? She said seven o'clock."

"Ten 'til, now." Billy doubted that Pammy would put on the show she had promised Franco at school. But, he had come along, just in case...

"There she is!"

"Damn it, Doo-nell! Not so loud! That damn man will hear you and come after us again!"

"Sorry, Franco."

"Sorry, hey-ull! Just keep your damn mouth shut and watch."

Without warning, there she was, raising the window shade. She was smiling, her ash-blonde hair toppling luxuriantly past her slightly freckled shoulders.

"Let me look!"

"Shut the hell up, Donald!" Franco's eyes were glued to the binoculars. "I'll let you look in a few minutes!"

Pammy swayed from side to side, unbuttoning her shoulder straps and stepping out of the sleeveless dress she had worn at school that day. She fingered her throat, cupped her apple-sized breasts and proceeded to quickly work her hands to her crotch, her hips and thighs convulsing in simulated intercourse. Faster and faster her pelvis pumped the air. Her head rolled around and around in ersatz ecstasy.

"I want to look, too! Now!" Donald implored.

"Shut up, pisser!" Franco hissed. "I ain't through!"

With great effort Billy glanced sideways. Franco held the binoculars in one hand and gripped his swollen penis in his other, matching Pammy's motions with his own strokes. Pammy unexpectedly turned to the side, stripping off her underwear. Then she kneeled, obscuring most of her torso from view.

"Damn! Now I can't see her big old titties!"

Franco's disapproval was forgotten when Pammy's long tongue poked out from between her overly rouged lips. Farther and farther she extended it, bobbing it up and down, a tantalizing, tasty, wet torment. She knew exactly what she was doing and what she was exciting her worshipping male audience to do, also.

She jumped to her feet and whirled like a well-heeled stripper to face the window and teasingly wagged her long adolescent tongue from side to side in her open mouth, a deliberate cascade of hot young female saliva falling from it to the floor which Billy wished he could be lying on to catch the sweet flow with his own open mouth.

"I can't stand this," Billy gulped. "I sure want to make out with her. Goddamn it, this is too much! I'm going to have to beat my damn meat, too."

"Uhhh! Uhhhh!" Franco moaned, falling to his knees while his seed spattered the crumbled forest carpet. The binoculars lay beside him, having been discarded a moment earlier. "Ahhh..." he sighed with the relief of release. "Feel goooood," he approvingly muttered, squeezing out a last milky white drop of semen and adding, "Poo-sy would be a lot better, though. I just got to foque her. Feeeeel reeeeeal goooood."

Donald scooped up the binoculars and offered,

"You want to watch first, Billy?"

"Nah, little bro'. Go ahead. I'll watch in a minute," Billy responded, carefully unzipping his jeans which had become unbearably tight in front.

■　　■　　■

"I'll go if I get drafted...but I sure ain't volunteering for no Viet-Sheet. Foque eet. All that sheet's going on over on the other side of the day-um world. They ain't invading us or nothing, so why in the hey-ull are we over there invading them?"

"Something's got to be done about the communists, Franco."

"Yeah, bro', that's what Daddy says. You know he's wanting to run for that state representative job again. He tries to be friendly and all that sheet, acting like he knows this and all that, but he don't know nothing about anything he says. He just wants to be a big shot. He says he likes so and so, but he don't, really. He lies about a lot of sheet. Are you going to the rally with your folks tonight?"

"Nah. Tonight is what they call an organizational meeting, whatever that means. Momma and my stepdad usually like for me to go, and it's a lot of fun, all the buttons, posters, bumper stickers you get to keep, and shit like that. You remember when your dad ran for state representative last time, and we helped with catering? We got to meet people that most folks get to see only on TV. That was really cool. I got a couple of state senators' autographs. You ain't going, either?"

"Nah, not this time. Foque eet. Come on over. I know where Daddy's done hid his naked women books, thems whats got really big titties. You can beeeat- yo'- meeeeat!! Feeeel goood, sheeety bro'!"

"Can't. I'm going to stay with Mr. And Mrs. Mills tonight. Boy, Mrs. Mills looks good. I'd rather beat off thinking about her, for sure."

"How old is she? She looks pretty good. I seen her a couple of times."

"She's about twenty-five, I reckon. She's always hugging and kissing on me, but not like I wish she would. I'm just a little punk kid to her."

"Maybe you could talk her into giving us some poo-sy. Feel good."

"I wish," Billy parried. "But back to what we were saying… we ought to support the president and win over there. You know, for the country. And I don't like these hippies running around. We even got a few of them here at Gilmore. Stepdad says if you choked one, fifty dicks would pop out of his throat."

"I don't like them hippie queers, neither, but, Bee-ly, we don't need to be over there in Viet-Shit. What good does shit like that do, fucking around in somebody else's day-um country? It ain't none of our business. Where was it your daddy died?"

"Korea," came the somber response. Billy's confident countenance instantly darkened. He dropped his fork onto the pressed vacuform plastic dinner tray holding his plate of school food. The noise in the cafeteria became impenetrable to Billy's ears as he tried to imagine what his father's voice must have sounded like… not like a Southerner such as himself or his mother, but still… Dad…. and a real Dad, at that.

Franco knew he had said the wrong thing, noticing the blankness in his friend's eyes.

"Sorry, bro', I didn't mean to ruin your appetite. You never got to know him, did you?"

"Uh-uh," Billy answered, shaking his head. "I was too little to… shit… I wasn't even born yet."

"Wasn't he a Marine? Some kind of sergeant or something?"

"First Lieutenant. Platoon leader. His last battle… they know he killed forty Red Chinese himself. No doubt about it. Momma said when I turn twenty-one, she'll give me his Congressional."

"Ain't that the highest medal you can get?"

"Yep," Billy answered, too softly for Franco to hear plainly.

■   ■   ■

Billy's doleful remembrance of his rambling lunch conversation with his best friend vaporized in the reverberations of the school bus's backfire. Several dozen elementary grade kids screamed with excited enthusiasm which continued as the blast echoed off of the buildings fronting the intersection. There, on the right, was the office of G. C. Campbell Homes, Inc., where the political meeting would be held in a few hours' time.

Gosh, if I could only go to the rally tonight, Billy wished. *Maybe later in the year...all that good Brunswick stew... Stepdad acts proud of me, although he won't say it, when I wear a bunch of candidate buttons... Yeah, I guess I like that. Can't wait...*

Billy speculated why Franco wasn't on the bus.

Bet he got put on detention again. He's always messing up... he never gets anything right.... Damn, I hate these ugly damn glasses... they're heavy as hell... they make me look like shit...

Billy removed his despised spectacles and gently massaged the grooved bridge of his nose with a thumb and forefinger, cursing the glasses anew as he thought about having parallel indentations on his nose for the rest of his life. Three seats forward, Pammy and her pesky little sister argued loudly over the ownership of a makeup kit mirror.

Who fucking gives a shit? He angrily wondered. *It doesn't mean shit!*

A prickly nervous sensation crept up from Billy's ankles to his knees, and higher to the pit of his stomach when he realized, with sudden alarm,

Lou's not on the bus, either! Oh, no...

Billy sighed, wondering why Franco always played any and every situation as stupidly as it possibly could be.

■ ■ ■

"Why didn't you meet me after sixth period and tell me?" Billy demanded. "You could have got really messed up bad! We could have both took him down."

"Ah, I'm alright, he just hit me a couple good licks. My upper lip's a little swolled up but besides that, I'm okay. Big Red come out of nowhere and made him quit. I got to say this. I owe him one."

"What's Lou look like?" Billy asked, trying to imagine Franco's lip. He didn't sound any different over the telephone.

"Ah, hell, I didn't even hit him once. Sumbitch's damn arms are so long. I couldn't get close enough to him to hit his ugly ass face."

"Da - - dadgum," Billy said, softening his intended expletive when his mother entered the kitchen.

"William," she interrupted, "Get your books and take your blue blanket with you. In case we're late, Mrs. Mills says you can sleep in their TV room."

Billy remembered the night last year when he and Mrs. Mills' cousin spent the night in the tiny cubicle, barely large enough for the color TV. Half the night, anyway. They had sneaked out, met Franco at the pipe, and rocked roofs until two or three A.M.

"Yes, ma'am," he said. "Franco, I got to go. Later, bro." Billy hung up the phone without waiting for a response. He smiled at Mrs. Capler, who did likewise. She looked ten years younger during the campaign functions. Her sapphire eyes sparkled. She could have easily passed herself off as a younger, healthier relative.

"You look real good, Momma."

"Thanks, Will," she said, surprising her son with both the shortened name and a curtsey. Mr. Capler also came into the kitchen, and except for the perpetual sunglasses, presented the image of a totally different person.

"'Bout ready, Betty baby?"

"I reckon," she informed him, eyeing her sharply clad husband with pleased bemusement.

"And you look real good, too, Step - - " Billy, curious about how his stepfather would react, finished his compliment with, "I mean, you look great, Dad."

Mr. Capler, surprised with his new title, gave a truncated laugh and stated,

"Well, thank you, boy. Thank you."

Why will this change? Billy agonized, heading upstairs to get his blue blanket. *Why does it have to change? What am I doing wrong? What is wrong with me?*

■   ■   ■

"Gosh, this is fun."

"What's fun? Being here alone with me on a lonesome Friday night?"

"Yeah... I mean no... I mean, yeah, but..." Billy stammered. The plump but attractive blonde with seductive sea-green eyes had really thrown him a verbal curve. He had worshipped Janet Mills for the entire three years she and her salesman husband Dwight had lived beside the Caplers, and Billy figured that she had to know it. He had to pass below the Mills house on the way to the pipe, and he couldn't help but think of her. How nice it was when she hugged him and kissed his ears! Billy loved it, even though it was torturous teasing, but this sounded different. Her directness was somewhat frightening.

Mrs. Mills laughed as she set the boy's drink on the bar. It was a half and half mixture of coke and sweet tea with an extra squirt of lemon juice. She looked at it with feigned curiosity and said,

"Woops, I forgot the taste test. I know how much you love my special tea, and I want it to be just right... for both of us." She raised the glass to her mouth and stirred the contents with her long pink tongue for two or three seconds, all the while studying the enraptured teen with her penetrating eyes.

All Billy could think of was how much he wished his lips could be the rim of that glass. The insides of his testicles felt like they were bubbling over with carbonated seltzer water. Before he realized it, he was sliding off the bar stool. His hands shot out and caught the counter's edge, preventing him from tumbling in embarrassment to the hardwood floor.

"Don't fall off the stool, sweetheart," she chortled. "Dwight won't be home until way, way late, and maybe not at all, tonight. I don't want you to be scared of me. You aren't, are you?"

Billy steadied himself on the stool and blustered, "Naaah," with a strained macho growl vaguely reminiscent of the type his stepfather made. He took a healthy draught of his coke-tea combination, hoping it would cool him off enough to erase his crimson blush even though he was trying desperately to catch the flavor of her mouth on the glass.

"So... how's tenth grade?"

"It's okay, I guess."

"I hated tenth grade. It sucked big dicks, to tell you the truth about it."

A shard of crushed ice spurted up into Billy's nasal cavity. *Did she just say what I think she said?*

"Bet you've got a pack of hot little girl friends," Janet ventured, intently studying the boy's face. Her pink lips turned up at their corners and she added, "Can't keep their hands off of you, can they?"

"None of them look half as good as you." Oh, nuts! Billy immediately grimaced. *How corny! I didn't mean to say that!*

"How sweet of you, Billy!" Janet cooed, obviously impressed. She came out from behind the bar and stripped off her white cashmere sweater to reveal a very thin blouse, thin enough to plainly advertise her bra style. She kept smiling and queried,

"Glad you've already done your homework?"

Billy nodded. "It was just a few math problems I had left. I didn't even need the book. I got it in my back pocket."

"You are so smart! Come on. I'll teach you crazy eights." Seeing Billy hesitate, she explained, "Crazy eights is a card game, Billy. And it's not strip poker!"

Clumsily, Billy attempted to shield his aroused condition with his left hand and carried his coke-tea mixture in his right. He could not take his eyes from her buttocks, aimed at him and so alluring as she bent over to clear the coffee table. *Wonder what they feel like? Are they hard or soft?* he mutely asked, sitting on the plush carpeted floor while she took a position across from him on her second-hand sofa.

"Now here's what you do," she directed, dealing herself and Billy eight cards apiece. The adolescent was thankful that her flirtatious tone had changed, but hoped that she would feed his expanding ego with another innuendo or two later in the evening. *What if she kisses me good night?* he suddenly wondered, trembling at the prospect of her lips wetly touching his.

"Billy, are you listening to me? You haven't heard the rules of the game! How can you play with me if you don't know how?"

■   ■   ■

Oh, my God! They're soft! Billy discovered, his fingers daring to wander, to lightly touch the cleavage bisecting Mrs. Mills' backside. Billy expected to be slapped and pushed away at any moment.

She had started the dance lesson with fast '50s Elvis tunes. *How the heck have we gotten to this?* Billy asked, mentally retracing the evening's events to the darkened living room awash with slow dance music.

"Mmmmm... Billy, you're a very good dancer. You haven't stepped on my feet once!" she whispered. Janet unlocked her fingers from his and threw her arms around his neck. She began to rub his back, telling him, "You're so tense, Billy. Bad day today? Hmmm?"

"Nah, not..." His words hung uselessly. *If she keeps this up, I'll cream in my pants!* he perceived worriedly. *Does she know I'm on the hard?*

"You're so - - stiff!" She tossed her head to clear the hair from her face and pressed her thighs more firmly into Billy's. Janet ceased her leisurely gyrations and ordered Billy,

"Hold still a minute, hon. Hmm-hmm, your shoulders feel like iron. You gotta relax, babe. Or do you lift weights? Bet you do. Your shoulders are growing big and strong enough for any lucky girl to hold on to."

"Oh, Mrs. Mills, that massage is great."

"Call me Janet tonight, sweetheart," she directed, followed by some words Billy didn't quite hear.

"What?"

"Your mother. Is she still making you feel guilty about liking girls?"

What a question! Billy studied Janet's face, so extra pretty in the moonlight coming through the windows. Billy had to force himself to concentrate so he could answer.

"Yeah. No matter who I like, there's always something wrong with her. And if she doesn't find something wrong with the girl, she cuts down her family. Or me. If nothing else, she takes it out on me. So I don't tell her nothing no more. Nothing!"

"Nothing... at all?"

"I can't. Never. Mrs. - - Janet, it's always my fault, no matter what. I can't - - "

"Poor baby."

Janet's mouth was also soft, but her lips pushed hard into his. Billy was stunned and his glands shifted into overdrive. Something entered Billy's mouth, wagged from side to side, then withdrew. Janet's face pulled away. Her hands gently rubbed his face, her thumbs digging slightly into the teenager's cheeks. Her tongue licked around her lips several times and she breathed out heavily, stating,

"You taste so good, Billy. You're not going to tell your mother I kissed you like that, are you?"

"No way!" Billy replied hastily, unable to control his quivering. He pulled her closer. "I used to dream about us doing this," panting as he added, "I - - I still do. A lot."

"Do you? Maybe I dreamed about you, too. You are so handsome."

"I am? Really?"

"Sure are. And I'm not worried about you saying anything about our kiss."

"I won't. I swear!"

"Mm-mm. I know you can keep a secret, hon. You've never told a soul I was a diabetic, have you?"

"Well, no, but, Jan - - Janet, that's nothing to be ashamed of. You're - - you're so - - - " Billy stammered, hesitant about saying the word, "- - sexy," but letting it out anyway.

Janet's sugary tongue returned, exploring Billy's inner mouth for over a minute while she moaned and burrowed her face into his.

Billy's knees began to buckle from this new, incredibly unimaginable pleasure.

"You're going to make us fall down, sweetheart. Let's sit down on the sofa."

They sat and Janet draped her right leg over Billy's lap. With one hand she cupped his head and with the other she unbuttoned his shirt and rubbed his stomach.

"Like it wet?"

"Uh-huh," Billy affirmed without having any idea of what she meant.

Janet lathered his face and neck with her skilled, slippery tongue, lapping on his lips repeatedly.

"I love to lick and lick and lick a man. It makes him beg like a dog. I'm very dominant. You just lay there and enjoy this. Ever had the come jerked out of you? I'm good at it. Real good. If you beg me enough, I might even suck it right out of your balls. I know you'd like that."

Billy was overcome by her aggressive onslaught, sliding under her into a prone position. Her nimble fingers unzipped his pants and seized control of his love muscle, pumping it with surprising gentleness.

She eyed his penis in the semidarkness, remarking,

"You've even got a handsome dick."

Billy couldn't speak. Overwhelmed by her actions and the heavenly flavor of her flood of sweet saliva, he lay helpless, unable to avert the eruption of his geyser. For six seconds that seemed like a minute, he felt as if he was coming apart with an ecstasy beyond description.

"Whoa!" Janet said loudly, aiming Billy's penis toward the living room's tenebrous interior. The essence of the boy's masculinity spurted over the coffee table and splashed the woolen carpet. Billy lay crumpled and drained to exhaustion, gargling Janet's spit.

"You sure had a lot of it in you. Don't you feel better getting it out?"

"Yes, ma'am," he wheezed.

"Always polite. Billy, you are so sweet." Janet stood beside the spent and vanquished boy, firmly centering the sole of the patent leather flat on her right foot over his bare navel and simulating walking on him.

"I'll have you back up in no time, honey boy. You will become a man tonight," she demanded, grinding her smooth-bottomed size seven into his midsection so hard he felt his intestines spread.

"Leaving my shoeprints on you means you belong to me, sweet cake."

She discarded her blouse. It fell unceremoniously onto the semen-splattered coffee table, followed by the lace-lined bra. Janet guided her pear-shaped breasts close to Billy's face, her subjugating foot still mashing him into the sofa's softness.

"You think my tongue tastes good? Try these. They're luscious. Suck them while I stomp your balls flat."

■　　■　　■

He knew he was about to awaken. Images of Janet's body atop his returned freshly to his hormone-drenched brain. His eyes opened and he saw, as he remembered impaling Mrs. Mills from below, that he was alone in the tiny TV room. *How did I get here?* He foggily wondered.

"Come on, sport! Your momma just called! She wants you to come on home to do your chores!" Mr. Mills, putting on a blue paisley tie, said from the doorway.

"Does he have time for breakfast, Dwight?"

"'Fraid not, Jan-Jan. What's the matter, Billy? Don't remember where you are?"

"Yes sir! Yes sir!" Terrified, Billy hastily dressed, expecting gunfire, or worse, at any second. He heard the squeeze of air being pushed out of a bar stool, then Mr. Mills' voice, followed by that of Mrs. Mills. Billy held his breath. Her words were unintelligible but her tone was nonchalant.

Thank God! Thank God! Billy gratefully discerned. *He doesn't know! I got to get out of here before - - if she says something - - he'll cut my dick off - - and my nuts!*

"Don't you want some toast for the road?"

"No, sir. Thanks anyway. I got to get on home!" Billy replied, ignoring the ache in his full bladder and hitting the side door almost at a run, his blue blanket completely forgotten.

"Billy!" Janet called as the youth's speeding feet touched the Mills' gravel driveway. He reluctantly spun about to see her comely round face. She flicked her tongue from corner to corner of her mouth and with feigned innocence invited him to,

"Come again... and I mean real soon."

6

OCTOBER 16

FRANCO FINGERED HIS enlarged upper lip gingerly. The swelling was already much reduced but his hatred still burned hotly. He smiled with the thought of his cunning ersatz revelation to Pammy, but not too widely. His lip was very sore.

"I told Pammy we was fighting over her. She thought that was cool."

"Why'd you lie, bro'?"

"Might get her to liking me enough to give me some poo-sy. Like I say - - feel good. Hey, might as well try. You won't get none if you don't. You know it?"

"Better use a rubber."

"Shit, naw. I hate them damn things. Look at that. There's a damn rubber right there beside your foot. Some nasty son of a beech has done used it and blown it up like a damn balloon. Must have been a damn nigger."

"Aw... you don't know that."

Franco surveyed the area around them. The kids called the place The Glade, just a few yards down the street from Gilmore High at the end of a dusty road, more accurately termed a path. Here anything and everything went on. Shattered beer bottles lay about and used condoms were in abundance, weekend trophies of pubescence. Some had been proudly hung on the bushes.

A female blue jay swooped down to investigate the boys, then, convinced they were no threat to her nest, darted between some low pine limbs. Curious, and sounding somewhat offended, Franco asked,

"How come you're always taking up for them niggers?"

"Franco! Somebody's coming!"

"Is it Lou?" Franco demanded to know, tossing the remainder of his Winston onto a pile of weather-cracked tires. "It's gonna end up different than it did the other day, bro'!"

Billy strained through his hastily donned horned-rims to see up the path. In a few seconds the three noisy teens approaching them were identifiable.

"Nah, it's Johnny Kimbrell and a couple of eighth graders. Did you tell them about the fight?"

"Uh-uh, naw," Franco denied, brandishing Billy's newly opened knife. "Damn Lou kept saying he was sorry and all that shit. I told him I'd meet him here again and I'd kill him. He's a chicken shit. He knew you'd be here too and we'd both show 'em all something! We'll kill him, sheety bro', won't we?"

"It's three-thirty, bro'. He ain't going to show up."

"He's a chicken shit!"

"Chicken shit or not, he's already got what he wanted. Big Red let him into his little in-group. Don't you see? He don't care nothing about bothering you now."

"Hey, y'all!" cried out a newcomer. "Where's Lou and his bunch? And Big Red?"

"Yeah," another chimed. "We want to see Big Red Pinson! Tough guy!"

"They ain't coming!" Franco boastfully responded. "Lou knew I'd kill him with this." Franco slashed the air with several figure eights. "He knows he can't beat me in a knife fight."

"Gol-lee shit," the shortest eighth grader murmured, very impressed by Franco's dexterous showboating.

"We'll wait a few more minutes, okay, bro'? Say, three-forty-five, then we'll get on home."

"How 'bout four? He might had to take him a long shit or something."

Billy assented with a mumble and turned away. He didn't have the heart to tell his friend that he had seen Lou heading for their bus after the last bell of the day, but he did not relish the prospect of explaining to his mother why he was so late getting home, either. *What would she say?* he conjectured. *Been at the pool hall again? Hanging out at the college to watch all the little hot tails?* What would he be accused of this time? And if he even mentioned The Glade, it would be instant trial and conviction for drinking beer with older kids. Forlornly, Billy decided, *Who cares? Why not wait? Franco's got an audience, a regular fan club from the looks of it, and he's having the time of his life. Besides, it keeps him from aggravating me to ask Janet to give him some, too. No way...*

■　　■　　■

"It's almost five o'clock, William! Where have you been? I've been worried sick about you! You don't care about anyone but yourself!"

Billy halted and looked at his mother. Her face evinced more lines than usual. She did love him, that he accepted, but he had constant trouble dealing with how she showed it. *Damn it, Momma, why do you do this to me?* he wanted to say.

"Momma, what do you want me to say?" was what came out.

"William, I want you to at least call me. There's a pay phone at the pool hall - - "

"I wasn't at the pool hall, Momma, remember, I promised I wouldn't go there any more? Anyway, I don't have a dime. I never have a dime!"

"Go on! Just go on up to your room!" she spat, waving him past. "You don't love me enough to give me a goddurn phone call, you don't have enough consideration - - "

"I told you, I didn't have a dime! You got to have a dime to make a phone call!"

"Lower your voice, William. I know you were carrying on after school with that grubby little Sharee Post, weren't you?"

"What?" Billy, astonished, stood motionless, his mouth agape.

Mrs. Capler's expression reshaped itself from one of hurt into one of smugness. She took in another menthol puff and elaborated, spouting smoke as she did so,

"Well... somebody saw you. You and Sharee behind the gym. You two were... making out, all over each other like a couple of dogs in heat... disgraceful and... well, sordid."

"You have got to be kidding me."

"There you go. Somebody saw you."

"Who?"

"Well... I got eyes everywhere. People tell me stuff. That's more than my own only son will do."

"Momma, that wasn't me. Anyhow, Sharee's a good girl. She's not a slut."

"William," she uttered, slowly for effect, "It's a matter of... social standing. She isn't on your... economic level. You should date up... not down. People know you by the company you keep."

Billy snorted angrily. Mrs. Capler had him on the defensive, and she wasn't about to let off the pressure.

"No, you don't understand, William. Nice girls don't let boys feel them up behind the gym like little white trash."

"That couldn't have been Sharee. I saw her working in the library after sixth period. She works there until four-thirty every day."

"Uh-huh, so where've you been for the last two hours?"

The screen door shuddered under the rapping knuckles of Franco Campbell. Mrs. Capler's accusing visage wilted just slightly.

"Come in, Franco," she practically barked. "What can we do for you?"

"I won't be but a minute, Mrs. C.," he said, very aware of her inhospitable mood.

"Come in, bro," Billy beckoned, thankful for his appearance.

Mrs. Capler's daggerlike gaze and the words "company you keep" hung in Billy's mind all the way to his room. Franco had to give his opinion,

"Gee, bro'- - don't get mad, but - - "

"I know," Billy stated, draping his jacket over his desk chair. "It's okay."

"Your moo-ther sure is foqued up. I mean, really, really foqued up. I heard all of that bool sheet she was saying. Ain't none of it true."

Billy chuckled. Franco's deliberate mispronunciations were usually spoken in an attempt to soften a hard point. Billy never tired of hearing them. Sometimes they were unbelievably funny... sheet for shit, deek for dick, foque for...

"I know she is, bro'. You don't have to apologize."

"I gotta get on home, but I had to tell you again... I hate Lou. I hate that mo-la- - - hey, you know, we laughed at Doo-nell for talking about burning his house down. Hell, let's do it. You know I'll never tell nobody. Burn him up! Keel heem!"

Suddenly warm, Billy cracked open the window over his desk. He noticed a tear at the lower right corner where the screen mesh joined the aluminum frame. *Better tape it down later*, he resolved, *or Momma will surely blame me for it.*

"That would be a good Halloween trick. Or are you talking like… really doing it?"

"Naw. I mean it, bro'. He needs to die."

No longer distracted by the torn screen, Billy felt fear gnawing at his insides as he realized his friend was very serious.

"What if somebody innocent gets hurt?" he barely heard himself ask.

"Foque all of them. They're all sheet. We can sneak into their crawlspace tonight and torch them up. Let's sneak out tonight about midnight. Meet me at the pipe and we'll go do it. All you gotta do is get in the crawlspace and set a fire under where the kitchen is. The cops will all think it was a day-um accident like somebody left the oven turned on. Okay?"

This is crazy! Billy told himself, his stomach twisting as if in rebellion from having been overfilled with raw peanuts. *I got to get him out of here! Momma's already pissed off enough at me and I don't need for her to hear him talking like this!*

"Okay, bro'. We'll burn him up, but not tonight. My stepdad's going to Richmond soon and I have to really watch myself."

"I heard Daddy say you can get somebody to do anything you want done, long as you got the money for it. Too bad we can't pay somebody to torch him up."

"Yeah, that would be nice," Billy falsely agreed, trying to diminish Franco's rage. "We'll talk about it tomorrow."

"We'll plan it right and do it this Friday night so we can sleep late without anybody getting suspicious. Hey-ull, I'll do it by my day-um self if I have to."

Franco spun about to leave, his air of determination frightening Billy. Speechless, Billy watched him walk out of sight, closing his eyes in relief as he heard the screen door shut with his friend's departure.

■　■　■

While visions of sugar plums danced in his head…

No, they're not sugar plums. Billy scrutinized the spheroid scarlet objects descending from a bright and cloudless sky. Ten… fifteen… dozens, maybe a hundred… they sound like classical music… almost like that Beethoven stuff they played at the auditorium last month… what in the…

Billy… need you… friend…

"Who is it? Where are you?"

Billy stood alone in the center of the road, directly over the pipe. Nothing moved in the bushes or on the surrounding lawns. "Where are you?" he asked again.

Need you… Billy… friend…

"Oh, shit…" Billy jerked off his horned-rims. They'd sat so uncomfortably on his nose that they'd given him a headache, the kind of piercing pain that sets in behind the eyes for a day's duration. "God almighty… I hate having to wear these…"

Gift... Billy... gift...not wear more!

Billy's fingers opened, and he watched his glasses fall.

"Ah, fuck," he uttered, hoping they wouldn't be scratched by impacting the street. He'd never hear an end to it if they became scratched or an arm snapped off.

They never hit the ground. The arms, then the lenses, dematerialized without a trace. Above, the discs drew nearer. Billy could make out fine details on their short wings and underbellies.

"Hold it... I can't see this good without..."

Not ready... not ready... friend...

The saucers dissipated as the glasses had. Their symphonic harmonies evaporated with them. For a few moments all was quiet.

No, not ready... yet. Gift...take gift... not wear things on face any more... ever....

The cool sheets soothed his whole body. Billy stretched and rolled, breathing deeply.

"Whooo," he exhaled, thinking, *I've had some screwy dreams, but this... Still,* he reflected, *the dream had felt really good, like anticipation of something longed for, but what?*

Billy faintly heard sirens. In a few seconds their mournful wailing hushed.

Billy thought he had begun to dream again, hoping to fall back into the previous one, and lapsed once more into a muddy slumber.

Gift. Now take gift! Take now!

Stabbing pain behind his eyes prompted Billy to partially waken. Something moved on his chest.

Rémy was poised atop the blanket. He wasn't moving, but his posture was changed. He wasn't in his sideways-facing stance. To the right, intermittent flashes of red danced on the window panes, highlighting the little manikin's expressionless face.

Yeah, Rém, Billy groggily thought. *Your head's looking forward. Good boy...*

Gift... You have it now... You will be ready... soon...

Billy rolled toward the wall, further shaking away the effects of torpor. He thought, *Thank God my headache's gone... Sheee... even that was a dream.*

Billy sat up, and his bedcovers toppled onto his lap. The early twilight was as dull and gray as it ever was, but there was something extra this Saturday morning. The cyclic red flashes were still there on the window panes.

The boy roused himself to full consciousness and surveyed the neighborhood. Over the hill, a wide column of black smoke curved upward into the stratosphere. Someone, somewhere close by was in some kind of trouble, and serious trouble at that. A frigid and humid breeze crossing through the netting in the window screen carried a tangy odor of burning building materials into Billy's nostrils. He tried to close the window as quietly as possible and spied a familiar shape at the edge of the sill.

"Crap. I thought I put you up last night." The window's closing thud was loud. Billy feared it would surely wake up his mother, but he was more concerned with hiding Rémy than with the certain accusation of masturbation. The boy rapidly replaced his favorite plastic man, being careful not to drop him and make more noise. A small dark form wrapped up in the string mass atop his desk caught his attention.

"Blue boy," he recognized, untangling the little spaceman from the oddly wet, thin cotton coils. His left arm hung much lower than Billy knew it should. "When did I bend your..."

No base! He wasn't standing on his flat base! Rémy, Louie, and two kneeling soldiers were the only ones who didn't have bases! Where was Blue boy's base?

And where the hell are your pistols?

Billy, with great care, dislodged the paperbacks concealing the other dolls. Fingering each member of the plastic platoon, he found Blue boy's base. It was so cleanly separated that it appeared as if he had simply stepped off of it.

"I know I didn't cut this off. Well... it is over ten years old... I reckon it could break off... maybe the pistols somehow fell out or broke, too... hey... Little Yaller's bazooka's gone... how did... oh, shit..."

Where the hell is Louie?

Billy eased the books back into place, flipped Blue Boy's severed base onto his bed and put his glasses on, wondering if he'd gotten up during the night and done things he couldn't recall. *Got to find Louie,* he was certain, *or Momma will throw him away.*

Gift. Why couldn't he get that word out of his mind?

Opaque fuzziness filled his field of vision. For a tenth of a second a sharp pain touched the rear of his eyes.

"Oh! Crap!" he sputtered, squinting in inexplicable surprise.

Gift is yours! Not wear things you hate any more!

What the hell is going on with me? Alarmed, Billy removed the horned-rims. Outside, through the lifting haze of fog and smoke, the neighborhood's details were outlined in twenty-twenty clarity.

Gift.

"Am I going nuts? Am I still dreaming?" Billy slapped his jaws. He looked out again into the gathering light.

"No! This is real! I can see perfect!"

Billy tested the evidence. Spectacles on, cloudiness on. Take them off and, *Yeah,* he thought, smiling. *This is the last time I ever take your god-awful-ugly ass off of my face.*

"William, did you hear the fire engines?" Mrs. Capler's skeletal form trudged into the room, her bedroom shoes flapping on her heels. She searched the horizon. "It looks like somebody's house up the hill is on fire."

"Fire?" With apprehension mounting, Billy remembered, *Franco... Lou...*

7

October 21

GOOSEBUMPS CARPETED BILLY'S skin and the cold wind swept under his plain brown jacket. As he pedaled past the Casses' driveway he noticed Jimmy and one of his sisters on their front porch. Sara was looking toward the smoke pillar, now steamed white by the fire department's aggressive water assault. Jimmy stood with an arm hooked around one of hers. His unsightly right eyelid was closed and greenish blue, hiding the mutilation underneath. Jimmy's equally inutile left orb rotated wildly as it had done since his birth.

Billy's foggy breath surged from his lungs and he topped the hill's crest. He kicked a heel back, bringing his vintage 1957 Deltawasp bicycle to a stiff halt.

It was the Jones house.

Rather, what was left of the yellow wood frame home. In the front yard Billy counted three fire engines, two rescue-ambulance vehicles, a chief's car, two county deputy's cars, and half a dozen sheet-covered bodies.

A black-coated fireman emerged from the gutted shell, tears etching twin rivers which flowed through the layer of soot masking his sobbing countenance. In his arms he cradled a small sky blue bundle.

"Oh, God, Franco... you asshole..." Billy's Deltawasp fell over onto the asphalt, clanging loudly. The numb boy stepped into the aggregation of crisscrossing hose lines, their woven cotton jacketing straining to the bursting point, and watched the firefighter hand the dead child to a rescue man. The pair helplessly shook their heads with sullen sobriety.

Billy coughed up sweet-tasting phlegm, the same type of carbon-permeated mucus the firemen were publicly expunging from their sinuses. The boy's stare fixed on the six bodies lying in a row between a pumper engine and an ambulance.

"Look out, son! This place is dangerous. You'll get hurt here!" a fireman warned, using a hooked pole to snap blackened, smoldering boards off of the ruined front wall. Dazed, Billy veered toward the bodies.

A cold burst of wind lifted the sheet off of the corpse closest to Billy. Lou Jones' lifeless form lay roasted pink and bent, with huge yellow rips in the skin. His only clothing was a charred remnant of cotton underwear. His mouth was open in a silent scream, the hair he had so assiduously tended totally singed away and the skull blotched and bare. His teeth jutted from baked gums, their roots showing hideously in the blue-grey haze coating the neighborhood in a blanket of stink and death.

Reflexively, Billy recoiled, tripping over a hose connection coupling. Billy bounced, wheeled around in mid-air and attempted to run, tripping twice more, wetting and staining his denim jeans with dew-drenched grass. Voices barked,

"Get away from there, boy!"

"I told you, go on, son, you'll get hurt!"

"Get out of the yard, kid! This is a fire scene!"

Billy mentally cursed, *Goddamn you, Franco, goddamn you! This is the worst thing you've ever done!*

Neighbors on their lawns and at their windows watched the drama with morbid curiosity. Mrs. Clayton's mouth and eyes opened with what seemed like a reaction to her husband's comment. Old man Folkes, next door, alternated his interest between a bowlful of bran flakes, the tragedy, and the morning newspaper. Yet, none of them would cross that invisible border marking the Jones property. They stood there in their housecoats and curls, tee shirts and robes, with ogling, inquisitive faces begging answers to unspoken and unbearably morbid questions.

They were looking at Billy also. The boy could sense their comments:

Get out of there, stupid kid.

Go on, boy. You're too young to see this.

Why aren't you home watching cartoons?

Getting your kicks, kid?

Ain't like the movies, is it, boy?

"Fuck you. Fuck all y'all," Billy gasped coarsely, the stench of charred human flesh clawing at his nasal mast cells. *What the hell am I going to do about this?* he agonized. *I can't tell on Franco... no matter what... but this...*

Nearby, the Jones' collie jerked his chain taut upon recognizing Billy. Sheppie's body quaked all over. He paced furtively in front of his doghouse, whining pathetically. His paws rapidly and nervously churned up the well-worn earth, kicking up popcorn-sized mud balls.

Billy staggered over and hugged him. The terrified pet responded by licking the boy's face in gratitude and imprinting mud all over the front of Billy's jacket.

"Sssh, Sheppie. Sssh. Franco used to say you were the only Jones worth half a shit, and only because you're adopted. Now you're the only one left." Billy squeezed Sheppie tightly to him, trying to comfort the both of them. The wretched animal's shudders vibrated through Billy. "Sssh, Sheppie, it's gonna be all right. It's - - "

Behind Sheppie's rear legs lay a mangled blue object.

Billy's soul froze.

■　■　■

Rick Wayman knew he needed to scoot the boy out of the area. When he saw him trip repeatedly as he retreated from the dead Joneses, Wayman figured the kid was out of his hair. But then Billy had gone to the dog. *Time to go, son.*

The detective's dun trench coat flapped brusquely as he walked up behind Billy Beaudet. Tall, forty-three years old, showing some gray at the temples, Rick Wayman looked very much the authoritative figure striding through the yard, a moving piece of order on a puzzle board of absolute chaos.

He had seen it so many times both in World War II as an infantryman serving in Italy and in the two decades he had afterwards served as a city policeman. *A boy gets traumatized and nine times out of ten he'll go to an animal, a pet. Well,* Wayman shrugged, *this one's no different...*

Billy's back slammed hard into Wayman's chest. Surprised, Wayman grabbed him and pulled him away from Sheppie. The dog resumed barking and snapping, fearing that the detective's purpose was to hurt the boy.

"Whoa, son. Take it easy."

"It's Louie! It's Louie! I'd know him anywhere - - there's no way there could be another one like him - - see - - " Billy's wide blue eyes glazed in near-panic and his hands wrung uselessly. The investigator patted the teen's shoulders.

"Calm down, son."

"No! No, sir, I can't! If it is Louie - - then - - "

"I'm sorry, son, but it is your friend Louie Jones. Who are you?"

"I'm - - I'm - - " Billy dared to take another glance at the chewed up chunk of plastic. "I ain't nobody, sir."

"Okay, kid. Calm down." Wayman's presence was magnetic. Billy, seeking the man's approval, swallowed hard and breathed deeply, trying to comply.

"Sir? Who are you?"

"Name's Rick Wayman. I'm a cop. Do you need a ride home or anything? You can't stay here."

"No, sir. No, sir. Thanks anyway." The air was thick, leaden, and Billy stumbled through it as if it was physically resisting him. *Don't look back!* He reminded himself. *That guy's a cop! He'll get suspicious! That couldn't really be my legionnaire, could it? I wouldn't have, I couldn't have done this... could I?*

Wayman knelt and rubbed the collie's neck. Sheppie's whines grated the detective's ears.

"Weird kid," he told the uncomprehending dog as they both watched Billy pick up his bike and mount it. Another man in plainclothes perhaps twenty years younger than Wayman walked up behind them and informed the detective,

"The fire marshal says it probably started under the house in the crawlspace. He found what's left of a one gallon or so gas can turned over. He's studying the burn progression pattern now."

Wayman nodded to his young partner, a man radiating energy and enthusiasm. "Well, Paul, you might have here your first arson case as an inspector. Ah, hell, I hate multiple homicides."

■   ■   ■

"There's a lot of day-um people's got them army men, bro'. Me and Doo-nell had a bunch of them once. Ain't no telling who the hell's it is. How do you know it's yours? And why would you take it with you to burn a day-um house down?"

"How do you explain my Louie being gone?"

"Louie?" Franco's face wrinkled.

"I mean, if I did it, why did I take him with me? How'd I get out of and back into the house without Momma hearing me? Am I going crazy?"

"Maybe your moo-ther throwed him out."

"Hah - - she'd have thrown them all out. And how come that other one was off his foot piece? What the hell is going on?"

"Hey-ull, I don't know. I don't know nothin' 'bout nothin'. Aw, foque eet!"

Donald barged into their large upstairs bedroom. Franco acknowledged his coming with,

"Get the hell out of here, Doo-nell!"

"Why?" Donald wanted to know, smiling a greeting at Billy sitting on the lower bunk.

"Donald!" When Franco used his brother's name properly, he meant business.

"Shit on you!" the younger Campbell angrily snapped, slamming the door behind him.

"Thanks, Franco." Billy watched his friend open a window so he could smoke undetected. "This is serious shit. A little kid doesn't need to hear this kind of shit."

"Hey-ull, yeah. Like I say, foque heem. I do hate it that the rest of them got burned up, though. I didn't know there was so many of them day-um Jone-shits."

"Lou's uncle and his family were staying there. They're - - were - -from Kentucky. I heard Momma tell Mrs. Wolfe on the phone. Damn, I wish I hadn't seen Lou. Man, he was really fucked up. And the smell! Momma made me take a shower and change clothes when I got home. She said she might have to throw the clothes away, because the stink might not come out."

Donald again crashed in and headed for the tiny TV sitting on the floor in a corner.

"Damn it, Donald!"

"Shit on you! I want to watch cartoons! Momma said for you to come downstairs any damn way. Want to watch cartoons with me, Billy?"

"Nah, thanks, little bro'. I got to go home and look for something."

"What for, Donald? You tell on me for running you off, you little pisser?"

"Nope," Donald replied matter-of-factly, turning on the television to fill the room with Saturday morning squelch. "There's some guys downstairs that want to see you. Might be from school about you skipping classes all the time. Daddy said you'd get in trouble with the - - uh - - the - - "

"Truant officers?" Billy offered.

"Yeah, that's it," Donald confirmed emotionlessly. "And one of them's some old turd. Looks mean."

Franco arced his half-smoked cigarette out of the open window and asked Billy,

"Foque 'em. Wanna cut hell? I don't give a day-um about them whatchacallits wanting to see me. We can cut hell right out of the window."

"Better not. They'll just come back later," Billy said, heading for the wide beige-carpeted steps which led downstairs. Franco grumbled, trailing him. Billy added, "I got to get on home, bro."

"Come on over later."

"If I can." Billy turned into the kitchen and stopped cold, his neck hair stiffening at the sight of the tall plainclothes investigator.

"Go on, Billy," Franco ordered.

Rick Wayman's eyes squinted in recognition.

"Well, well... so which one of you boys is Franco?"

8

October 22

"GRAMMAW?"

The elder Mrs. Capler's slow but steady gait halted and her gray head turned to reveal a wrinkled brow. She detected a thread of desperation laced within Billy's inquiry.

"It's something very important, isn't it, Billy?" she returned, speaking with hard-earned wisdom visibly etched into her septuagenarian features.

Beyond them the Caplers sat in the kitchen eating their Sunday lunch. Billy's grandmother had just taken an old blue sweater from the cupboard locker and had lain it on the small table there in the foyer. The boy involuntarily glanced in the direction of the kitchen. Grammaw Capler smiled comfortingly, reminding him, lowly,

"You know whatever we say stays with us."

"Well, Grammaw, I was thinking. Uh, if you pray a lot and all that shit - - I mean - - stuff - - "

The old lady could not help but smile more broadly. She'd been through a similar conversation forty years earlier. She hoped that what she anticipated saying would have a more beneficial effect on Billy than it had had on Jack Capler. Maybe, she conjectured, this one would in time become the preacher she so earnestly desired in the family.

"Yes, Billy. You should pray every day. Every chance you get. It never hurts."

"Well, uh… if you pray to God for Him to kill your enemies, will He do it?"

"Whooee - - you threw me a curve ball there. I didn't expect that. But the Bible has an answer."

"Where in it? What does it say?"

"In the Gospels. Jesus said… the best way to destroy your enemy is to make him your friend."

"But, some people, you just can't, Grammaw. Some people are just too rotten."

"It takes time, son. Rome wasn't built in a day."

"I wish it could work, but things just don't. Not that way, not in real life."

"That's what Jack said, too, a long time ago, and it's what he still says. Just between us, is he still calling you those hateful names?"

"No, ma'am. He hasn't called me Little Lord Fauntleroy or Dolly Boy in, I guess, a year now."

"Good. I used to fuss after him when he'd say those things."

"One day he'll regret it. He'll get old, need me, and I won't be there."

"Oh, I think you will. I hope you and him and your mother can settle all your differences. It's so hard being your age. Especially these days… with the war getting worse and all this immorality and meanness in the world."

"But… Grammaw?"

"Hmm?"

"Can… will God kill your enemies if you pray for Him to?"

"Well, He did it in the old days for the Israelites. But Jesus came and he told us in no uncertain terms that we are to - - "

"Mom!" intruded the voice of Billy's mother.

"Yes, Betty?"

"Come on back in here. You've got to hear this!"

"I'm coming, Betty," she told her, adding with a whisper to Billy, "Get rid of whatever is bothering you. Sometimes you don't know what it is, but once you do, get rid of it. Even if it hurts."

■　■　■

"Billy is so bright, Betty… Jack… but he needs guidance."

"He doesn't want to listen to us. He's hardheaded like all young 'uns are these days."

"Betty, he needs you. And you, Jack, you completely ignore him."

"Mmph," Capler came back neutrally, his attention riveted to the cars racing across the television screen. "Dadgummit, he let him get the lead. He can't win the race now."

"When I was a teenager, kids were tough. Kids these days are… soft… like jellyfish."

"I don't think so, Betty. The needs stay the same. Times change."

"I beg to differ, Mom. Times don't change… people change."

Behind the door in the next room, Billy kept his face predictably buried in his grandmother's fragile copy of *The Odyssey*, but his ears stayed cocked in the direction of the adults. He breathed lowly,

"Thanks for trying, Grammaw, but all you've managed to do is get me a really bad lecture later."

"He's just… immature," he then heard his mother say.

The doorbell rang. Billy could tell by the footsteps that his beloved grandmother had arisen and was ambling to the side door.

"Oh, Lord," Betty Capler spat. "It's that old goddurn nigguh."

"J. D. Davis?" Mr. Capler asked. "He's all right."

"He's making his door to door… begging rounds again. He could get some kind of a job. Gateway or Helping Hands hires a bunch of retarded people who are… trainable."

"I ain't too sure J. D.'s retarded. He pushes his little grocery cart around, collects cans and bottles and sells them. He's his own man, his own boss…"

"He'll never… have… anything."

"Well, maybe he doesn't want much. He eats. He's not starving. He doesn't have the problems most people do. He might be a lot smarter than most people."

"Jack… he's not a… productive member of his community."

"Productive? It's his life. He can live it any way he wants."

Good for you, Stepdad! Billy silently congratulated. *Bravo! You do surprise me sometimes. Keep it up!*

Mr. Davis's baritone laughter caused Billy to smile. The man said earnestly,

"Thank you so much, Miz Capler! This here is a sure fine sweater! And it's so big! I'm a-gonna put it on right now! Thank you so much!"

"I'll say this for him, Jack. He's grateful for what he does get."

How about that? Billy's eyebrows lifted. *Good for you, too, Momma! Maybe you can keep it up and - -*

"That's more than young 'uns these days are. Kids today… have… too much. They don't appreciate nothing!"

Billy frowned, his mother's painfully acidic words lingering in his ears. The teen, still sitting, craned his neck and saw, through a front window, the gentle, frosty-haired old man contentedly pushing his cart down the driveway.

■ ■ ■

We've gotten this far. Maybe she won't say anything about it, Billy hoped. The Buick Wildcat wheeled onto the main road leading to Garden Pines and Mrs. Capler said the words her son had dreaded since leaving Grammaw's house five minutes earlier.

"William… what goes on in our household is nobody's business but our own."

"Not even Grammaw's?"

"No, William," she made plain, glaring through her horridly odiferous tobacco smoke cloud. "Not even Grammaw's. If you've got a… problem… you know you can come to me or, if it's a… male thing… you can come to Stepdad with it."

"Umph," grunted Capler, the translation of which Billy read as: *No, not now. Not ever. Don't bother me.* His stepfather's huge head swiveled right and left, and the boy read the action as pretending to be concentrating on the traffic, now sparse and not warranting that level of actual caution… or so it seemed to Billy, who told himself,

Yeah, and get put down again.

■ ■ ■

Even if it hurts, she said yesterday, Billy thought, remembering his grandmother's sage advice. Marilyn and Marilee, the eight-year-old Squeed girls, and Al Gates were with him at the bus stop, a misty rain chilling them all to the bone. Billy couldn't keep his eyes off of the trash can flanking the Caplers' driveway. Rémy and the other little fellows lay in a crushed paper grocery sack near the top of the can where Billy had sorrowfully consigned them the night before. *Get rid of it. Even if it hurts.*

No! Need you, Billy... friend...

What is this? Billy grimaced. *Why can't I quit feeling this in my head? They need me? The little boys need me? Ah, sheee- yit.... I must be going crazy. They're just...*

Al broke Billy's reverie.

"What are we doing on Halloween night?"

"Huh?"

"Are we going rocking houses or trick-or-treating next week? We can do both, can't we, Billy?"

"I don't know, Al," Billy answered, in anguish over whether or not to fetch his figurines. The school bus was visible at the top of the next street. In mere seconds it would be too late. Billy looked across the pavement at the windows in his house. Was she watching?

"Fuck it!"

"Fuck what?" Al asked, grinning at his own vulgarity. "We gonna fuck some girls tonight?" he added, trying to irritate the Squeed twins who had no idea what he was talking about and cared nothing for anything the boy said anyhow.

Billy didn't elaborate. He dashed to the trash can and, not daring to see if his mother was watching, extracted the crumpled grocery sack and secreted it inside his cheap jacket. Returning to the stop as the bus approached, he felt the enclosed figures through the paper to ensure he had retrieved the correct sack. His expression showed relief.

"What you got, Billy?" Al asked in his eager-beaver manner.

"Ah - - stuff to make wine with," he answered, explaining, "Stepdad leaves some of the, uh, the ingredients and I store them in my locker at school."

The Squeed girls stared. Al maintained his grin and gave them a very impromptu elaboration.

"See, Billy's dad makes homemade wine. We drink it all the time, don't we, Billy? We're gonna get drunk on it tonight, too, ain't we?"

"Sure," Billy popped back, much to Al's delight. The Squeed twins boarded first, and Al followed Billy, who quickly spotted his best friend.

Billy sat by Franco, who snarled when Al joined them.

"Why don't you go on back yonder, you leetle queer?"

"I'm not a queer," Al defensively stated, his face exposing his self-satisfaction with the lie he'd told the Squeeds. He went further, "And I didn't tell on y'all that day y'all shoved me out in that boat."

"Got to hand it to you, Al," Billy helpfully said. "You were smart enough to ditch the nail gun in the lake, get to shore - - "

"That lake was cold!"

"Uh-huh, and even though you were froze solid, you outran old man Meyer."

Franco remained unimpressed. "That old fartbag? Hey-ull, even Doo-nell could outrun him. A damn titty baby could outrun him."

"And I didn't tell on y'all! So am I in the club now? I did what y'all told me to! Y'all said - - what's our club's name?" Al's body pressed against Billy's side, pushing plastic limbs into the latter's ribs.

Gift... remember my gift to you!

"The Little Boys," Billy let out off the top of his head without knowing why.

"That's us?" Al queried. "We're the Little Boys?"

Franco could stand no more. "You ain't no Little Boy! You are a leetle queer! Why don't you and Stanley Marx start a Little Queer club? That'd be just right for you!"

"I ain't no queer!" Al objected.

Billy's mind drifted to the previous night and his mother's blunt interrogation.

■ ■ ■

"These look like the things your little dollies stand on. You still got some of your little dolls? Why did you cut them off the flat pieces they stand on?

"I don't know what they're doing on my floor, Momma. I don't have any army men left, anyway, and I didn't cut off any bases or anything else."

Mrs. Capler was unconvinced, and her stabbing stare made the fact clear that she believed him to be lying. She noticed something else.

"Where's your glasses? How come you haven't been wearing them?"

"I don't need them any more. I see just fine."

"Well," she admonished, leaving the dismal fluorescence of the room behind her, "your eyes are just going to get worse. Don't come crying to me when they do."

The flapping of her slippers hitting her heels receded into the distance. Billy recalled sadly the words: *Even if it hurts.*

"Sorry, guys," he said, full of regret. He dropped the figures one at a time into a small grocery bag. He couldn't bear to look at Rémy, who entered the sack last.

"So... I see none of you have your foot pieces now. I don't know where they are. I am sorry, but if I'm doing crazy stuff I don't know I am, especially - - God, I'll never forget how messed up Lou was. And that baby, that was the absolute worst part of it, that poor baby - - "

No... Billy, no... love you, Billy... need you... not throw away!

"God, fellows, I'm sorry... please forgive me." Billy tearfully rolled up the sack, unsure who he was asking forgiveness from, certain of nothing except the fact that he would get little if any sleep that night.

■ ■ ■

You... need me! Never leave me!

Billy was startled by the jostling elbow of Franco.

"Cheer up, bro! At least that day-um mo-la-foquer ain't around no more. You know it?"

"Yeah, bro," Billy replied before realizing that Franco had referred to Lou Jones. The roofless ruin of what had been the Jones home loomed starkly against the morning sky's lifting foggy mist, and the now empty doghouse looked glaringly misplaced.

"Where are we going to meet after school today?" Al asked.

"Wherever you ain't going to be," Franco bluntly informed him.

"Couple of days," Billy muttered. "I'll leave them in my locker for a couple of days."

"What?"

"Ah, nothing, bro'. Just thinking about something."

"Think about poo-sy. Feel good."

The chilly morning's autumn mist moistened Billy's face through the open bus window. Try as he might to think of Janet, he couldn't block those pervasive words hopping from neuron to neuron in his youthful brain:

Love you... Billy... take me home with you again.

"You know those cops that come by the house the other day?"

"Yeah. What did they want?"

"Cops? Cops are after us?" Al was instantly excited.

"Shut up, you leetle queer, or I'll beat your god-day-um ass right here on the damn bus!"

"Sssh, Al. Go on, bro'."

"They'd heard I was trying to get Lou to knife fight me. They didn't come out and say it, but Momma said from the way they was talking that the fire had been set."

"Set? Do they have any proof of that?"

"Set? The fire at Lou's?" Al intruded.

"I told you to shut up, you little quee-arr! Anyways," Franco continued, his rage softening as he switched his address to Billy, "naw, they can't prove a day-um thing on neither one of us."

"Us?" Billy asked with a reflexive spasm of fear in his tone.

"Yeah. That one, the old one, asked who you was, too. I didn't tell them nothing. You know I ain't going to say sheet. Momma told them you wouldn't never do nothing to hurt nobody, so they didn't push it."

"Great," Billy spoke flatly, a nagging loosening spreading through his bowels.

■ ■ ■

Billy regarded the whole day as having been a total waste. He had been unable to do anything right or think straight in any of his classes, even gym class. He had even avoided Sharee Post in the lunchroom. Billy kept imagining his mother's face floating above him, her bony right index finger shaking at him. The mental apparition kept scolding him mercilessly with words such as "unproductive," "disappointing," and "not living up to your potential."

Damn! he silently cursed. *It's like life is one big bus ride in a circle going nowhere. And that other voice! Who... what... is it? Am I falling apart?* Billy was nearing a state of emotional trauma and he knew it.

"Grammaw said, 'even if it hurts.' Why didn't she tell me it might just hurt too much?"

"Say what, bro'?" Franco demanded. "What the hey-ull are you talking about now, sheety bro'?"

The bus brakes groaned painfully as always, and two seats ahead of the boys, Sara Cass stood up. She brushed her straight black hair over her left shoulder and said something to the small child who sat next to her by the window. Sara smiled and stepped into the aisle. She had long, strongly formed legs and was wearing patent leather black flats exactly like the ones Janet had worn the night she trampled him into submission and then deflowered him. Billy stared hungrily at her shoes for a few seconds, wanting to taste their leather in his mouth and to beg her for domination, unaware that Franco had just asked him,

"Hey, Bee-ly, are you okay?"

Someone else came from behind them and into the aisle. It was Sara's younger sister, and she had blocked Billy's view of Sara's sexily shod feet. He snapped out of his wishful daydream and had a sudden idea. He rose out of his seat.

"Where the hey-ull you going?" Franco wanted to know.

"I'm getting off a stop early. I'll call you about it later, bro.'"

"Gonna try to foque Sara, sheety bro'? She looks pretty good. Bet it would feel good," Franco said with an impish grin.

■ ■ ■

"I thought you had gotten off with us to come see how Jimmy was doing."

"I should, Sara, but... maybe I will later. Tell him 'hey' for me, okay?" Hiding the bundle lodged between his shirt and jacket was the reason he had dismounted the bus one stop ahead of his own. The two Cass sisters eyed him with suspicion as he walked toward the swamp, his gray suede shoes picking up and dropping coarse lumps of reddish brown mud.

"I should have said, 'Fuck him, he got what he deserved.' Right, Rémy?" Billy eased through the maze of thorn bushes and came to the pipe's entrance. "Sky's really overcast," he thought aloud. "It's a good night to rock houses, but not tonight. Not this Halloween, either. Too much shit going on and me and Franco don't need to get blamed for nothing else, at least, not for a while."

Billy stuffed the sack under the tangled old oak root, perceiving a troublesome hesitation within himself and the unspoken words,

Friend... Billy, we need each other...

"Come here, Rémy!" Billy snatched his favorite manikin from the sack, carrying him to the outflow end of the pipe, saying, "I got to get home but I got to set you down and tell you - - you ain't real! You ain't real! You can't be! You're a plastic doll!" He laid Rémy on his back near the coursing stream of water and screamed,

"I am not going crazy! I am not going crazy and you cannot be real!"

Billy... friend... no... don't leave me...

"I feel affection from you! I feel it! But it cannot be real! It just can't because it's impossible! Rémy - - you are just a chunk of fucking plastic!"

Love you... friend...

Rémy stood erect. It was a smooth movement, effortlessly executed.

Billy's knees went numb and the boy collapsed into the stream. The icy water gushed up his back. His breath was knocked out of him. He slid his buttocks upstream over the slimy pipe's bottom and watched the unbelievable continue to happen. Rémy steadily strode forward, his arms outstretched.

Billy... Billy...

The shocked boy flipped over onto his stomach and tried to find some sort of traction in the numbing raceway assaulting him. He coughed out a mouthful of foul water and slipped twice in the slimy algal layer beneath the rapidly moving stream. He managed to take one step and fell flat again, for a moment no longer mindful of its coldness.

He stood spread-eagled and began to hopscotch on the lower side of the pipe's interior arcs, not daring to look back. At the entranceway he halted, spotting the grocery bag off to the side that he had to step over to get away. He tried to see every crease of the bag, straining to detect any sign of movement within.

"Rémy?" he called warily, weakly, turning about carefully in the entrance and seeing no Rémy, but hearing within his own brain,

Billy! Here! Come! Get me! Please! Friend! Billy get me! Need you!

A burst of wind bit through the freezing boy, yet the rapid onset of the cold came as much from having seen Rémy stand by himself as it did from the air and water soaking him to the bone.

"No... this ain't real... it just can't be."

Billy! Please! Remember gift! Rémy need you...

Without thinking, Billy charged low toward the outflow end, taking care not to strike his tousled head but misstepping back into the thick subsurface algal layer and falling once more to slide the final eight feet of concrete pipe into the shallow circular pool a yard below, its surface coated in bubbles created by the cascade of laundry soap effluents and the gases from billions of decaying microbes.

Billy hit the pool hard on his left side, barely aware that this water felt warm for a heartbeat's time but grateful that he had not broken a rib on one of the charred foundation stones. The sensation that his testicles had abruptly frozen on impact with the water caused the boy to stagger to his feet in a half crouch, peering with dripping desperation into the brittle, dead grey brush halfway encircling the meandering creek, trying to spot Rémy.

Billy! Here!

To the teen's left, knee deep in a mat of blotched rockbound mosses, the four inch high object he was looking for stood waving its arms.

"Oh, fuck, this is real!" he gurgled, becoming once more oblivious to the painful cold piercing him to his core. Between rapid breaths, he asked, "You are real, aren't you, Rém'? Please, Rém', please be the answer to my prayers!"

Gift... Billy... You and I...

Rémy extended his molded arms and placed his hands palms up. Dazed and still in shock, Billy picked up the telepathic figure and turned, telling Rémy,

"We can't get back inside this way, Rém'. Too slick and wet. Come on, let's go this way over here."

The boy worked his way to the grass through the thick, oozing slime of the muddy shore, nearly losing both of his plain suede shoes as the pliant earth seemed to want to suck them downward. He scrambled up the bank and stopped at the edge of the roadway, looking at Rémy very closely and continuing to implore,

"Please, Rém', please be real! Don't just be some crazy as hell shit I'm imagining. If you're not real, don't tell me you are. Show me again so I'll know for sure."

Rémy's eyes flashed green, the same iridescent shade of green Billy had seen snaking around the figure's head when it had been perched with its companions on the window sill in Billy's darkened room.

"Thank you, God," the boy muttered repeatedly as he crossed the two lane asphalt road bisecting the subdivision, making sure to hold Rémy where he could constantly see him. The boy reached the pebbly surface at the rim of the other side and looked down at the grocery sack still wedged firmly under the oak root. Billy asked,

"The others, Rém'... are they alive, too?"

No, Billy... not others, but Rémy can move them. We go get others now. Leave in bag behind house. Put Rémy in pocket.

"I'm so cold I can't stand it!" Billy complained, slipping Rémy into his dripping jacket's right slash pocket. He slid down and through the crusty hard red clay clods of the embankment until he reached the tough old oak root and the light brown grocery bag locked in its dead wooden grip. The sack audibly tore a bit in response to Billy's tugging. The boy quickly glanced inside and saw they all appeared to be still there. He crumpled the sack into his drenched clothing and said aloud,

"Let's go home, Rém'!"

Good boy, Billy!

■　■　■

"What do you think you're doing coming in here all wet like that?"

"I, uh, I took a shortcut and fell in the creek, Momma. That's not a crime, is it, slipping and falling in the creek? That could happen to anyone."

"Well, where did you get off the bus at?"

"I got off up at the Casses' stop. I thought I'd try to see if I could cut through the brush and stuff and get here just a little quicker."

"That's the most goddurn ridiculous thing I ever heard of," Mrs. Capler snapped in her usual harsh tone, firing up a cigarette even though another one, not half finished, burned noxiously on in the thick amber glass ashtray to her left. She took a long drag and slowly blew the cloud toward Billy, a hint of a smile belying the cruel nature of her intent in the question, "You got the hots all of a sudden for one of Jimmy's sisters? I hope it's the older one. That little one is pretty but she's... jail bait."

"No, Momma," Billy fired back, feeling the familiar anger at her hurtful prying manner he knew so well begin to offset his discomfort at being cold. "Sara's just a friend, Momma. Don't you know that? Anyway, who cares how it happened? I feel like I'm made out of ice!"

"Well, there you go. Serves you right. Better be careful... Sara Cass will get you in... trouble."

Ignoring the judgmental caveat, Billy began to peel off his jacket, then he remembered Rémy ensconced in the slash pocket. Billy hesitated a moment, numb with cold and indecision as what to do next.

"Take off your shoes and socks, William."

"Yes ma'am," Billy answered flatly, trying to hide his gratitude for her having unintentionally alleviated his concern. "Guess I'd better finish upstairs," he added, noticing his mother's disapproving grunt as his saturated socks released a double torrent of filthy water onto the floor. "I'll get the mop, Momma."

"No, you go on upstairs to the bathroom and get the rest of that mess off. Now I'm going to have to wash all these clothes and then dry them," Mrs. Capler complained, taking a long and deep puff before continuing in short bursts of smoky exhalation, "Electricity and water cost… money. Washing and drying don't come cheap, but you don't know anything about that, do you?"

"Leave my shoes and socks here in the kitchen, Momma?"

"Go on, get the rest of that stuff off before you get sick. Lord knows you don't need to miss any school, especially as bad as you're doing so far this year."

Billy! Do what woman says! Not speak more! Go!

"You can't hear him, can you, Momma?"

"Hear who?"

Smiling, the barefoot teen wasted no time with giving an answer he could not explain to a mother who had no capability of believing it even if she saw it with her own eyes. Billy whispered as he negotiated the corner facing the three steps to the upper section of the split level house,

"Please keep being real, Rém'! Please don't let this be another stupid ass dream. If that's all this is, I don't ever want to wake up from it. Dying couldn't be any worse than living in this shitty place."

Billy entered the hall bathroom and gingerly helped Rémy out of his pocket. The khaki man hopped from Billy's hand to the tiled floor. He landed with a clatter and rolled. Springing to his feet and sensing Billy's alarm at his action, Rémy thought,

Falling not hurt Rémy, Billy. Rémy not feel pain in body.

"That's a relief, little bro'. That scared me when you jumped like that."

Billy! You do as you must! Do as woman told you!

"What are you going to do now, Rém'?"

Rémy get others from bag and bring them all back to you.

"How are going to do that? I mean, get them all inside the house again? I could get them tomorrow. They're not going anywhere down by the basement door, right?"

No. Not wait. Rémy put string back through hole in window screen.

Billy smiled broadly in unexpected realization. At last, things were beginning to make a very crazy kind of sense.

"So how are you going to get up on top of the desk all by yourself? Don't you want to wait for me to set you up there?"

Rémy climb up lamp cord behind desk.

Without another thought, the animated figurine darted from the bathroom. Billy marveled at how effectively the carpet muffled the clicking of Rémy's rapid footsteps. A barely discernible tap and creak told Billy that his new "gift" had pushed his bedroom door open wider than the bare crack it had been left in and had gone on inside.

"He's a fast runner," Billy mumbled, adding as his tossed shirt hit the bathtub with a soggy splat, "Thank you, God. I won't let You down for this! I swear to God - - I mean - - I'll be good from now on."

9

GUIDED BY RÉMY'S mind waves, ten tiny figurines climbed into their bookcase sanctuary, their plastic limbs wedging progressively higher in the thin voids between the books. Max, the squat red robot, was the last to topple over the rim of the paperback row.

"Let me understand this. You're the only one who's actually alive, but you can make them all move, too?"

Rémy raised his right fist, signaling yes.

"How long have you been alive? Is it because of all the praying I've been doing? You control all the others, I know that, but, I mean, if God sent you to me, how come you killed all of those Joneses? And, did you stick that pencil in Jimmy's eye?"

The right fist rose once again and gave a single terse shake.

"I got so much to tell you, Rém'..."

Billy leaned forward in his chair and extended his right forefinger. Rémy took a step forward on the desk and reached to Billy, offering his own small right first digit. They touched lightly, and a warm, loving sensation traveled up Billy's arm.

"So how exactly did you get to be alive? When? No, no," the boy hastily countered his own query. "Just tell me this. I got to know this. Don't get pissed off at me for asking you, okay? The... the damn Devil didn't make you come alive, did he?"

Rémy's left hand, palm down, traversed the space in front of his molded hips. *No,* Billy understood and every muscle in his body relaxed. He slowly let out a breath of relief.

"That's the only thing I was really worried about, Rém'. I guess you just didn't know any better doing all that bad shit. Well, from now on, don't do nothing to nobody else unless I tell you or... or ..." Billy thought of some advice his stepfather had given him on several recent occasions. Bitterly, Billy considered his inability to fit in with any group at school and how he could never do anything quite right at home. "You know, Rém'..."

Anything for you... Billy...

"I feel like you're trying to tell me stuff, too. Sometimes, Rém', Stepdad says you got to take every advantage you get in this world. And a lot of times you've got to make that advantage yourself because you won't get it any other way. Rém', how long are you going to live? Do you know?"

Always be with you... always love you, Billy... Rémy not die.

"Don't you ever leave me, Rém'!"

Never leave you. Never.

The door swung open. Billy's vertebrae tingled in fear at the idea of his mother seeing Rémy moving. Would she drop dead of a heart attack? Billy knew that if she was gone, he'd have to leave also. Before he could shield Rémy with cupped hands, Mrs. Capler emotionlessly informed him,

"Suppertime, son."

"Okay, Momma." Billy pivoted in his chair and glimpsed the trailing edge of her housecoat. When the flapping of her bedroom shoes was no longer audible, the boy turned back to see Rémy in his former position of lifelessness. "Well, Rém', you're my advantage. You and me. Forever."

Forever...

Billy rose and watched while Rémy reanimated and worked his way to the Little Boys' lair.

"At least, this explains the cut screen. It explains a lot of things. But we will definitely find a better way out and in for you. We can't keep the window open all winter. Hey, I know... I'll show you a crack in the hall closet floor later. And best of all," he continued, "I ain't crazy!" Billy grinned all the way to the kitchen, not caring to note the pile of wet clothing still in the bathtub, pleased that at this moment the only problem he was concerned with was how to keep from showing this miracle from heaven to Franco and Donald until Saturday morning.

■ ■ ■

"Ohhh... uhhh... uhhh..."

Billy froze in his steps, straddling the often-crossed and badly loosened barbed wire fence. Someone was in the bomb shelter.

"Dang, Rém'... wonder if it's Franco and Donald?"

Rémy turned around in Billy's jacket pocket.

"Ummm..."

"That sounded like a girl that time, Rém'!" he whispered, easing over the wire and carefully descending the slickened path to the shelter entrance. A familiar voice demanded,

"Kiss me!"

Billy peered into the angulated corridor. Franco and Pammy were standing up, having intercourse. Pammy's bare buttocks repeatedly slapped the cold concrete blocks in response to Franco's sexual pounding. Franco's pants and underwear lay crumpled around his ankles.

"Kiss me!" Franco again demanded.

Whap! Whap! Whap! Whap!

Pammy's head rolled and she saw Billy's silhouette. Behind her thick glasses her eyes glazed and went blank. Her puckered mouth twisted downward, forming an embarrassed frown.

Whap! Whap! Whap! Whap!

"Ahhh! Ummm!" Franco smeared his lips across Pammy's for a few seconds and withdrew from her. He unloaded his liquefied protein toward Billy, who jumped backward to avoid the pulsing, weakening shots.

"Aw, bro'... you foqued me up," young Campbell complained, firing his final salvo, much reduced in range, into the air.

Billy laughed heartily. Franco pulled his pants up while Pammy slipped farther into the shelter's depths, her backside reddened by repeated impacts with the corridor wall, her panties clutched tightly in her hands.

"I heard somebody down here. If I'd have known it was you and Pammy, I'd have waited until y'all were finished."

"Aw, that's okay," Franco said, filled with lusty pride. "Hey, Pammy! Come on out here! Pammy! Come on!"

"No!" she replied with hushed urgency.

"It's alright. Bee-ly won't tell nobody. He won't tell nobody at all." Franco added to Billy, quietly, "Maybe she'll give you some, too, bro'. If you want to, we'll throw her down and you can fuck her whether she wants to or not. Who gives a day-um?"

"She don't have to come out, Franco. Come on, let's go on up to your house. You ain't going to believe this, maybe not even after you see it!"

Franco urinated on the corridor wall. The porous blocks greedily soaked up the fluid, releasing a tart ammonia odor that bit at Billy's nostrils. Franco disinterestedly asked,

"What you got?"

"You're gonna have to see it to believe it. You'd never believe it if I told you. It's a miracle, man, a gift from God! First He cured my eyes, now He's sent me this! Come on, I can't wait!"

"Day-um, Bee-ly, let me fee-nish pee-sing. All the spaaarm I didn't shoot out is clogging up my deek inside." Franco commented, making a final squirt and zipping his jeans. "Must be something really important."

The boys left the sour odor of nitrogenated earth behind them as they walked the sixty yards to the Campbell's screened-in back porch. Billy had to know,

"Is anybody home?"

"Daddy's out building a house in Henry County. I'm afraid we might move into it and rent this one out. Sheet, I don't want to move no damn wheres."

"Man, that sucks."

"I know it," Franco agreed, opening the meshed door for his friend. Billy looked back and saw the tall dried grass move near the bomb shelter.

"Pammy's gonna go the long way home," he observed. "She don't want me to see her."

"Took awhile, bro," Franco chortled, "but I deed eet! I foqued her. Feel gooood!"

"Your momma home?"

"Nah. She's done gone to the grocery store."

"How about Donald?"

"He's up in the bedroom. He won't do sheet when them day-um cartoons are on."

As the boys passed, a very old banjo hanging on the living room wall sounded a dull note. Billy halted as if he had been struck and remarked,

"You know, I figured you all were just hearing things when you said that once in a while your great-granddaddy still played on that thing."

"I told you it was true. It's my great-granddad still playing it."

"I believe you now. But you're going to see something a lot weirder in a minute."

"What is it? Must be really - - "

The banjo's leftmost string emitted another note.

"Damn, it ain't never hit a note twice this close a time together before. Least, I hadn't never heard it do it." Franco fired up a cigarette and carelessly tossed the still smoking match aside onto the shag carpet. Billy followed him up the steps through his friend's exhaled noxious plume. They could hear Donald's little hi-fi record player playing a twanging song which the elder Campbell brother passionately despised.

"Turn that shit off!" he snapped, kicking the door open with such force that it vibrated audibly.

"Hell, no! Kiss my butt! Hey, Billy!" Donald was dancing to the country music tune, a comic book rolled up in each hand. On the television screen, animated creatures, presumably fanciful rats, danced likewise, their antics muted by virtue of the volume button having been turned to the lowest setting.

Billy smiled at the sight as the hi-fi ground out the lyrics of the Campbells' father's last campaign theme:

"G.C. Campbell is his name!

Building houses is his game!"

"I said, turn that goddamn shit off!" Franco took a baseball bat from the closet and waved it threateningly. "I hate that shit!"

"I'll turn it off, bro," Billy offered.

"Naw, hey-ull, naw, I been wanting to do this for a long time!" Franco thrust the bat downward twice, sending the hi-fi's arm through the air as the crushed body spun floorward. The despised record exploded into innumerable bits of useless polyvinyl and Donald warned that,

"Momma's gone be mad as hell!"

"Aw, to hey-ull with it," Franco tossed out blithely. "Foque eet." His anger assuaged, he pitched the bat into a corner where it clattered a moment before rolling to a stop under the window sill. Donald complained,

"You ain't gonna be able to listen to your Elvis record or that help-me-Rhonda one, neither, now."

"I said I don't give a day-um," the older brother responded blankly, watching his friend walk over to the aluminum frame bunk bed and pull his jacket zipper down all the way while stating,

"You won't believe this even after you see it. It's all I could do to keep from telling you until now."

"Telling us what?"

Billy, ignoring Franco's question, came out of his jacket. He stretched it gingerly across the lower bunk.

"Whatcha doing?"

"You'll see, Donald. Now, no one would ever believe this in a million years, so it don't matter if we tell anyone or not."

"Tell what? You know we won't say sheet."

"Franco, I know. Rémy! Come on out!"

"You ain't got another one of them big ass black snakes like you had last year?" Franco wondered aloud. A form buried in the brown jacket rose to nearly four inches in height under the jacket's fabric before emerging into the light. Rémy's unblinking eyes coldly surveyed Donald, then Franco.

"Neat!" Donald squealed. "Cool!"

"Is that a damn robot? Day-um, that can't be real!"

"That's what I said, too, at first."

"Sheee-yit!" Franco sat on the floor, his cigarette dangling from his lower lip. He vainly looked for a switch or battery door somewhere on Rémy's body. "How in the hey-ull - - is he alive? I can't believe this sheet, sheety bro.'"

"My bro's…" Billy triumphantly announced, "Meet the newest member of our gang. From now on we really are the Little Boys."

10

NOVEMBER 7

"I'VE GOT SOMETHING for you, Sharee, but you have to promise, I mean, like, swear to God, never to say how you got them. This is just between us, right?"

Sharee Post smiled at Billy across the lunch table. Her admiring attention was broken by the sight of two familiar people in the food line comprising a very unlikely duo.

"There's your friend Franco and Mr. Broward."

Billy looked over his shoulder. There was Franco clad in his denim jacket. The words "liTTle BoYs" were scrawled across the back in white chalk. A scowling Bull Broward trailed young Campbell. The vice principal's mouth sneered as he issued a stern directive to his charge who sullenly but obediently took a seat at the faculty dining table. Broward threw back a coat flap in a gesture of triumph before sitting beside the boy. Billy didn't envy his friend. The intimidation power of the man behind whose back the kids called Bull was electric.

"I heard on the intercom, 'Franco Campbell, come to the office,'" Billy informed Sharee, "but I didn't know it was anything serious enough for him to have to eat with Fatso."

"I know he skipped Latin," Sharee revealed.

"Hey, brother!" Arty Johnson and John Marston sauntered to the table's end. Billy beckoned for them to come closer. Pleased, they did so and Arty continued, "Your main man done messed up, Billy-Bo."

"What'd he do this time?" Billy grinned in spite of the question. He loved the nickname Arty had given him several years past.

"Him and that Eddy Mundy boy done got caught smoking beside the gym. Coach Hale caught them and sent their asses to the office."

"Apparently Franco didn't go," Billy ventured.

"I'll bet you Eddy Mundy didn't go, neither," John tossed in, reasoning, "See, he think he's some kind of Elvis or something. He be thinking he's cool, but he's a fool. Always be talking 'bout getting a gun and going and robbing dudes."

"Oooh, that's stupid," Sharee shuddered.

"So how come Eddy Mundy ain't over there eating with them?"

"Probably he took off, Arty. And I agree with you, John. Eddy Mundy's a punk. Franco don't need to be hanging around him." Billy let the subject go as more kids arrived, filling the table. The girl who had flirted with Franco threw Billy a sweet smile. Billy raised an eyebrow in return recognition, and Sharee observed,

"You've gotten a lot more confident, Billy. You're more different than you've ever been since I've known you. Remember back in third grade?"

"Yeah? Really?" Billy softly asked, Franco's plight forgotten.

"Um-hum." Sharee plowed the applesauce with her fork. "What was it you were saying?"

"Oh... yeah, like I said, just keep this special between us. I want you to have these because you're my friend." Billy reached for the diamond earrings hidden in the customized interior pocket he'd crudely sewn inside his jacket. Plastic hands within shoved the jewels between his fingers. Billy handed the earrings to a very impressed Sharee.

"Billy! They're beautiful! Thank you! Are they real diamonds? They couldn't be, could they?"

"Yeah." Billy nodded. "I do think they are."

"Whoo-ee! Where you get them from, Billy-Bo?"

"Hot, Arty."

"Oh," the larger boy acknowledged. The group of black kids seemed to, in unison, throw a protective curtain around the table. Billy felt safe, but Sharee was concerned with what Billy had said to Arty.

"Did you - - "

"Steal them? No, gosh, no, I didn't." Billy saw Arty wink at him, a between-us-guys sign of understanding. *Well, I didn't,* Billy rationalized. *Rémy did. From somewhere. Who cares from where?* Billy thought about the coin and jewelry stash hidden behind another section of his bookcase and of Rémy's nightly exploits which were steadily increasing the take of loot. "Like I said, this is because you're my friend."

"Just... a friend?"

Oh, hell, how do I answer this one? Billy agonized. *What do I say?*

Special... friend.

"Thanks, Rémy."

"Who?"

"Ah, I meant... you're a special friend, Sharee."

She showed her bubbly smile. She really is a wonderful girl, Billy knew, but maybe that answer will hold her for now.

■   ■   ■

"That day-um Stanley Marx has been telling me a bunch of god-day-um bool sheet."

"What's he saying now, bro'?"

"That son of a shit bitch has been saying some grown-up woman's been giving him poo-sy every Wednesday after he finishes his paper route. What a bunch of sheet!"

"Look at him, Franco," Billy directed. Stanley Marx, a few seats behind them on the bus, was loudly bragging to Al Gates and a much younger boy about his newly found studship.

"Hey-ull, I don't want to look at that skinny little bastard. Stanley's lying, any day-um way. What woman, even an ugly old pig twenty-four hundred years old, would want to mess around with a deek soaking queer like him?"

"Tell you what, bro'... me and Rémy will meet you at the bomb shelter tomorrow, and we'll go see if it's true."

"Naw. It's a lie. It ain't worth fooling with."

"So we'll be able to prove it's a lie. Hey, I'll bring my camera. We'll hide somewhere and, just in case there is something to it, like if some ugly old hog woman shows up, we can take pictures of them."

"We can blackmail him! Hey-ull, yeah!" Franco was suddenly interested. "We can make him give us his paper route money!"

"Sixty bucks a month. What do we have to lose?"

■　　■　　■

"This is where he said he laid her down." Al Gates grinned, pointing to a crumpled mat of grass ringed by cigarette butts. "Me and him came up here yesterday. That's when he told me all about her. He says she's real pretty."

"Shit!" Franco spat.

"And he said she's married and he's the one who's done got her pregnant." Al displayed his ear to ear grin and asked, "Are y'all gonna take pictures of them while they're doing it? I want to watch them real bad!"

Billy had been busy studying the undeveloped terrain around the lonely, narrow dirt road, his little white camera dangling by its cord from the boy's wrist. He pointed to the knoll across the road.

"We can hide in that tall grass. We can put our bikes in it behind us. I can get a couple of pictures. It's a clear view."

"Will you be able to tell who's in the pictures from over yonder?"

"They'll be small, but, yeah, Franco, I think so. You'll be able to tell who it is."

"Gooood. Did you bring that sheet you got to rub on the pictures after you take them?"

"Yeah, I got it. You want to rub the pictures?"

"I guess."

"I'll do it!" Al eagerly volunteered.

"Shut the hey-ull up!" Franco snapped, then turning to Billy, he asked, "Why'd your moo-ther get peesed off about that pocket you made? Hell, I might sew me one in my jacket, myself."

"She said it looks tacky because I used red thread on a brown jacket and you can see the stitches I made with it."

"Umm." Franco refocused his attention upon Al. "You done showed us the place, so now you can go on and get the hey-ull out of here."

"I don't want to go. I want to see Stanley and that woman doing it. I want to watch how to - - "

Franco's well-aimed fist crashed into the deltoid muscle of Al's left shoulder, knocking the younger boy onto the muddy ground. He whimpered,

"Why'd you do that? I didn't say nothing for you to do that to me! Little Boys don't beat each other up! Ow! It hurts!"

"You ain't no god-day-um Little Boy! Now get the hey-ull out of here while you still can and you better not say nothing to that other queer Stanley Marx about us being here!"

Al hesitantly stood, fearful of what the enraged Franco might do to him next. His numbed shoulder ached fiercely. He looked pleadingly at Billy.

"Don't hit him again, Franco. He's leaving. And he won't say nothing about none of this. Right, Al?"

"No, sir! You betcha I won't!" Despite the pain, Al managed to grin at Billy as he mounted his bicycle. "Will you bring me back some pictures?"

"We'll try to. 'Bye, Al."

"'Bye, Billy. 'Bye, Franco."

"Get the hey-ull out of here!"

■   ■   ■

"I'm getting cold, bro'! We're going to have to get on back to the house soon. He ain't coming no way! I told you it was all just a bunch of bool sheet!"

"Let's give it a few more minutes, Franco. He's got to be done with his paper route by now. I'm cold, too. I can't take much longer laying down on our bellies on the ground like this. My feet are freezing!"

"I'll bet you he's been through with his paper route for a long while."

Billy smiled at Rémy sitting on the developing wash cylinder lying between the boys. "Hey, look at him, bro'... Rémy don't get cold."

"Must be nice. Hey, what's that I hear?"

The sound of a bicycle chain snapping in response to pedal-pushed gears grew in volume. Breathing with some effort, Stanley Marx pulled his Schwinn over, gave his kick stand a boot, dismounted, and sat on the flattened grass mat. He took off his coat and furry hat, despite the chill, and lit a cigarette.

"I didn't know he smoked," Franco murmured. "Hey-ull, he just comes up here by himself and smokes weeds. What a damn liar. Let's whip his ass and take his weeds."

"Whoa. Wait."

Stanley lifted his head. A car was coming slowly up the road. Young Marx smiled. The vehicle pulled over and stopped just outside of the hidden boys' view. A door opened and shut. Stones crunched under heavy feet and Stanley rose to his knees.

"A man! Look! It's a damn man!" Franco sneered in disgust.

"Wonder what's going on?"

The well-built middle-aged gentleman, clad in a flawlessly tailored blue wool pinstripe suit, bent over and kissed Stanley on the mouth.

"This is gross!" Franco whispered. "I always told you he was a damn queer! Billy, take a picture! Come on!"

"I wonder if I ought to. This is not what I wanted to see. "

"Take a picture! Come on, so everyone will know he's a damn queer! Billy, I'll swear I took the pictures! Come on! Do it!"

Billy raised his Land 20 and sighted in his target. The man was unzipping his trousers and Marx eagerly awaited what was coming next.

"Here's your supper, Stanley. Be a sweet boy," the man laughed, his accent definitely not Virginian.

"This is really sick," Billy muttered, taking three pictures. Franco accepted the cylinder from Rémy and carefully washed each down with the development fluid.

"These look good, Billy. Can I have them?"

"Sure. You ain't going to show them around at school, are you?"

"Reckon I will."

"It'll mess him up for good."

"I don't give a day-um. He deserves it. He soaks deeks. He is a leetle queer."

"Just don't tell nobody how you got them and definitely don't mention my name. Okay?"

"Alright," Franco quickly responded.

Billy believed him. Franco needed to accomplish something on his own, or at least be seen as doing something by himself, even if that something would be seen as, as his mother would say, sordid. Billy chuckled at his maliciously grinning friend, trying to foresee all the attention Franco would be getting for carrying out his planned act of cruelty.

Stanley and his slightly gray-haired lover had finished and were walking, hand in hand, in the direction of the woods. Billy felt a sudden flash of mischievous inspiration.

"Rémy! Go let the air out of his tires!"

"Hey-ull, yeah! Make all four of them flatter than day-um pancakes!"

A buff form raced forward in immediate response. Within half a minute the boys heard air hissing out from its pneumatic containers into the environment.

"He's a fast leetle mo-la-foquer, ain't he?" Franco asked, his voice laced with uncharacteristic anxiety. "Bee-ly... is he the vice president of the Little Boys or am I?"

"You are, of course, bro'. Don't worry about that. Rémy's like... he's our secret agent man."

"Just wanted to be sure. And Al Gates ain't no Little Boy. I mean, if you say so, he is, but - - "

"Tell you what, bro', Al Gates ain't a Little Boy as long as you don't want Eddy Mundy to be one, neither."

"Aw, Eddy Mundy's cool."

"Sheeee-yit. Hey, you want to see something really funny, bro'?"

"Hey-ull, I already have."

"Well, what I mean is… I saw you and Pammy doing it. You want to see me and Janet? If her husband ain't home, you can watch us doing all kinds of neato stuff. You won't believe some of the things she does to me!"

Franco smiled, his anxiety dissolving in a rush of purile expectations.

■　　■　　■

"Billy, Dwight will be home any minute! I can't now!" Janet Mills reluctantly exited her basement door. From the woods at the edge of the swamp, in the gathering darkness, Franco and Rémy watched as Billy begged the adult woman for spit and sex.

"Please, Janet, please! Help me out somehow. Just kiss me a couple of times, at least, and please, please, beat me off, too!"

"Oh, okay, if you have to. Sit down, honey boy!"

Billy obeyed and Janet's mouth covered his. The boy turned into jello while Mrs. Mills' tongue choked him and her hands expertly manipulated his maleness to an orgasm.

"Well, hon', we'll have to do better some other time. For right now, you'll have to settle for fertilizing my back lawn." She stepped lightly on his midsection, mashing a groan from deep inside the boy.

A hundred yards away, headlights signaled Mr. Mills' approach.

"Shit!" Janet exclaimed, going into the basement doorway. "Don't move, Billy. He might see you! Damn it all, I know my mouth is all red now. I hope he doesn't ask why…"

Her words departed with her as she went into her basement. Billy felt somehow shortchanged. Dwight Mills' car passed by and Franco, standing near Rémy, stepped close, stating,

"We couldn't really tell from back yonder what y'all was doing."

"She beat me off, that's all."

"Hey-ull, that's better than nothing," Franco reasoned, handing Billy the white Polaroid camera. "Still feel good."

"Yeah, but I'm going to get chewed out bad now for being out past dark."

"Foque eet. It's worth it, ain't it? I'll see y'all tomorrow."

"Okay, bro."

Franco's shape blended into the night and Billy realized that his intensely homophobic friend still had the photos of Marx and the unknown man.

"Damn, I guess he's going to mess Stanley up, Rém'. Ah, fuck him, anyway. Like Franco said, after all, he's a queer. You better go ahead to the house up through the closet door when you can, Rém'. I'm going to catch unholy hell from Momma."

11

November 9

Billy's stomach rumbled fiercely. As the dismissal bell rang, he gratefully shut his doodle-filled notebook and, as he had done so many times previously, made his way with his classmates to the door under the watchful gaze of Coach Hale.

Across the chaotic hallway Sharee, just out of her Latin class, chatted with a very lithe and tall brunette wearing a gaudy excess of rouge on her lips. *Yum yum*, Billy thought. *Wonder what her name is?*

"Hey, Beaudet! Grab that queer! Grab him!"

Glancing to his left, Billy saw the husky eleventh grader who had yelled to him, a football player with two missing upper front teeth and a face like a squashed clam. The big boy leered maliciously, as did his two equally brutish halfback companions. All three wore their varsity football jackets. Billy was surprised. Most jocks never spoke to anyone but other jocks. Seeing that Billy would not comply, the boy called out to others,

"Johnny! Willie! Get that queer before he gets away!"

Through the pubescent crush reeking of an overabundance of hormones, Billy spotted the rapidly bobbing thin head of Stanley Marx. The pursued boy looked backward at his tormentors. Tears fell copiously from his oversized eyes to the corners of his mouth. His face conveyed a hunted desperation. Quickly, Marx struck the double exit doors and vanished into the swelling jumble of young bodies headed for the lunch line.

So, Billy figured, *Franco's been showing the pictures. Well,* he resignedly thought, *I hope he keeps my name out of it.*

Billy felt strangely selfish. He knew that, morally, he should have pity for the aggrieved Stanley. Questions churned in Billy's brain: *Why don't I care? Even if Stanley is what he is, he's still a human being and someone I've known since third grade. Why don't I feel any concern except for keeping my own part in this sickening mess a secret?*

"Going to lunch, Billy?"

"Yeah, Sharee," Billy responded, happily noticing that the brunette had come with her. An uproar of laughter at the building's upper level distracted him. "What's the big deal up there by the office?"

"I can't tell. Debbie, you're taller than me or Billy. What's going on?"

"Let me get these on." The brunette fumbled for a few seconds in her pocketbook, donned her glasses and, on tiptoes, craned her neck to peer over the pedestrian traffic. "Ah… there's a bunch of people looking at something on the bulletin board, I think."

"Come on!" Billy grabbed Sharee's hand and began to pull her after him.

"Billy! Wait! I've got to go to my locker first!"

Releasing her, Billy pushed onward. The crowd around the bulletin board had grown. He could not see what the object of their curiosity and mirth was, but he feared the worst.

"Come on, people, let's move on! What's the problem here?"

Bull Broward's words exploded the levee, their authoritative gravity forcing the human sea to flow along. Mr. Broward's usual frown metamorphosed into an expression of deep concern when he saw what had been added without authorization to the bulletin board.

Billy caught a sparing glimpse of a pair of small black and white photographs pinned near the bottom of the board's cork face. Broward's hands darted out and removed the pictures. The vice principal dropped them into his coat pocket and retraced his path into the office. He took a black telephone receiver off of its hook and began to dial a number, ignoring the elderly secretary whom he had bothered.

"Did you find out, Billy?"

"Huh?" Billy whirled, lying, "Uh, no, Sharee, I didn't."

"Hmm," Sharee answered, letting the matter go. "Is it okay if Debbie eats with us?"

"Sure, sure, glad to have you."

"Maybe your friend Franco will sit with us," Sharee speculated, tacking on the humorously offered qualification, "if he's not in trouble again. He didn't make it to Latin today, either. He's going to flunk for sure."

"He doesn't care if he does or not. Let's just hope he hasn't done anything too serious," Billy said, more to himself than to Sharee. "He's always pulling something stupid off."

■　■　■

"Nice. Nice."

The rapidly rotating emery wheel's motor ceased its monotonous whine and Billy's forefinger moved from the on-off switch to the tip of his sharp new creation. He tested the tightness of the cotton string securing the straightened fish hook to a three inch long strip of bamboo.

"This ain't coming off, little bro'!"

Rémy came from behind a desktop vise and accepted his javelin from Billy. The legionnaire held it horizontally at hip's height and stroked it as if it were a pet, admiringly nodding with approval and gratitude.

"We can't have another situation where somebody gets chewed up. This will protect you and the others, but don't use it unless you absolutely have to. It was bad enough losing Louie. I don't want to lose anybody else. I could, if I had to, replace everybody but you, Rém'. You're the best friend anyone could ever have."

Billy's face neared Rémy's. The boy felt their souls touch, almost to mingle. The one's inner essence briefly grazed that of the other, and both of them swayed in the resulting upsurge of emotions. Recovering, Billy told his companion,

"I don't know what I'd ever do without you, Rémy. You did some bad things, but that's not your fault. You didn't know any better. I've got to teach you these things. I don't ever want to be without you. You and me, we're it, right? Forever, like Damon and Pythias."

Love you... Billy...

"I love you, Rém'. More than anything."

"William!" Mrs. Capler's intruding summons found Billy's ears all the way from upstairs.

"Ma'am?" he shouted, blatantly irritated.

"What are you doing?"

"Making something in the tool room!"

"Better not make a mess! You know what happened the last time! You're not on a papier maché kick again, are you?"

"No, ma'am!" Billy let out a nervous breath and opened the flap of his jacket. "Jump on in, Rém'. I got Rubberbuster and Blue boy in my britches' pocket, and my bike's out back by the basement door. Franco's been talking about an important mission for the Little Boys, and we can handle it, right? We're regular secret agent men, ain't we?"

Rémy showed Billy a single shake of his right fist.

"Yeah, that's the spirit. Give me the spear until you're all fixed."

Rémy set his gig between Billy's fingers and scampered into the inside pocket. Billy dropped the tiny weapon butt first after him and said, walking as softly as possible to the basement door,

"Probably going to miss supper and get bitched out again. Ah, fuck it. Little Boys come first. I ain't no little kid any more, so why should I stay here at home after school every day and do nothing?"

■ ■ ■

She's bound to find out sooner or later, a terrified Stanley Marx knew, his white-knuckled fingers interlaced between his uncontrollably shaking knees. *Why? Why? And who? Who could have been so cruel to do this to me? I've never hurt anyone in my life! Why does somebody hate me so much? And... do they know who Bobby is?*

He had tried to call Bobby as soon as he had arrived home, pumped so full of adrenaline after a three mile plus run that he was not even winded. *This is all a nightmare,* he kept telling himself. *This hasn't happened! This can't be real!*

But it had happened, and real it was. Stanley also knew it was not just going to go away.

"Bobby! Please answer me! Please!" he had pleaded, screaming into the telephone to no avail. "Bobby! I'm in big, big trouble!"

Then he had heard his mother's car pulling into their rough gravel driveway. She had come home directly following her shift at the hospital.

Stanley's bright blue eyes again filled with tears and he fled from the kitchen table to his room at the other end of the little wood frame single story house, hiding like a rabbit in the brush amid the piled up collection of stuffed toys and dolls on his bed.... a collection he never let anyone see...

... except for Bobby. Bobby had made oral and anal love to him over and over there in his bed while Mrs. Marx was pulling a double work shift. Bobby had shown him things he had never dreamed of, ways to release the welled up adolescent passions within him, ways that did not require, and in fact mandated the absence of, a girl.

Surely, Stanley prayed, *Bobby, smart Bobby, will figure a way out of this for me. Bobby was a teacher once... and teachers know all the tricks... right?*

He heard the door shut and the sound of his mother's white nurse's shoes shuffling across the floor tiles in the kitchen with their soft rubber soles. *What am I going to tell her? She must know I'm home! The door was unlocked and my down jacket is on the kitchen table.*

He cradled his vertically compressed-looking, sandy-haired head in his bony hands and listened as his mother set down what he thought was surely her tote bag. There was another telltale interaction of medical shoes with kitchen linoleum...

... and the telephone rang... only once.

Stanley, his nape hairs on end, strained to make out the words his mother was saying. She never spoke loudly, even when angry and telling someone, in fact anyone who would listen, how Mr. Marx had abandoned her and her son for a much younger and prettier woman. He had simply left without any explanation to live with her. He had not seen Stanley since shortly after the boy had begun second grade.

Mrs. Marx had made a lot of sacrifices and had done the best she could, proudly obtaining her nursing license and managing to find this snug little house at the western end of Garden Pines. Still, she hated Stanley's father, his trophy wife, and even their four daughters who in all probability, she guessed, did not even know they had an older brother.

It had been she and Stanley against the world for ten years. *What will she think of me now?* The tormented youth wondered. *Is someone telling her what happened today? Is it the same one who took the photos? Is it the same person who flattened Bobby's tires? Is there more than one of them?*

Who are... they?

"Son, call Mr. Hoffman at his gas station," he remembered his mother telling him after hearing the story he had told her about encountering a man with four flat tires. "He'll send someone to come help him out right away."

Stanley had dutifully done as his mother directed, but in his zeal to rescue his adult lover, he neglected to notice his mother listening. He hung up the phone after telling Mr. Hoffman where Bobby was stranded, and felt icy fear in his gut when his mother asked,

"How did you meet up with this man over there on the other side of the hill? That's not on your route and there aren't any houses there yet that I know of."

"I don't know, Mama," Stanley had lied. "I guess I just had a lot of nervousness to get rid of, so I biked on over that way to work it out. I've done it before. You know… whenever I'm nervous."

His mother's only response was to look down as if to say: *You're as bad a liar as your father.*

Breaking his reverie, Stanley raised his head, anchoring a shock of sweat-matted hair in the shape of an ash-blond spike. He thought he had heard the telephone receiver being put down and for an unforgivably long minute the boy tracked his mother's deliberately slow footsteps by the creaking of the floorboards. She was approaching, but was hesitant.

She must know, he feared. *She must.*

The door opened and Mrs. Marx sat on the bed facing him, their knees touching slightly.

Mrs. Marx was a plump woman in her forties, not really fat, but her cherubic face and closely set lips showed deep inner concern, even dread.

"Son, that was Mr. Broward at school. He said he'd called earlier. He wants to meet with both of us tomorrow morning, but you're not to go to school like you usually do. We'll meet him in his office at ten-thirty. Tell nobody, son, and I'm very serious about this."

"Do—do—do you know, Mama?" he whimpered, still fearful, yet relieved at having asked.

"I've known for the past couple of years, son. A mother can tell things about her children they don't even know about themselves."

"I feel ashamed, Mama," Stanley moaned, looking away from her toward the wall pasted with cartoon ducks, a decoration one would expect in the room of a much less mature child.

"I don't understand it, son," she sighed deeply before continuing, "but I want you to know I love you. I always will, no matter what." She squeezed his hands in hers.

Stanley's cheeks instantly wetted anew. This time his beloved mother was there to throw her arms around him and cry as hard as he.

■　　■　　■

Stanley came to groggily. It was nearly dusk, and Mrs. Marx had told him she was going to fix his favorite supper of meat loaf and French fries smothered in onions and ketchup.

He eyed his watch. He had cried himself to sleep nearly four hours earlier.

"Come on down, son, it's ready!" Mrs. Marx called, to Stanley's delight no differently by her tone than usual.

Stanley stood too quickly, and his skinny body sat back hard. He waited a moment for the blood to refill his head. He arose again, realizing with alarm,

What about the paper route?

As if she had read his mind, his mother assured him loudly from the kitchen,

"I told Mr. Evans you were ill, so he took care of your deliveries."

"Thanks, Mama!" Stanley yelled in her direction.

"Clean up and come on, son. Your meat loaf and fries are waiting for you!"

Stanley's legs seemed heavy, slow to move. Because I ran so much today, he reasoned. He kept wishing he would wake up and he would be a small child with an intact, happy family. *If I had that,* he thought, *nothing else would matter... not even Bobby.*

He ambled toward the tiny mauve bathroom at the end of the hall, casting a glance to his left, looking at the pink bedroom his mother slept in. Maybe now, he hoped, he could paint his own bedroom pink, too, maybe get some frilly covers for his own bed, maybe decorate the...

Then he saw it.

At first it looked horribly ugly to him, the shotgun butt barely protruding from under his mother's box springs mattress. For the first time in his young life, however, he had an urge to hold it, to be in command of the one article of his father they still had.

He quickly pulled it the rest of the way out of its half open leather sheath case and hefted the weapon up, studying its curved twin percussion hammers and with curiosity pressing one of them backward until it unexpectedly cocked with a loud click.

Oh, no! You idiot! he chided himself. *How do you undo it?*

He regretted that he would have to show his mother who would undoubtedly, after uncocking the hammer, assume he was contemplating getting it all over with.

"No, we'll be okay," the boy said to convince himself. Life was about to change in ways he could not guess about, he felt, but like his mother had told him several hours earlier, this was not the end of the world. They would make a new beginning together, he and his mother, away from the ignorance and petty hatreds of Gilmore High and Garden Pines.

"Now if I really was going to do it..."

He sat at the edge of the bed and put the muzzle in his mouth. He licked and sucked on the double steel barrels for a moment to warm them, fantasizing about going down on two muscular, athletic older boys at once.

"Mnnn," he pleasantly moaned at a feminine pitch, imagining himself on his knees begging his two make-believe Adonises for the hot, salty man-juice he loved to gargle and swallow slowly, then feeling its thickness as it entered his stomach. *Love relish, as Bobby calls it.*

His thumb touched the front trigger and he sensed excitement from his perception of danger. *But of course I would never really do it. This is as far as I would ever...*

"Stanley!" his shocked mother, standing in the doorway, screamed.

Reflexively, he began to jump to his feet, his hands automatically moving downward to steady himself. His right thumb became hung between the triggers and without thinking, he jerked it downward to free it, his mouth still fellating the barrels.

Stanley's head exploded in a deafening blast and scarlet cloud from which flew high-velocity skull fragments and dentin missiles. A hole opened in the ceiling and as brain shards painted the attic, plaster fell in chunks from around the aperture's bloody corona. The plaster clattered mockingly around Stanley's decapitated body, which twitched for several seconds on the floor.

Mrs. Marx, wearing in front a new crimson coat made of her son's flesh particles, collapsed forward, bouncing hard on her knees with a loud double crack before kissing the tough-fibered carpet. She flailed helplessly in the mess on the floor, screaming herself hoarse until only short sobbing hisses bled from her strained throat.

■　■　■

"Let's cut hell on through here fast just in case Daddy comes out right now. That'd be just my luck."

The cabled stop light swinging in the wind turned yellow, then the bottom light lit red, and Billy followed Franco's urgent suggestion, pumping the Deltawasp's pedals hard. In a few seconds they were clear of the intersection and out of the line of sight of G. C. Campbell's construction office window. They pulled behind the local hamburger joint and Franco lit a cigarette, contemptuous of the disapproving, leering adults watching him from the drive-through line. He vigorously shook his match and as ever, without bothering to ensure that it was extinguished, unconcernedly tossed it into the dark green dumpster behind them. He blew double jets of smoke from his nostrils and smiled.

"Tastes gooooood, Bee-ly. Wanna weed, keed?"

"Not now."

"Aw, come on! You ain't had one all day!"

"Oh, alright. But I ain't going to throw the match in the dumpster like you did."

"Foque eet, bro," Franco countered, laughing as Billy clumsily lit up. "Damn fire department's right here. They can put it out. It'd be good practice for them."

Twenty yards away at County Station Six, three short beeps pierced the air. A mechanical rolling door clattered as it rose in the gray light of the chilly November afternoon. The boys saw two streaks of dark blue dash inside the station. Doors slammed and red lights flashed and an orange and white ambulance surged from its ready position. Its siren wailed sadly and the vehicle turned left onto the highway.

"Damn," Franco admitted, "I thought for a second they was after us. Thought I might have done set the damn dumpster on fire, after all."

"It's headed down the main drag the way we came, bro.' Look at that! Half the damn people ain't even getting out of the way! Wonder if they're going to a wreck? When we go back by, we might see something."

"Maybe they're going to rescue Stanley."

"Stanley? Why?"

"He's probably choking on a beeg deek."

The two snickered crudely. Franco blew away a lengthy plume and continued,

"Hey, bro', after we scare the hey-ull out of Bullshit Broward, we can get poo-sy from any girl in school. Even them damn stuck up cheerleaders."

"How do you figure that?"

"Easy. We make up a story about us having magic powers or some kind of sheet like that, then we show Rémy to any girl we want to foque. We tell her we'll put a curse or something on her if we don't get no poo-sy. Nobody'd believe it even if she says anything about it. Hey, Donald's done told a couple of kids in his own class about Rémy and even them little farts don't believe it. I wouldn't believe it neither if I hadn't seen Rémy alive, myself."

"What does Donald think about Rémy?"

"Doo-nell thinks Rémy's cool. He's been praying like hey-ull every night for one for himself. Hey, be thinking about which girls you want Rémy to scare for us."

"I can't think of nobody right off," Billy quipped, attempting to sidestep the proposal. "Anyway, we got to get on and drop Rémy and them off. Not much daylight left and we've got over three miles to go home. I'm catching hell when we do these missions," he hastened to add, complaining further, "I heard Momma tell Stepdad she was looking into sending my butt to a military school if I didn't straighten up."

"That's really bad, Billy. I'd hate that if it was me. What'd your stepdad say?"

"Well, I was listening to them at the vent in my room, so I didn't hear everything they said, but he sure ain't against it. He doesn't want me around."

"Hmmph. And Daddy's serious about us moving, too."

"Oh, shit! When?"

"Don't know. I wish they'd let just me live at the old house. You and Rémy could run away and move in, too. We could have us some hey-ull raising parties. Get lots of poo-sy. Feeeel gooood."

"Come on, let's cut hell and finish our mission! Tu say?"

"Hey yay! Oh-oh-seven all the way!" Franco catapulted his cigarette onto the asphalt and orange sparks flew helter-skelter. "There's old Bullshit's house over there. Think he'll see us?"

"We'll drop our men off at the bushes beside his driveway. I told Rémy to be safe and take his time getting home."

The boys pedaled past the fire station, pausing a moment to observe the empty bay area under the still open door. In ten more seconds they were at their destination. Billy gently placed Rémy and the two automatons in the cold-deadened grass beside Broward's gravel driveway.

"Let's be planning on what girls we want to foque," Franco insisted while the three figurines darted under the cover of the plentiful Chinese privet hedge forming a living border of Broward's front yard. "Hey, y'all! Scare him good!"

"Rémy! Don't get caught! Stab him only if you have to! Just come on home safe!"

"Scare the hey-ull out of him!"

"Yeah, scare him to death!"

The adolescents chortled as they walked their bikes uphill, just off the roadway in the dimming light. An uncomfortable recollection came to Billy.

"Dang, Franco, maybe I shouldn't have said that."

"Said what?"

"I shouldn't have said for Rémy to 'scare him to death.'"

"Foque Bullsheet. So what? Then we'll be rid of him."

"Maybe I ought to go back and tell him not…" Billy stopped and stared at Broward's front yard. Something was disturbing the grass near the cracked concrete steps of the small, red brick house. "Too late, I suppose."

"Yeah. Let them do their day-um job. We'll have him thinking he's crazy in no time. You know it?"

Billy squinted as the double beams of an approaching car's headlights turned on, brightly illuminating the pair.

"Reckon so," he slowly answered with extreme reservation.

■　■　■

Bull Broward let the towel fall from his thick waist and stepped into his boxer shorts, thinking about his coming rendezvous with the married civics teacher, Mrs. Edge. His smile turned downward when he felt an extruding drop of warmth under his chin.

"Crap."

Broward went back into the bathroom, still awash in steam from the bachelor's shower. Broward spied a touch of unwanted red where the warmth was.

"Crap twice," he mumbled. "Thirty years shaving and I still manage to get razor cuts."

In the spartanly furnished bedroom the telephone sounded a demanding summons. Bull haphazardly tore a bit of toilet paper from its wall-bound roll, placed it on the cut and had the receiver in his hand midway through the third ring.

"Yeah… Oh, Sue, yeah. At Mac's. No, the one west of Amelia. Uh-huh, seven-fifteen. That'll give us time to eat and get back here. Sam working until eleven or twelve tonight? Ah, the heck with his mother. It's none of her business where you go. Baby, anyone can take advantage of you… if you let them. What's that? Oh, leave it to me. I'll handle Waters. He can't even wipe his - - "

A loud hollow smack vibrated down the adjacent hallway. Bull held his breath. Alarmed, he told Mrs. Edge,

"Ssh! Got to check on something! Be right back!" Broward's eyes locked on the open doorway. He set the phone on a pillow and groped for the wooden bat beside his bedstead. He flexed the muscles rippling under his hair-covered arms, moving his beefy frame cautiously to the bedroom door.

"You kids playing games again?" He warned, "If I catch you in my house this time, it won't be just a couple of afternoons in detention. I'll get the sheriff to take you to jail! I don't care how young you are!"

No answer.

A bead of sweat formed over Broward's swarthy brow. He worriedly considered: What if it's Sue's husband? How could he possibly have found out?

"Sam?"

Silence.

Broward peered into the hall. There on the throw rug lay his .22 caliber rifle where it had obviously toppled from its position in the closet corner.

"Sheee!" Bull sighed, thoroughly relieved. To reinforce his peace of mind, he looked down the hall again. Several very rapid movements around the rifle caught his attention.

In the narrow confinement of the hall the .22's bark was deafening. Broward's left foot jerked sideways out from under him. The vice principal's face met the wall so hard that the sheetrock was crushed. His breath escaped him as his stocky body bounced off of the hardwood floor.

"Damn!" he cursed. "How could it fire by itself?" In his instep he saw a small crimson hole. His left ankle burned as if it had been stabbed with a glowing iron poker. He tried to raise his leg without success. "Damn it! Damn rifle!"

He gave the smallbore an angry sideways glance and spotted the tiny body of Blue boy wrestling with the muzzle end, like he was trying to aim it.

"What in the name of..." With disbelief, Broward watched Rémy's arm flash downward and strike the trigger. The bullet impacted on the bridge of the man's nose, sped up through the ridges of his maxillary sinus, and ricocheted repeatedly inside his cranium, transforming his brain into almost four pounds of useless mush. Bull Broward reflexively sneezed a bright scarlet mist and his dying bowels released their contents with a massive relaxation of smooth muscle.

Rémy studied the downed Broward for a full minute. Beyond the soiled body, Sue Edge's electronically transmitted demands to know what was happening were squeakingly audible. Rémy hoisted his spear and walked up to within an inch of Bull's face. He carved a diagonal slash across the corpse's forehead. Rémy's own head cocked to one side, then the other, his quick mind taking note of the relative lack of blood flow from the cut.

Half of his assignment was complete. He pivoted smartly and marched toward the living room, willing Blue boy and Rubberbuster to dutifully follow on either side. Rémy scanned the coat ahead, draped carelessly over a sofa arm.

Blue boy, assisted by the cupped hands of Rubberbuster, clambered up to the sofa seat nearest Bull's coat. At Rémy's psychokinetic order, Blue boy disappeared into a coat pocket and immediately pushed out two small gray photographs which Rubberbuster speedily retrieved and punctured with the barbed tip of Rémy's extended spear.

Rémy swung the photos aloft and his plastic mouth twisted into a laconic smile. He would discard these damning pieces of evidence in a drainpipe somewhere en route home. His dear human friend would be happy. With every plasmatic iota of his alien existence the Being knew that he had at last attained a personal goal, a necessary goal he had longed to accomplish for over three hundred unbearably lonely years...

Love you... Billy...

12

"I TALKED TO Mrs. Edge's husband's boss. Mr. Edge was at work. Apparently he suspected something was going on all along. He's on his way home right now."

"Ahhh, that's just great. Better get somebody on the way to her house fast or we might have yet another body on our hands tonight."

"On the way, Sarge."

Despite the grisly scene, Rick Wayman couldn't hold back a smile. Years earlier, he had trained the policeman who was now headed for the rear door. *Anticipate trouble*, he had told him so often. *Well*, Wayman hoped, *you'd better get there before Mr. Edge does.*

Several other officers were busy checking and rechecking measurements in Broward's hall and bedroom. A young rookie retched from the pungent odors of bodily excretions permeating the house and turned, grateful for a burst of fresh air as the back door opened to let one officer out and another in. Wayman asked the plainclothes newcomer,

"All wrapped up at the Marx house?"

"I guess so. Procedure's complete, anyway."

"I hated to bail out on you, leave you there by yourself, Paul," Wayman apologized, nodding to the prostrate form lying in the hall, "especially with a hysterical mother to deal with, but as you can see, the corn is popping tonight."

"Sure is." Paul Ross drew near to view the scene and continued, "The Marx case looks pretty much like a cut and dried suicide. And a messy one at that. The kid blew his brains and hair through the ceiling, all over the attic. Goddamn, it's awful what a twelve-gauge shotgun can do to a human head! A big chunk of skull stuck to the underside of the roof fell back out right on top of Mrs. Marx. She had to be sedated."

"The father show up?"

"Nah. He cut out a lot of years ago. We're trying to locate him."

"Any reason why the kid would drop the hammer on himself?"

"Nope. All Mrs. Marx could tell me was that Stanley had left school early and walked home, and that he was too torn up about something to even talk. She couldn't calm him down." Ross put his hands on his hips and added quickly, "I don't think she was being straight with me."

Wayman halfway smiled. *Yeah, he might make it as a detective after all.* He probingly asked, "Think she's hiding something, maybe? Like what was eating the kid up enough to make him kill himself?"

"That's exactly what my impression was, Sarge, but circumstances being what they were..."

"We'll check it out at the school tomorrow. This is, or was, his vice principal."

"What's the story here?"

"Nothing. That's the problem." Wayman shook his head. "No sign of entry anywhere. The doors and windows were all locked. The only tracks around are cat tracks going into a rat hole behind the back porch. No sign of any struggle, either. It's like the squirrel gun there fell out of the closet and shot him twice all by itself."

"Twice?"

"Yeah!" Wayman's face contorted with disbelief. He leaned over and asked the nauseated rookie, "Done with the muzzle measure?"

"Yes, sir, I mean, Sergeant."

"Okay. We'll check the throw rug for cordite. If forensics wants the gun, be sure to tell them to take the rug, too. And I have got to, absolutely got to know if this gun's been filed down at the sear."

"At the... the what, Sergeant?" the rookie queried, still green in the face.

"If he cut down the sear, it means he converted this rifle to a fully automatic mode. That means it could have fallen and fired two times. Write it down if you have to, son!"

"Yes sir... Sergeant, I mean!" The rookie produced a small writing pad and groped for a pen he didn't have. He ducked into the bedroom, hoping his partner had overheard and would remember Wayman's words.

"Who called it in?"

"The civics teacher, Paul. She was on the phone with this guy and pow, pow, she hears two shots a couple of seconds apart. She seemed to think he'd heard somebody out here."

"Are we looking at a love triangle here?"

"Yeah, but the husband is rock solid."

"Doesn't mean he didn't have someone else do it."

"You're catching on, Paul."

Ross carefully stepped between the rifle and Broward's corpse. After several moments of study he asked,

"What's this?"

"What's what?" Wayman rhetorically replied.

"It looks like there's some kind of a scratch on his forehead."

"We can't figure that out, either. Nothing on the wall he could've hit to cause that."

"Man, look at the dent he made. He sure kissed it hard."

"He might have scratched it himself before he was shot. He'd been shaving. That much is sure."

"Shaving? His forehead?" Now it was Ross's turn to smile.

"We'll have forensics check the surrounding tissues. And take his razor. It could be possible evidence… and any stray blades lying around."

"Wonder if any of the kids hate him enough to do this to him?"

"Good question. We'll check that angle at the school tomorrow and see if any of the staff can help us. I called the principal, guy named Waters, right before you got here. He couldn't help us over the phone but we'll be sure to check the disciplinary records. You never know what you'll find. Then again, even if this is a murder, it might not have a blessed thing to do with the school. Here's the techs. Time to move out of the way, Paul."

Two specialists carrying their kits stood behind Wayman, impatiently waiting for the investigators to step aside. The balding older one asked,

"Photographer done his thing yet?"

"Yeah. He popped a lot of flashcubes. He's in the living room now."

"Any place or thing special, Rick?"

"The gun, of course, and the sink and mirror in the bathroom. And also dust the phone in the bedroom and all the door facings and knobs. Give me a call if anything shows, Bob. Hey, don't kick the gun, Paul."

"Sorry."

"Give special attention to the razor and any loose blades. Find out if you can what made that cut over his eyes."

"Okay."

"And Bob, I don't care what time it is, call me if anything shows."

■ ■ ■

"Where's the picture, Al?"

"Oh! Franco, you're gonna get my jacket all dirty! I'll get in trouble!"

"You're already in trouble! Now answer Bee-ly, you leetle queer!" Franco Campbell pinned Al Gates hard against the dingy back wall of the coal bin. "Only one who seen me put them pictures up was you, and you done admitted getting one of them down right before fourth period. Where the hey-ull is it at?"

"Don't hit me! Just don't hit me!"

"Lay off a little, bro," Billy interceded. "Al, the whole school knows Stanley Marx killed hisself last night. We gotta have that picture or we'll all go to jail."

"It's under my chest o' drawers, in a yellow envelope. I'll bring it to you. Just don't let him hit me!"

"I'll beat the god-day-um hey-ull outta - - "

"Okay, Al. You bring it to me after school. Let him go, Franco."

"You been running your mouth everywhere telling all about being a secret agent man for the Little Boys. You ain't no god-day-um Little Boy!" Franco pressed the helpless Al harder into the bricks.

"I didn't say nothin' about y'all! I said I took the pictures! Nobody knows nothin' about y'all!"

"And nobody better find out! If I have to go to jail, I'll kill you! I had to wash 'Little Boys' off of my goddamn jacket because of you!" Franco's left hand found Al's Adam's apple and made the eighth grader cough painfully. Young Campbell's right hand reached into his pants and grasped the red-handled pocket knife. Billy said,

"No, bro', don't pull it on him. He'll be all right. Let him go."

"You better not say sheet!"

"I won't! I won't!"

"Nothing, you leetle queer!"

"I won't! Swear to God! You can trust me!"

"You can go on to class, Al. And Al, you don't know a thing. Right?"

"Yeah!" Young Gates frantically scampered up the dirt trail behind the gymnasium. Billy made a quick visual check of the gym windows to ensure there had been no witnesses to the drama. Franco stated,

"That leetle queer'll fall apart if a cop starts asking him questions. He ain't tough like us!"

"I know it. I'll put Rémy on it. He'll figure out some way we can keep Al from talking. I hate to say it, bro', but if we're going get out of this one, we might have to get more than just that photo. Bro'... I didn't want to tell you on the bus, but... Rémy shot Mr. Broward dead last night. He told me he made it look like an accident."

Franco smiled broadly and immediately suggested,

"We'll get him to kill Al, too!"

"Franco, Rémy killed Broward to protect me. We never should have taken those damn pictures. Anyway, Rémy found the two Mr. Broward had and destroyed them. I'm just worried about anybody having seen Al get the third picture."

"Hey... they'll blame us for shooting old Bullshit. Plenty of people seen us on our bikes last night."

"Maybe Rémy can convince Al he'll go to hell or something if he breaks down and tells what he knows."

"God-day-um, you know he will."

"He don't know anything about Rémy, so maybe..."

"Get Rémy to cut his throat while he's asleep! Hey-ull, yeah!"

"No! Not if we don't have to! There's been enough killing!" Billy swallowed hard. "Rémy will figure something out for us. If no one gets hurt, that would be best, but, ah, let's just let Rémy handle it. He knows better than we do what to do about this mess."

A shape materialized atop the edge of the coal bin's gaping lip. A tenor voice proposed,

"Hey, you buttheads, what say we skip first period?"

"Hey, Eddy!" Franco called in greeting. "Sounds good to me! Got a weed, keed?"

"Shit, yeah!" Eddy Mundy grinned, showing his prematurely decaying teeth. He dropped a filterless cigarette which Franco deftly caught.

"Man, he's your friend, not mine," Billy softly informed Franco with no uncertainty of disapproval. Billy spun on his heels and walked toward the main building as the first bell sounded. He ignored the entreaties of his friend and young Mundy to stay.

"Aw, come on, Bee-ly!"

"Yeah, man. Stay here. We'll show 'em!"

"Can you believe it, Rém'?" Billy bitterly asked his companion, sequestered as usual in his jacket pocket. "Can you believe how much they look alike with those damn peroxide streaks in their hair?"

▪ ▪ ▪

"Yes, I do remember. Mr. Broward usually asks, uh, that is, you see, he asked to use my phone even when he was in a hurry. But he didn't ask yesterday. Why, do you know he almost knocked over my nail polish? What a mess that almost made! He wasn't nice at all!"

"Do you remember who he called, Mrs. Quigley? What he said? It's very important!" Wayman's characteristic diplomacy was wearing thin. The elderly secretary was frustratingly slow in recollecting the vice principal's words of the previous noon.

Paul Ross nodded and smiled to his partner and mentor as if to say, *Calm down, she'll come through, just give the old girl a minute*. But Ross was impatient, too. The morning report had revealed that the sear on Broward's .22 had not been filed, thus eliminating the possibility that the weapon had accidentally discharged twice. Ross had learned the mechanics of small arms in the green hell of Vietnam, as Wayman had in Europe a generation earlier. Worse, there were no telltale prints anywhere in the house except those of Broward. The pair was convinced that Bull's death was more than an unfortunate happenstance.

"I try my best never to pay any attention to personal calls," the gray-haired lady began, prompting Wayman's chest to puff out with consternation.

"It is urgent, Mrs. Quigley. Please!" Wayman, with a deliberate slowness, pleaded.

"Well, I did hear him ask to meet with them. The parents. It was something that Mr. Broward was very, very concerned about. Oh, he was rough with the boys and girls when they needed it, but - - "

"Whose parents did he want to meet with, Mrs. Quigley?" Ross asked.

" - - but he cared about all the kids. He really did care, you see - - "

"Whose parents?" the junior officer repeated.

" - - if he hadn't cared, he wouldn't have been the way he - - "

"Whose?" Wayman roared. The two other ladies in the front office, also staff assistants, stared in shock at the investigators.

" - - gone to the trouble he did," Mrs. Quigley continued, unruffled. "Whose parents, you ask? It was his mother he talked to. I know that."

Wayman's lips formed another, an unspoken, "Whose?" but this time Mrs. Quigley beat him to the punch.

"That poor little Stanley Marx's mother."

■ ■ ■

The unmarked sedan glided leisurely through the quiet leaf-strewn street. Paul Ross posed the question,

"So what if they are connected? And if so, how? Mrs. Marx is so torn up, she doesn't even remember Broward calling."

"Poor woman," Wayman muttered. "But tying the two shootings together right now would be jumping to conclusions. That's the hard part, Paul, keeping different possibilities open and resisting the easy route. You can't take a thing for granted or assume anything when people are involved. Logic alone don't make it. Look over there."

"Another petty theft. Getting to be common in this area," Ross acknowledged, seeing the patrol car parked several streets away, and adding, "A pro job like the others?"

"Yep… no sign of entry in that one either, I'll bet you, except maybe a screen barely cut on a corner. Paul, you won't see me connecting these thefts with the Broward case on the single common point of lack of forced entry. Yet, you've got to keep it all in the back of your mind."

"We do have to talk to the kids at school."

"Definitely," Wayman agreed to a point, "but not at school. I find that kids at school tend to dummy up no matter what. Some kind of image, a code, not to tell on anyone."

"Like crooks."

Wayman choked out a short laugh. "Kind of, in a way you could say that. We'll talk to the kids who were Stanley's neighbors first. I hope we can find out some possibilities as to why the Marx kid did himself in. If a Broward connection crops up, we'll take it from there. But like I said, don't force it. It'll only confuse the process."

"Let's see." Ross ran a finger down the column of names that the principal, Mr. Waters, had given them. "Where do you want to start?"

"Right there. Straight ahead in the curve. Remember that Campbell kid we questioned after the Jones fire? I'm sure he knew Stanley. We'll do this systematically, move on to the next kid, and so on. We'll go make a few preparatory calls and get right on it in the morning."

"I love working on Saturdays," Ross facetiously volunteered. Wayman said with equal waggishness,

"Welcome to investigations, the most regular and predictable part of police work."

13

"THE CHAPTER INTRODUCING the wondrous world of quadratic equations was handled, overall, I'd say, with your usual flair for half-heartedness," the ever-sarcastic Mr. Kline spouted, handing previously sorted sheaves of graded tests to each front row student. The girl in front of Billy took her paper and passed the rest to him. Billy imitated her action and saw with satisfaction the grade glaringly posted in red ink above his name.

"There was, however, one notable exception to this mediocrity which has served as this class's trademark so far this year. Mr. Beaudet, it seems, has buckled down. He has progressed from an average of just under a D to your champion of quadratics. Mr. Beaudet, please raise your test paper."

"Whooooo," came the universal response as Billy obeyed. The stiff-backed teacher resumed his praise:

"Let his one hundred per cent serve as an example. If Beaudet can do it, and he is, I concede to you, young sir, quite smart, then each of you in here can do as well. My main task would seem to lie in finding out what might motivate you."

The last dismissal bell of the school week shook Gilmore High's walls. Someone patted Billy's back in congratulations as he gathered his books. To his left John Marston smiled, saying,

"Billy-Bo, you're the one who might get me through this course now instead of the other way around. Man, these quads are pretty tough. How'd you max this mother?"

"I found a good tutor, bro'. He knows all about this stuff."

"Do I know him?"

"Nah, he's, ah, he's out of school."

"You must have worked on them quadratics quite awhile."

"Not really, John. He, well," Billy foundered to express the fact, "he kind of just pours it into my head. I don't have any trouble at all remembering equations and formulas and how to work them, any of them, anymore."

"I wish you could get him to pour it into mine," John obliquely hinted, moving out of the classroom. Billy was close behind him.

"Tell you what, bro'... one day," he said as the two stopped at John's locker, "... one day, I'll tell you all about it. John, you're my friend. I don't have very many. I can count them on one hand. I won't forget you."

John managed a weak smile. He liked the young misfit equally in return, but the nation was on fire racially and the boys were cultures apart. "Hey," John quipped, "Hee-hee, Billy-Bo, here comes your honey!"

Billy swiveled and saw Sharee Post emerge from the bustle. She appeared deeply pensive.

"Oh, Billy, I still can't get over the announcement on the PA this morning about Mr. Broward's accident. And people are saying those awful pictures are why Stanley killed himself. How could anybody be so cruel as to stick pictures like that up so everybody would see them?"

"Don't know," he lied, taking her hand. "Come on. I'll walk you as far as the library."

"Billy!" she gently admonished, pulling her hand downward so that only her fingers lingered on his. "We can't hold hands in the hall! Mister - - "

"Broward will see us? Not any more he won't." Billy took her hand again and they were soon by the library's double doors. Billy studied Sharee's expression. She looked confused.

"Billy, are you okay?"

"Yeah, babe. Why?"

"I kind of see a mean streak in you. Like you're almost happy about poor Mr. Broward being - - being - - "

"Dead? Nah! Not about him being dead." Billy struggled to assemble another prevarication. "It's just that, whenever I'm with you, no matter what else is going on, I'm happy. Yeah, that's it."

"Billy! I'm - - I'm - - aren't you the smooth one!" Sharee cooed, dovelike.

"Here!" Billy dug a gold wristlet from a trousers pocket and showed Sharee the inner surface. "See, babe, I had it engraved: 'To SP from WB.' I don't forget my friends."

"Oh, Billy, you shouldn't have! And you got it engraved for me! But is it really what it says? Eighteen carat... gold? Real gold?"

"Yep!" Billy exclaimed proudly, thinking about how skillfully Rémy had wielded the sharp point of the compasses he'd kept from last year's geometry course. "See, I've got this friend, my best friend, he's a really good engraver. The best. He got me a good deal on the bracelet, too."

"Franco can engrave like this? Why, Billy, this looks professional! I didn't know Franco could even spell!"

"No, not Franco. Another guy, you don't know him, he's out of school now, see, hey, I gotta catch my bus! See you tomorrow?"

"You bet!" Sharee arched her head back, letting her ash-blonde waves cascade over her black sweater. She waited a second or two at the doors, watching Billy walk backwards. "Don't trip and fall!" she warned bemusedly.

"Okay!" Billy turned as he exited the building. The stones in the bus parking lot crunched under the soles of his soft gray shoes. He whispered to his concealed comrade,

"Hope she doesn't say anything to Franco about having my best friend engrave that bracelet you brought in last week. We can't ever tell him you're my best friend. We can never hurt Franco's feelings. Okay, Rém'?"

A single gentle push under Billy's left breast answered in assent. Billy could not resist, adding, as he mounted the bus steps,

"But we know. Don't we, Rém'?"

■ ■ ■

Al Gates' knuckles whitened as he squeezed the cream-colored receiver. His nervousness affected his voice and he could barely choke out a trembling reply,

"Yeah, Billy. I'm down here in me and Joe's room. No. No one's around. Yeah, my momma said some cop is gonna come talk to me and Joe about something tomorrow. I know he's gonna ask about Stanley. I just know it! Should I go ahead and say I took them pictures? I don't want to now! I'm skeered!"

"No, Al, no!" Billy's tone was deceptively calm and reassuring. "Don't admit to a thing! They'll talk to all the kids around here. They're just going to ask if you knew if anything was bothering Stanley. Whatever you say, do not say anything about Franco putting those pictures up. They'll accuse us of killing Broward!"

"They said on the announcements that that was a accident!"

"Uh, yeah, well... shit, you know cops. They'll blame us anyway. You listen to me right now and don't you screw this up!"

"Yes sir!" Al quaked.

"You got the damn picture?"

"Wait... yeah, it's still in the envelope."

"Take it out."

"Okay... it's out."

"Put the damn picture on the ground just outside your window. Put something on top of it so it don't blow down to the damn Squeeds' driveway. And don't you let anybody see you!" Billy shifted his head so he could better listen to his mother at the other end of the house shuffling kitchenware in preparation for supper. Through the phone line he could identify the opening, then the slamming, of a window. He laid down the receiver and walked across his stepfather's darkened bedroom. Across the street he could barely distinguish an edge of a photograph between the ground-level window and one of the many holly bushes fronting the Gates home. A black object appeared to sit atop the photo.

Billy also spied the '56 red and white Chevy that Al's brother Joe was so proud of. *So far, so good,* Billy thought, stealthily returning to the phone in time to hear Al tell him,

"I done it! I put Joe's clock on top of it. You going to come and get it?"

"Yeah, later. Listen, Al. This is the most important part. Make sure you go to the bowling alley with Joe tonight. Me and Franco will meet you there and we can make plans on what to say to the cops."

"Joe won't take me with him. See, he just goes there to meet Donna and they go and eat or whatever. He don't never want me to come."

"Al!" Billy hissed, one ear still intently keyed on his mother's kitchen activities. "I don't care how you do it, make sure you go with him! Tell him some girls will be there to meet us, hell, I don't care!"

"Okay, Billy. I'll get him to take me. I promise. But how will we get back home?"

"Got that covered. Don't worry about it." Billy laid the receiver down on its pegged base and somberly went back to his room. Rémy came out from under the bedspread skirt and watched the boy kneel beside the shelves.

"Guess I'd better put all this jewelry in a bag and bury it at the pipe, just in case the cops do look around the house. You never know for sure what cops are going to do."

Rémy ducked back under the bed and quickly reappeared, brandishing a rusty hacksaw blade.

"The picture's laying outside his window." Billy sighed, staring tiredly at Rémy's blade. "Whatever you gotta do, Rém'..."

■ ■ ■

"I ought to have my head examined for letting you tag along tonight! Don't you think for half a minute you'll be able to hang around me and Donna and our friends!"

"No way, Joe! Me and the rest of the Little Boys are gonna have our own girls there!" Al bragged.

"Whaaat?" Eighteen year old Joseph Gates smirked in disbelief and pushed a brown curl away from his eyes as the Chevy ground to an uncomfortably slow halt at the intersection.

"Yeah. That's my gang. I hang out with tenth graders. Didn't you know? We're the Little Boys!"

"'Little' is right. Darn it, I just put new drums on her last month. Brakes are awful soft."

"Cut loose when we're downhill on Faron Road!"

"You listen to me, you little weenie! If you hadn't whined and cried as much as you did to Momma, you'd still be at home where you belong. You got any money?"

"Yeah. Momma gave me five bucks," Al replied. The Chevy's motor powered up as Joe wheeled it onto the local favorite downhill drag. "And Daddy gave me two more!" Al gleefully added.

"You little pootface! You've got more money than I do!" Joe laughed, his foot pressing harder on the gas pedal.

"Burn rubber!" squealed Al.

"Aw, what am I doing, trying to impress my little brother? Who gives a ... hey," Joe's ruddy face contorted. "Aw, no! No, it - - I ain't got brakes! The brakes are gone!"

"What? What are we gonna do?" Al opened his door slightly, the inrushing wind making it hard for him to hear Joe's command,

"Shut the door, Al! You'll fall out!"

"What are we gonna do?" Al again demanded to know, abandoning his plan to jump. The car was still accelerating. Eight hundred yards ahead in the night, one lane Faron Creek Bridge spanned the terrain cleavage at the bottom of the hill.

"Listen to me, Al!"

"I'm skeered, Joe! I'm skeered!"

"Listen to me! We're the only car on the road, so we'll cross the bridge, hang on, it'll be rough, then we'll slow down using the shoulder. I'll gear down when I can. Don't worry about - - "

"We gonna make it?"

"Sure - - ah, no! No! No! No!" Headlights materialized ominously in the darkness. "Looks big, like a tractor-trailer, maybe!"

Al screamed in panic, "We're gonna die!"

"No, we ain't! We'll make it to the bridge first!"

"Help us, God!"

The approaching vehicle's low rumble became audible. It was indeed a truck, at least a ten-wheeler and it was moving a good bit faster than Joe had believed.

"Hang on, Al! I might have to ditch it!"

"God! Oh, God! Yaaaaa!"

Joe Gates was about to meet the onrushing goliath on the bridge itself. He waited until the truck's blinding headlights flashed off and back on, its driver signaling that he was the biggest mother on Faron Road and by golly, he had the right-of-way.

"Brace yourself, Al!"

As Al's screams ripped his eardrums, Joe wrenched his Chevy's steering wheel hard to the right. The car smashed into the railing and a metal support hidden within a post hung the front bumper. The heavy automobile flipped in response and landed top down in the knee-deep creek. The last sound Al Gates heard was the muffled popping of his own neck bones being pulverized.

The ten-wheeler's engine wound down and the steel beast, having crossed the bridge as the Chevy was still airborne, slowed momentarily. Unexpectedly, it geared up and continued its journey on the lonely blacktop, its panicked driver's insidious secret securely shrouded in the thick darkness.

14

NOVEMBER 11

"I DON'T KNOW, Betty baby."

"Well, I thought you might have heard… something… about it, Jack."

"Umph," Jack Capler grunted, raking his roast beef back and forth across his plate like a cat playing with a mouse's dangling entrails. He paused to watch his wife light another cigarette. She whipped the sulfurous match sideways to snuff the flame, her wrist bones cracking in their small sockets with the effort. Capler's words came as the match hit his wife's uneaten supper and the wafting stink entered Billy's nostrils.

"All I know is, Sheriff Gibbons is thinking somebody might have cut the Gates boy's brake line. Damn brake fluid's all over the street out there. Just an idea they've got to look into."

"Teenagers!" Mrs. Capler moaned, aggravatingly louder than usual. Billy continued to devour his meal in silence, not caring to argue with his mother about her favorite put-down subject. He could feel the upwelling resentment emanating from not only his mother but his stepfather as well, who bluntly revealed,

"That detective wanted to talk to you, too, boy, about the Marx boy."

"Why?" Billy shot back as he lowered his fork. The boy saw redness in Capler's eyes, a redness he'd seen too often, one that could not be obscured by the sunglasses the man habitually wore everywhere, it seemed. *Careful,* Billy advised himself. *He's been in his goddamn bourbon again.*

"Stories are getting around that your buddy was a gayboy. Did you know that?"

"A what?"

"Ah! Don't shit me, boy! You know what a damn gayboy is!"

"Jack, don't speak to the… child… like that!"

"I'm not a child, Momma!"

"Well, you're not a man, either! Are you… boy?" Capler tauntingly spat, his brown orbs glowing with unprovoked anger behind their green screens. "If I didn't know the county sheriff so well, the detective would've come right over here like he did all the other little farts."

"William doesn't appreciate influence, Jack."

"Yeah! Yeah! Ain't that the truth! He even asked G.C.'s boys about the gayboy paper boy. Yeah, G.C. didn't pull no strings, and, ah, shit!..." Capler rambled, "I used to double date with Sheriff Gibbons, long time ago. Ah, hell, you don't care, do you, boy? You know it all, don't you? Got it made, right? A free ride off of me. Shit, that ain't going to last forever, I'll tell you that."

"Jack, why don't you go on upstairs?" Betty suggested, an unmistakable tremor threading itself throughout her words.

"Yer mommer and I - - hell, I had to take you, too. Little fuzzy-haired, useless - - you were part of a package deal. You eat like a damn horse and you don't do a damn thing to earn your keep around here!"

"He cuts the grass, Jack," Mrs. Capler offered, ruining her weak attempt at conciliation by adding, "... in the summer."

"Sure, I was part of 'a package deal,'" Billy bitterly blurted, unable to hold it back any longer. "You knew that, didn't you? I was what? Four, five, when you two got married? Looked real good, didn't it, Stepdad? That's where you left me, too. Momma, you call me a loner..."

"Well... you are a loner."

"That's what I've been taught to be by both of you! So I didn't ask to be born, okay?"

"William," his mother began calmly, "Don't play the suffering little - - "

"Lord Fauntleroy, Momma?"

"Now, you just wait one goddurn minute! I have never called you that!"

"No, let the boy talk!" Capler barked. "He'll hang himself. When you turn twenty-one, boy, your butt's gone!"

"That'll make you happy, won't it?"

"Well!" Capler, without warning, gave a belly laugh that sounded like the discharge of a twelve-gauge shotgun. "I've put up with you too damn long already, if you really want to know. I married your mommer because I love her. I'll tell you one damn thing, boy... you're just a... inconvenience."

Capler angrily crushed his greasy napkin into his lips and, as he always had, pitched it toward Billy's plate. This time, however, the boy was ready for it. He lifted his left arm to deflect the de facto gauntlet and, to his dismay, it bounced back onto Capler's plate, right on top of the man's beloved mashed potatoes.

Capler growled. It was a deep, primeval animal growl. It came from his gut. Billy knew he'd opened himself up for more than a momentary abusive swipe or two with the fly swatter. *Oh, the hell with it,* he accepted, mentally projecting an escape through the carport door.

"William, you go on to your room! Go on! Right now, while you're still ahead! Go on!"

"Yes, ma'am," Billy acknowledged dully, refusing to display any relief at or gratitude for his mother's intercession.

■   ■   ■

"Nah, Rém', we can never bump him off. Much as I'd like to, sometimes." Billy set the cigar box atop the moldy folding game board and started pulling chess pieces out. Rémy hopped off of the window sill and began to help his friend prepare the black and red battlefield. "See, Rém, if we kill him, where'll we go? I just wish he'd stop drinking. He's okay, I guess, when he's not drinking. Sometimes he's even a good guy. He really is. Wish there was some way we could get him off the booze.

"Back when I was a little kid, I guess about six or seven years old, he took me to a movie where we used to live, nearer to Grammaw's than this place here. The movie was about this astronaut that went up into space and when he came back, he turned into this really badass caveman. It was really cool."

Astronaut?

"Yeah, the guys that travel around the earth in capsules. They shoot them up into outer space and go around and around the earth. They call it orbiting."

Rémy know all about that.

"Anyway, he seemed to like it a lot, the movie, but then we told Momma about it. That was a real bonehead thing to do. She said it was all 'ridiculous comic book crap.' I remember her saying it just like that, like she was spitting or puking at us."

Man not tell her different?

"No. He got drunk right afterwards and wouldn't talk about it any more. Never took me to no more movies, either."

Rémy not kill him, Billy. Him hurt inside as much as woman hurt. This kind of pain no one can help. Not kill him.

"Good. Thanks, bro'. Hey! You know, Rém, I love these chess games we have. I never could figure out how to play it. Then I read the rules out of that encyclopedia article to you, and you taught me! Man, you're smart! I just needed someone, I suppose, to take the time and help me, you know, really explain it slow."

Love you... Billy...

"I love you too, Rém. Hey, you want to be black or white?"

No matter.

"Me neither. Here. Finish setting up white. I'll be black. Now, don't show me any mercy!"

No mercy!

"Because I don't care if you always win, as long as I'll be able to beat anybody else. See, when you win, I win anyway. Know what I mean, Rém'?"

Rémy shoved his final piece, the white king, into position, and shook his right fist as a ready signal.

"I used to imagine my real father and I playing with these pieces. I used to wish he was here to teach me... but having you here is even better. I can tell you anything, Rém."

The door creaked as it slowly opened. Rémy instantly became still. Billy twisted around and saw Mrs. Capler wearing a look of troubled frustration on her lined face.

"Son, we don't expect... much... from you. Why do you disappoint us so?"

"Disappoint... you? I'm going out for a walk, Momma!"

"It's dark, William, and it's too cold. You've got no business going outside. You didn't go out to go to Stanley's funeral in the daytime, so why do you want to - - "

"He was just a gayboy, remember? Would you want me to be seen there?"

"Son, I just want you to be... normal!"

"Right!" Billy found his thin jacket hanging in its usual closet niche and made no effort to conceal his putting Rémy in the customized pocket.

"William, I'm tired of trying to teach you right from wrong. You ought to know better than to test me like you do. You do it constantly."

"It's all right, I won't be gone long, Momma."

"Don't you go to the goddurn Campbells' house!" she warned.

"I won't. I promise," Billy, somewhat cooler than he had been a few seconds earlier, informed her. He walked past his stepfather's room and took note that the man was snoring loudly, already sleeping off the effects of his whiskey. Billy knew that Capler might remember nothing of their suppertime confrontation.

Mrs. Capler stared for a moment at the abandoned chessmen, shaking her curly, thinning head of hair and wondering what to do about Billy's newly found boldness. Resignedly, she switched off Billy's gloomy fluorescent room light and went downstairs. There she would drown her maternal impotence in the murky abyss of a basement echoing with the canned nonsense and false mirth of Saturday night variety shows.

■ ■ ■

Rémy clung to Billy's jacket collar like a beggar lice. He gave a gentle tug, and Billy cautiously avoided the light which leaped from the windows to illuminate huge rectangular chunks of grassy yard.

"She ain't in the kitchen or living room. You think she might be downstairs? There's a car beside the carport, so she ain't by herself, dang it! Hey, I need some of her hot loving! Come on, Rém', let's look through the basement windows!"

Billy stooped low and approached the front basement window. He trembled when he saw the ghostly light of a television within.

"Dang, Rém', I don't see anybody in there, neither. Come on, I'll bet you she's on the other side!"

Billy's tennis shoes sucked up dank mud as he tried vainly to silently traverse the front of the door. His excitement mounted.

"I hear something, Rém'! There's a light on! Let's look under the curtain!"

Billy's heart sank. On the same bed she had so seductively led him to, Janet Mills rode atop a man Billy had never seen before. She rocked back, moaning with her impalement, as her partner smiled with an ecstasy which Billy felt rightfully to be his. Janet leaned forward and wetly smothered the man with her conquering mouth. Billy's anger mounted with his desire to be the one tasting her delicious, demanding tongue.

"Goddamn that fucking whore!" Billy furiously sputtered, backing into the ebony recesses between a pair of back yard maple trees. "I don't mind her doing that with her husband, but this is - - this is - - god-fucking-damn!" Billy stomped the moist earth and wondered what to do. "I'm so fucking mad, Rémy! How can we fuck these assholes up?"

Let out air in man's car tires?

"Yeah, Rém', go let out his air. Let it out of all his tires so he won't be able to leave. Mr. Mills will kill them both when he finds out about this bullshit. Hell yeah, he'll at least divorce the bitch! Goddamn whore!"

Billy hate woman?

"Yeah! Yeah! I hate her slutty fucking guts!" Billy hissed in reply, his jealousy uncooled. "Don't kill her, Rém', and don't burn the damn house down, but do something... something, you think of it, to fuck up the cheating bitch but good!"

Rémy leaped from Billy's shoulder and landed effortlessly on his styrene feet. Lost in the shadows, Rémy sent a telepathic question which entered Billy's head as easily as ever,

Not kill?

"No, Rém', but hurt the bitch bad! Get her caught, I don't care! I'm going on down to the pipe and get that necklace for Sharee. Sharee's not a cheating ass whore like Janet!"

The rush of leaves being swept aside told Billy that his friend was headed for the other side of the Mills' house. Billy's wrath lessened slightly as the fact that a certain measure of satisfaction was coming worked its way into his head. The boy cursed, stumbling through the dimly moonlit marsh pools en route to the pipe. Near the big twisted oak root, his nose discerned the unmistakable odor of exhaled tobacco smoke.

"Franco?" he called, his heart pounding. He prayed that the police weren't lying in wait to arrest him for receiving the fruits of Rémy's nocturnal escapades.

"Hey-ull, yeah!" responded a hollow but gratifyingly familiar voice.

"Damn, bro', I'm glad it's you! I was afraid the damn cops were down here!"

Franco Campbell's black silhouette moved vaguely at the pipe's far end. The glow of another cigarette puff illuminated his face with a blaze of orange lasting less than a second before he added, shaking,

"Sheet, bro', they grilled the hell out of me and Doo-nell. Did they come see you?"

"Naw. Tell me about it. What did they say?" Billy hop-scotched over the chilly inrushing creek and sat opposite his friend.

"It was them same two who talked to me back when Lou got burned up. We didn't tell them sheet. They wanted to know if Stanley liked girls. I said I didn't know. That old cop said they'd heard Stanley might have been a day-um queer. He didn't say queer. He said some other word that means it, preverter or something like that. I know he thought I was lying, but I don't care. They can't prove nothing!"

"Did Doo-nell say anything to them?"

"Hey-ull, naw. He done real good. He made them think he's retarded or something."

"Bro'... Rémy's the one who caused the Gates' wreck. He cut their brake line. Damn cops are really going to be nosing around here now."

"I heard only Al got killed."

"Joe's legs were both busted, but he'll be okay. Main thing is, Al ain't around no more to run his big ass mouth. And I burned that last picture up in the fireplace. No more evidence."

"You got Rémy with you?"

"Nah. I gave him something to do for me. You know that damn Janet?"

"Miz Mills?"

"Yeah. The goddamn bitch was screwing some man in her basement!"

"Ay, shay-it! That ain't worth a sheet! She's supposed to be your poo-sy, sheety bro'! Want a weed, keed? Make you feel better... foque that beech. Who gives a day-um? They're all a dime a damn dozen!"

"No, thanks. Anyway, I sent Rémy to fuck her up."

"Day-um, bro'! If she gets killed too, that'll really put the sheet on us! You know it? I hated talking to them cops. Sure don't want to do it again."

"It's okay. I told him not to kill her."

"Sure hope he don't," Franco spoke with uncharacteristic concern.

"Ah, shit on all of them!" Billy spat. "Yeah, why not? Give me a weed, hell yeah... as long as we don't say nothing, they can't prove nothing!"

"We're moving pretty soon," Franco stated, handing Billy a cigarette and match book.

"Aw, no! When?"

"Don't know. I'm afraid it'll be pretty soon, though. Daddy wants to get moved out and in the new place before the campaign gets started. He's going to try that politics sheet again. State repre – rep - whatever the sheet it is."

"You want all that jewelry Rémy's been getting? I got it buried under the bushes now. The oak root hole was too easy for someone to find." Billy ignited a match, the flash momentarily exposing the pipe's interior so brightly that it hurt his eyes. "I also got about thirty bucks in coins and sixty-eight in bills behind my book shelf. You can have all that, too. I just want to keep a necklace to give Sharee next week."

"She might give you some poo-sy. You need you some poo-sy, bro'. Feel good."

"Who knows?" Billy entertained the idea for the first time as a real possibility. "It's a shame you can't pack up Pammy and take her with you."

"Ah, piss on god-day-um old Pammy! She won't even talk to me no more. I don't know what's wrong with her, and I don't give a day-um, neither. Thanks for asking if I want all that sheet you got stashed, but Eddy Mundy's planning something that'll get us about a thousand, maybe two or three thousand dollars."

"What have you got in mind?"

"Eddy's got this fake pistol that looks real. He wants to rob Mr. Hoffman's service station up by the college. He's got it all planned out, man, we can't miss! He's even got some masks for us to wear, you know, them kind what you wear in the snow."

"I don't like the sound of it."

"Naw, see, we get a bunch of damn money, escape through the woods, take off the masks, cut hell home. Easy!"

"I'd still think about it first. Hey, thanks for the weed, keed!"

"You going already?"

"Yeah. Say hey to Doo-nell for me. I gotta get back home. You okay?"

"I reckon." Franco stared into the blackness past the shimmering, noisy outflow pool. His teeth chattered along with the hollow rushing of dried oak and maple leaves as an unexpected blast of cold wind suddenly swept in upon the boys.

Ignoring the discomfort, Billy rose and without looking back, exited the pipe, opting not to grope for the necklace in the cold, dank earth under the privet bush. Climbing the slope to the waiting street, he wondered what Rémy was up to and how he would handle the mission he had given him.

15

November 12

BILLY KNEW HE was only half awake, but he could not bear to rouse his adolescent body. The enthralling disks of scarlet were back, slowly lowering from his ceiling, an indescribably beautiful symphony accompanying their descent.

"Sheee... oh, no," he mumbled, seeing red flashes instead of disks, jumping about the room. A rush of adrenaline instantly broke his torpor. "Janet!" he said aloud.

Rémy sat motionless and cross-legged on the window sill, his face turned to the source of the commotion a hundred yards downhill.

"What did you do, Rém'? Please don't say you burned her house down. I sure hope you didn't. "

A police cruiser entered the Mills' gravel driveway and parked parallel to an ambulance partially hidden by the pine boughs extending over the fence. A scuffle was in progress, its combatant parties obscured by the tree limbs and the low-lying dawn mist.

Billy cracked the window open.

Rémy fuck woman up.

"Good... good." Billy heard shouts and threats. Dwight Mills was somewhere down there and he wasn't happy. "What's going on down there?"

"Get away from him! I'm not gonna tell you again! I'll have to lock you up!"

"Lock me up? Me? You can't be serious! That son of a bitch - - "

"What did he say to you, mister?" a different voice asked stringently. "You just calm down!"

"I'll kill you, goddamn it, I'll - - "

Billy gently lowered his window. Rémy still had not budged, but he answered his friend's next question before it was asked.

Rémy not kill her, Billy.

Billy looked into Rémy's khaki eyes and felt an encompassing pulse of protectiveness pass through him.

"It's okay, little bro'. For whatever it was you did, thanks. It's good enough for me. You know it's always good enough for me."

There were stirrings in the front bedroom. Mr. Capler had arisen as early as usual, even on Sundays. Billy heard his stepfather close his bathroom door, followed by the rapid gurgling of Capler's urine stream mixing with toilet bowl water.

The boy lay back. He could still hear the confrontation but was unable to make out the angry words. *It didn't matter,* he told himself. *Rémy took care of it.*

Rémy skipped off the sill and waded through the folds of bedspread. He flopped down at the edge of Billy's pillow and stuck his feet under the sheets, snuggling close and becoming still.

"Don't you ever leave me."

Always protect Billy.

■　■　■

"She's paralyzed from the neck down. Apparently she went to get some more beer or liquor for her boyfriend and fell down the steps. Her life is ruined because of... lust."

"Lord have mercy on her, Betty. I just don't know what this world's coming to."

"George said she slipped on a child's skate that was on the steps," Jack Capler told the two most important women in his life. "I can't understand that."

"That is odd."

"Why?" the elder Mrs. Capler asked, irritated when her son turned on the TV and twisted its channel knob in an attempt to find the car race. Betty Capler answered for him.

"The Millses don't have any children, Mom."

Billy listened intently to the conversation from the safety of the adjacent reading room, Homer's *Iliad* in his hands. He stretched his legs and stood, shaking out the numbness which comes from sitting too long on a hardwood floor. He walked to the doorway. Betty Capler sprayed smoke and eyed her son with what he interpreted as suspicion. Jack Capler's attention was glued to the event being broadcast from Daytona Speedway. Grammaw Capler smiled at the boy.

"Grammaw, can I show you this?"

"Why, Billy, you sure can. What is it?"

"It's in the *Iliad,*" he began, becoming aware that the old lady wasn't going to get up and come listen to him one on one. He suddenly felt selfish for having expected her to. After all, she was seventy-one years old. "It's about Diomedes. You remember Diomedes?"

"Oh, yes," his grandmother replied with genuine pleasure. "He was one of the very bravest of the Greeks."

"I was wondering... he had a lot of help from Athena..."

"The daughter of Zeus."

"Yes, ma'am, and he even wounded Ares..."

"Uh-huh. Good. I'm so glad you remember all of that. And your mother says she's proud of you. I hear your grades are going up. Way up. That's wonderful, son. I have so worried about you! It's important to know where we came from so we can wisely plan where we're going to."

"Kids today don't know or care where they're going, Mom," Betty interrupted. "And it's our fault. The teens and young adults like the Millses... that really bothers me... infidelity is so common now. There's no morals at all anymore."

"It's the wages of sin, Betty. The Bible says that in the last days these things will become common."

"I suppose so, Mom," Billy's mother passionlessly conceded, her slightly sunken blue eyes closing in synchrony with the next inevitable tobacco smoke inhalation.

"Grammaw, could God be who the Greeks called Zeus, and Athena, Apollo, and all them have been angels? I mean, if that's true, then I guess God does send somebody to help people if they pray long and hard enough. Reckon?"

Billy had barely heard himself blurt out the question and now he anxiously waited for her answer. The electronically transmitted roaring of car engines and the ticking of a grandfather clock were the only sounds in the room for a full ten seconds. Betty turned to her still smiling but stumped mother-in-law and opined,

"He's in his own little world, Mom."

Grammaw inhaled slightly, then coughed when an unexpected lengthy ribbon of the younger Mrs. Capler's hot smoke snaked into her aged lungs. Bitterly disappointed, Billy recognized that whatever she had been about to say in his defense had been literally blown away. He returned to the reading room, his quest for satisfaction once more crushed to pieces at the bottom of a high emotional wall. He sat heavily in the same still-warm spot he had occupied moments before and looked at the world beyond the frosty window. Boaz and Jachin, the two magnificent pines dominating the front yard, shielded Grammaw's little wood frame house from the sun's heat in the summer but they certainly didn't keep out any cold in the winter. Billy shivered, feeling as dismal as the cloud-swathed skies.

A plump feline body leaped onto the outside brick sill.

"Hi, Chubby," Billy whispered gently. "It's just me. What's Mrs. Peck doing, letting you out on a cold day like this?"

The unhearing calico watched Billy but couldn't recognize him through the condensed droplets covering the window panes.

Billy blinked and Chubby was gone. The boy heard his grandmother ask,

"Jack, when are you going to come and mulch the leaves in my yard? They'll smother the grass if you don't do it soon."

"Mnn?"

"The yard, Jack. When are you going to chop up all the leaves?"

"Oh, yeah." Capler recalled the annual duty he was two months negligent in performing this year. "I can take care of it tomorrow afternoon, Mom. I'm taking the day off."

"He's going to Richmond on Tuesday," Betty explained. "He'll be there ten days. Going hobknobbing with the big boys!" she boasted, eager to share the limelight.

"I am so proud of you, Jack. You have come a long way. Try to let some of that ambition and drive rub off on Billy, will you?"

Billy heard no reply, knowing his stepfather would have preferred the elder Mrs. Capler have never made the request, considering it not within his purvey to honor. Billy tried to telepath with Rémy, longing to feel his thoughts. After a few seconds he decided, "No use… too far, probably."

■   ■   ■

Jack Capler groggily speculated what he would do for recreation on his first day in Richmond tomorrow. He hoped for a repetition of last year's trip. His lawyer friend and fraternity brother had fixed him up fine. *What was that stripper's name, the one with the pink tassels, over at the Hondo Lounge? Jolene? Joanne? Damnation, she was real table grade…*

"Ahhh, shee-yit." *What does it matter? I'll never get any of that,* he thought, dazedly rolling out from under the pale blue sheets covering him. His bug eyes spied the bit of bourbon whiskey remaining in the open bottle on the night stand. The stuff reflected an odd combination of Monday morning sunlight and the cheap forty watt yellowness flanking it.

"Betty baby!" Capler moaned, sounding more like a toddler than a middle-aged man. "Betty baby! Come here!"

Capler collapsed back onto the bed, and it swayed precariously under the impact. He was still somewhat intoxicated and he knew it. He played with himself for a long moment and once more remembered the stripper.

"Betty baby! Come here!" he again demanded. "You know the best way to get over a hangover? Drink some more! Come on in here, Betty baby! Betty baby, ain't you home?" His large frame shook as he chuckled at his self-perceived wittiness. "Ah, hell, she ain't home. I'll get it my damn self."

Capler vaguely heard the sliding of glass across polished wood. There was a soft motion atop the mattress.

"Good, Betty baby," he stated approvingly. "Come here and give me a going-away present," he invited, continuing to manipulate his maleness.

He was startled by the cold spilling of Kentucky bourbon on his stomach and ribs.

"Hey, don't waste it, Betty baby!" Capler executed half a sit-up in reaction to the chilly aromatic liquid. He shook his tousled head, unable to accept the sight of Rémy upending the bottle as far as he could reach, assisted at the bottle neck by the tiny red robot Max.

"Sloppy little bastards!" Capler again reclined, foggily rejecting the scene.

A helmeted green soldier brandishing a ragged match book stood beside Capler's left arm. Rémy and Max dropped the bottle and Blue boy, holding a match as if it was a phosphorous-tipped miniature baseball bat, dashed up beside the soldier. He swung the match, hit the rough bottom of the match book, and tossed it onto Capler's stomach while it was still in the process of igniting.

"Gol-lee damn!" Capler sailed from the bed, his midsection swathed in a ghostly blanket of greenish-blue fire. He beat his stomach and ribs furiously, pounding out the flames before they could seriously injure him.

Panting from the effort, he looked away from his ribs. On the bed was the empty bottle and in mid-air, bounding from the mattress were Rémy and his mindless companions. They sped from the room with Rémy in the rear. The khaki warrior paused at the doorway and gave the stunned Capler a full four seconds of icy green-flash stare, then broke contact to join the others which had kept running as Rémy had ordered them to.

Capler forced himself to draw near the bed, its mattress steaming with the mixed aromas of oxidized alcohol and scorched linen. Slowly he raised the bottle and leered with somber disgust at his distorted image in the glass.

"That tears it... pink elephants, hell! I must have been out of my mind, playing with matches... what a fucking hallucination... umphh... little dolly men... that's it... no more!" Capler rechecked his reddened midriff for any real harm, then quickly dressed and took the now hated bottle outside. His powerful right arm catapulted it over the back yard boundary and out of sight into the woods. Without breaking, it loudly struck a tree trunk and plummeted to an unceremonious landing, rolling to a stop on the leafy ground.

16

EIGHTY-TWO YEAR OLD Nels Hoffman noticed Robert Mundy's familiar red and white 1957 Chevy pull to a halt across the street. As it stopped, it gave a single lurch as if the driver was unskilled in shifting gears.

That ain't Bob, the spry octogenarian noticed. *That's his boy. Why, he ain't old enough to drive yet...*

Nels started chuckling and considered calling his sole employee, his nephew, up to the front of the gas station to see some blatant juvenile delinquency in action.

Nah, he decided. *Let him finish changing those tires first.*

I bet that little fart took his daddy's car for a joy ride! Yep, there's G.C. Campbell's kid with him! Now I know it's stolen. If there ever were two peas in a pod...

Despite his age, Mr. Hoffman's eyes were as sharp as those of the boys he watched fumbling with two orange ski masks and putting them on clumsily.

Why, it ain't cold at all today, Nels thought. *And they're wearing gloves, too, and getting out and coming over this way.*

"Sheeeeeeit!" He knew what was about to happen and laughed aloud as Franco stumbled, nearly falling over the curb, trying without success to adjust his mask's eyeholes. Still laughing, Hoffman took his .22 caliber revolver from its nook under the cash register, emptied the cylinder into a nearby ashtray, and from a cigar box containing mixed bric-a-brac, found a pair of .22 blanks and put them in the cylinder.

The jingle of the bells over the door sounded as Nels, trying his best to maintain an even composure, set the revolver back in its place.

This, he said to himself, *is gonna be fun!*

■ ■ ■

"So that's why you didn't want to come to school today. That's a relief for me, Rém'. I thought you were getting tired of having to stay in the locker so long at a time."

No.

"Momma said Stepdad wasn't hurt but that he'd had the worst dee tee dream he'd ever had."

Man see us.

"I wish I could have seen his face! And that pot belly hanging out as long as his face! I bet you scared the living hell out of him!"

Man not hurt.

"Thanks, Rém'. That's probably the best part of it. See, me and Momma depend on him for a room and a roof, if you know what I mean. He's never wanted to adopt me and, hell, I'm a Beaudet anyway, not a Capler. When I'm old enough, I'll have to get my own place. For us. Damn, Rém', that scares me. Having to get a job and all. I don't know what I want to do. Being a grown-up is just around the corner. What am I gonna do? Shit!"

Billy not worry.

"Do you know something I don't?"

Rémy shook his right fist.

"You should have seen Sharee today. Man, she didn't know what to say about that necklace you also engraved." Billy stretched his legs and pushed the chair from his desk. He paused to listen to the television in the basement, the metallic corridor behind the vent tinning its sonic effect. "I like Sharee, Rém'. She's real." Billy smiled and leaned forward to rest his chin on his hands. "I gave it to her after algebra."

Rémy moved his black bishop a few spaces diagonally. Billy watched him sit again on the chess board and study the game situation. Billy offered Rémy his right forefinger. The legionnaire grasped it and the teen told him,

"Let's think back a few hours, bro'. Remember this with me. You weren't there, but you can see it in my head while I remember."

■　　■　　■

"Billy, how can you afford something like this?"

"Don't ask. Okay? It's taken care of."

The crush of students heading for their busses pushed by the pair. The library doors stood silently a few yards away, waiting for Sharee to arrive at her afternoon job. She glanced again at the immaculate pearl string.

"Billy, I... how do you do it? I'm worried you might get in some kind of trouble."

"Sharee, one of these days, I don't know how yet, but I can feel, just feel, that one of these days you'll be able to have anything you want. If I can make it happen for you, I swear I will. I've got a friend who can, well... he can take care of anything."

"Anything? Who? Do I know him? Is he a grown-up?"

"Don't worry, Sharee. You're too fine to be worrying."

"Billy... that's the sweetest thing anyone's ever said to me. Thank you."

"One day all these stuck-up kids around here and their ignorant parents who think they're so sophisticated are going to pay for looking down on - - looking down - - I mean - -"

"You do not have to apologize for your mother."

Billy's lips grazed Sharee's. It was the shortest of contacts but its effect was electric. Billy's face pulled back, showing a deepening red. Sharee was beaming.

"I've waited a long time for that!"

"Me, too. I got to go. Tomorrow, babe."

Sharee headed for her job at the library, still beaming.

■ ■ ■

"Yeah, Rém', you should've seen her. Guess you have now seen it in my head, right? Man, I can't believe I kissed her right there in the hall! And I don't care if Momma finds out or what she'll say about it."

Cut yard soon. Rémy released Billy's finger.

"Yard? Oh, yeah, Rém'... Grammaw's yard. Great idea! Stepdad didn't do it today, and he'll be gone 'til late next week... yeah, tell you what, bro'... we'll bike on over there Saturday morning. She goes to her old folks' church club early every Saturday morning and stays most of the day. We'll ride my bike over there, get there after she leaves, get her electric mower out of the shed, mulch the yard up, and take off before she gets home. We won't even leave her a note. It'll be a super nice surprise. Stepdad will be glad we took care of it for him. Course, we won't tell Momma, neither. I definitely do not want Grammaw to feel like she has to be grateful."

■ ■ ■

"Agh." Rick Wayman reached under his coat and adjusted the two shot over-and-under derringer on his belt. "I got to get a better holster for this little .32. Tell you what, Paul, it may not be departmental procedure, but my backup pistol gives me a lot of peace of mind. You should invest in one."

"It sure is real quiet here in the station today," Ross observed, sidestepping the subject.

"So far, Paul." Wayman let the matter go, as he had so many times before. *He'll learn*, the senior partner figured. "Wait until later, It'll be busy enough."

Ross nodded in recognition to the desk sergeant who had been one of his instructors at the police academy. The sergeant dropped his pencil and addressed Wayman.

"He still ain't worth a shit, is he, Rick?"

"Maybe he'll get there," Wayman laughed. Ross shared in the levity until the partners entered the pale green corridor abutting the station's holding cells.

"Why would anyone want to bump off an eighth grader? Even if we could be a hundred per cent sure about the brake line, I'd still think it was Joe who was the target."

"We might be a little closer now. While you were talking to the teachers, I had another long chat with Principal Waters." Wayman stopped and jabbed a thumb at the solid wooden door marked with an elongated red "6". "Seems this kid in here was at one time wearing a jacket with the words 'Little Boys' chalked on the back."

"'Little Boys'. That's the name Joe Gates mentioned. That's the name of the club he said his brother told him he was in. Said it was a bunch of tenth graders. It's a shot in the dark, Sarge."

"Maybe. But we won't need an introduction."

"Oh?" Ross's interest rose. "Who's in there?"

"Franco Campbell. Him and another punk by the name of Eddy Mundy decided to… tell you what, let's go back out front and I'll show you the report. Let this little bastard stew awhile longer. He'll keep."

"I never would have guessed this area would have so much juvenile crime. It's worse than downtown," Ross said as they retraced their steps.

"I know. See, Paul…" Wayman paused to ask the desk sergeant, "Got the Hoffman 211? Thanks, Bob." He continued to Ross, "Take a quick peep at it and then we'll talk to the Campbell kid."

"Whoooo… real smart guys," Ross said, bemusedly scanning the report. "If they'd had half a brain between them, they'd be dangerous." Ross shook his head.

"Yeah. What dummies. Old man Hoffman, the service station owner, knew who they were even with their ski masks on. He'd watched them, hell, he'd watched their fathers, grow up."

"I can't believe this. The Mundy boy pulls a pocket knife and demands money. But since he can't open the knife with his gloves on…"

"He was afraid we'd get his fingerprints," the desk sergeant interrupted, chortling gleefully.

"… so he just shakes it at the old guy."

"Keep reading. It gets even funnier."

"Damn, Sarge!" Ross bellowed, for a moment barely able to maintain his composure. "Campbell says, 'Shoot him, who'd you say you was?'"

"They'd cooked up aliases they couldn't remember. Anyway, 'shoot him' with what?" Wayman asked rhetorically. "That's when Mr. Hoffman pulled the revolver out of the cabinet, popped off two blanks, and the James brothers there took off like scared rabbits."

"This says they jumped into a car which was parked out front! Oh, hell, it was Eddy Mundy's father's car and the father had just reported it stolen! Brilliant m.o.!"

"Ain't it? Sounds like some kinda horse shit caper you'd pull off, Paul!" the desk sergeant teased. "Hey, Rick, Mr. Hoffman isn't going to press charges. I think G.C. must have squared it with him or something."

"Wouldn't doubt that one bit. A regular brotherly thing to do. Thanks again, Bob."

"Sure." The desk sergeant took the folder from Ross and the pair retraced their previous short trek. Wayman remembered his partner's last question.

"The way I see it, Paul, it's a conflict between the old and the new."

"Old and new what?"

"Look at these new neighborhoods, all the development going on. New people, from up north, mostly, are moving in, and it seems to the natives like they're getting the pick of the jobs. Progress, they call it. Causes a lot of friction with the old, established families, most of who probably didn't and still don't have a pot to piss in. It shows. The hostility comes out through the kids."

"I think I see what you're saying."

"The new kids, well, they've lost their old friends, roots, sometimes their family connections, and the ones who've grown up here, they hear their parents bitching about the newcomers getting all the breaks. They're not all wrong, either. Remember that Hasler kid, the real fat-ass one at Central, that we busted for selling marijuana?"

"Oh, yeah. What a loser!"

"He's got two brothers and four sisters. His dad was a door to door scissors salesman in New York City. Here, he's a plant manager supervising local folks, some of whose ancestors chartered this county, who make the same kind of scissors for minimum wage."

"Kids aren't dumb. They pick up on that kind of stuff fast."

"You know, Paul, I wouldn't be a teenager again. Hell, no, not for all the pussy in Hong Kong harbor." They were back at Door Six. Wayman's hand hesitated on the knob and he added, "Don't say anything about Hoffman not pressing charges. We've got to let him loose, remand him to his folks, but I want to pump out his head first."

Ross agreed and followed Wayman into the long but narrow room painted the same color as the corridor. Franco Campbell, wearing a bulky gray county-issued set of coveralls, sat fearfully at a heavy table which was so large that the men were hard pressed for space. Wayman struggled with a chair and Ross wisely opted to remain standing.

A dun-hued one-way mirror dominated the far wall. Wayman wondered if Franco suspected its purpose and if so, would it prevent his talking? The sergeant knew he had to get the boy's mind where he needed it and get it there fast.

"Okay, Franco. You know why you're here?"

"Yes sir," came the weak reply. Franco interlaced his fingers, trying to keep them pinned still. "We tried to rob the gas station."

"Son, I'm not going to beat around the bush. You know you could go to jail for a long, long time."

"Yes sir," Franco repeated, his lower lip shaking like a spoonful of warm rose jelly.

"I can't speak for the judge or the gentleman you tried to rob..."

"It was Eddy's big idea!" Franco's eyes opened wide.

"I'm going to cut to the bottom line here, son. Are you the president of a club called the Little Boys?"

"No, no. No." Franco was visibly shaken and surprised.

"Then who is?" Ross demanded.

"I – I don't – I don't know." Franco looked at Wayman, then at Ross, not knowing who or how to answer. Wayman's visage darkened and he warned,

"Don't piss down my back and tell me it's raining, boy! Your buddy Eddy Mundy said you were the president of a gang of real tough guys, or so you think you are, called the Little Boys." Wayman stretched out the last word, studying his captive's reactions.

"That son of a bitch! Eddy wasn't supposed to say nothin' about that! He ain't no Little Boy no way! Billy wouldn't let him be one!"

Wayman's lips curled upward in a smile. A shot in the dark, indeed, but some kind of nerve had been touched.

"Who's the president, then? Your buddy Billy Beaudet? Hmm? Was he supposed to help you guys rob Mr. Hoffman?"

"No, sir, he didn't know nothing about it." Franco groped in his coverall's chest pocket for a pack of cigarettes which had been confiscated the night before. Ross tossed him a stubby nonfilter type that bounced on the table. Franco grabbed it greedily and put it between his lips, puffing on it even before Wayman's fingers flicked open his lighter.

"Help me out here, son, and I might be able to put in a good word for you. Tell me, do you or your friend Billy know anything about all these burglaries in your area? Anything going around at school you know about?"

"No, Billy don't know nothing," Franco lied, dropping his guard as he nicotine infusion relaxed him somewhat.

"Let me ask you this, then. Was Stanley Marx a Little Boy?"

"Hell, naw! Queers can't be Little Boys."

"I see. Well, then, was Al Gates a Little Boy?"

"No sir. He wanted to be, but he was too much of a sissy."

"Who cut the Gates' brake line?"

Franco's body froze. Wayman's verbal torpedo had hit hard and the boy knew he was cornered. Wayman pressed the issue, his tone still gentle but very resolute.

"Son, if you know anything… anything at all, you'd better tell me and tell me now. If we find out later that you held back, I'll make damn sure you go to the state penitentiary for the rest of your life. I promise you, son, you'll never see the light of day. And do you know what big, mean prisoners at the Big House do to young, pretty boys like you?"

Paul Ross listened, ill at ease. *Should I intervene?* he silently asked himself. His partner, although the senior, was stretching his rope so tightly that it was fraying. *No*, Ross decided, *keep quiet. Rick knows what he's doing.*

Choking, Franco whispered,

"He'll kill me."

"Who'll kill you? Billy?" Wayman kept pushing, still calmly, watchful for any opening.

"He'll do anything for Billy. He's already done killed a bunch of people. He'll kill me, too."

"Who killed a bunch of people? What people?"

"Rémy. Billy calls him Rémy."

"Who is Rémy? Franco… don't quit on me now. Tell me… who is Rémy?"

"You ain't gonna believe me!"

"Son, I've been a cop since way back before you were born. I've heard it all. Try me."

"He's a - - he's a - - he's a - - a thing."

"'Thing'?"

"You ain't gonna believe me. You'll think I'm crazy."

"I said, 'try me." Wayman was becoming impatient.

"He's - - I don't know what he is. He's about this tall." Franco tried to estimate Rémy's height with his hands. "And he's got, he's got, you know, powers and shit. I told you you wouldn't believe me," the teenager groaned, tears welling up in his eyes as his distress mounted into near panic. "Rémy will kill me, too, 'cause I'm a traitor now. Traitors gotta die, don't they? I know that much! I'm dumb, but I ain't so dumb I don't know I gotta die for what I just said!"

"Does Billy Beaudet tell this Rémy what to do?"

"I ain't saying nothing else! Lock me up for the rest of my life! I don't care! I don't care! At least I'll still be alive! I don't even want no bars on the windows. Rémy will just come in right between them!" Franco's tears rained on the table and his voice grew in volume as he pleaded for protection. "I got nothing else to say! Lock me up! I don't know nothing, you hear? Nothing!"

"Mental case," Ross said softly.

"Franco," Wayman cajoled, struggling for the right words. He watched the adolescent cry out of control and was convinced that Franco was in terror, in genuine fear for his life. "Franco… you're doing really, really good so far. Don't quit on me now. Listen… nobody is going to hurt you, Franco…"

"You don't know him! Rémy can do anything!"

"Who has Rémy killed? Al Gates? Mr. Broward? Who?"

"I don't know nothing, I told you! Nothing!"

"Is it really Billy you're scared of?"

"Billy don't know nothing, neither. And there ain't no such thing as the Little Boys! It was just another stupid kid club! I just made it up! And Eddy Mundy don't know shit like he thinks he does!"

"Have to agree with you there," commented Ross.

"Son, if I told you I could cut you loose right now, would you tell me the truth?"

"I'm dead." Franco shook his head. "I'm dead if I walk out of this jail."

"Who is it you're really afraid of, Franco? Talk to me, son. We can protect you."

"You cannot protect me! You can't! And I did tell you the truth! I did!" Franco laid his head on his crossed arms and cried hysterically. His cigarette slipped from his fingers and rolled away, dropping to the linoleum floor. "You can't catch Rémy! Never! He's got hell powers! Hell powers!"

Wayman motioned to the observers he knew were on the reverse side of the mirror. Ross went out first. A uniformed officer waited for Wayman to exit, then he brought out the wobbling Franco. He held his arm, supporting the boy as they moved toward the freedom light shining at the end of the corridor. Franco implored the man to keep him incarcerated and to stay with him.

"Is he bullshitting us, Sarge, or does he believe his own crazy pile of poop?"

"He really is scared of somebody, Paul. I was wrong."

"Wrong? About what?"

"About having heard it all. That story not only takes the cake, it takes the whole damn bakery. Damn, I really thought for a minute there that we were going to shake something loose." Wayman released a long tired sigh.

"So now what?"

"I got a gut feeling that the Beaudet boy can fill in a lot of the blanks about a lot of the stuff going on. Damn it all, I hate having to walk on eggshells with the sheriff! Fucking politics!"

Wayman's face showed a mixture of anger, frustration, and behind it all, hope richly laced with determination. "This is the real world, Paul. This is stuff you weren't taught at the academy."

"Want me to watch the Beaudet boy's house at night... just between us two?"

"Only if you want to. Man, you couldn't pay me enough to do that if I had a wife as pretty as yours."

"Hell, I was only planning for a night or so, and then only for a few hours... just to see if the kid's sneaking out."

"I do need a concrete reason to lean on this one. Give me any good reason. Suspicion of burglary will do it. I'm just sorry we'll have to justify it up through the loop."

17

NOVEMBER 14

"LET'S DROP BY the library right quick and see if Sharee's here and say hey to her before we call it a day."

Billy noticed to his left a hand-painted sign draped on the wall beside the typing classroom door. He read it aloud to Rémy,

"Chess club final matches in progress."

Sharee forgotten, Billy edged to the open door and spotted, once more at the closest table, Bob Grizzle locked this time into a very, very serious match with...

"Chet Baldwin. Rémy, I really hate that butt wipe. Let's give him an ass whipping in chess as soon as he clobbers poor old Bob there like he always does. Who gives a shit if we miss the damn bus?"

Billy walked up to the duel in progress, slightly bothered that neither contestant took note of his approach. *Oh, well,* Billy reasoned, *these are the match finals and they do have to concentrate.*

Billy! Rémy urgently called. *Billy! Say out loud "Black Queen's knight to King's rook," then say "Check."*

"What are you talking about, Rém'?" Billy whispered, seeing that his tiny friend was at the edge of his jacket and eagerly studying the match in progress. Billy shifted his loaded book bag to a less uncomfortable position and asked,

"Hey, Rém', is that butt lick vulnerable?"

Billy! Listen! Say now "Black Queen's knight to King's rook!" Hurry! Other boy about to fuck it all up! Other boy not see!

"Black Queen's knight to King's rook."

Instantly, Chet Baldwin's eyes opened round and wide but his stare did not leave the board as he spat venomously,

"Shut the fuck up, Beaudet. Nobody wants to hear your dumb ass. You don't even know the rules. Everybody's always known you're a piss ant loser and I'm tired of you coming in here and being a pain in my ass. Get the hell out of here."

"Oh, yeeeeaaaah! Yeah!" Bob Grizzle's lens-magnified eyes lost their squint under the thick glasses and he flashed the silver braces girding his teeth to all present. Bob sat up straight, his face full of surprise and unanticipated hope. "Why didn't I see that before?"

"Maybe you'd gotten so used to getting beat, you couldn't see it," Billy hypothesized aloud, trying his best to suppress the delight in his voice.

"How's this feel... Chetster?" Bob uncharacteristically needled his opponent with the hated nickname, triumphantly lifting Baldwin's rook and replacing it with his sole remaining knight. He acknowledged with a chortle that the exposed white king was now a single and inevitably fatal knight's move away.

"You're in check," the happy Grizzle announced loudly, more to the crowd that had spontaneously assembled around the small table than to the aggrieved Baldwin, now shaking uncontrollably, vainly scanning the board in a frantic, desperate search to find any piece which could knock this interloping horse-headed assassin away from his sitting duck of an immobilized king.

"Billy," Bob beamed, "together, we have climbed and conquered the mountain top. He was so used to beating me and everybody else, he didn't leave anywhere for his king to run off and escape to."

"Of course not. He never thought he might have to."

The club members chimed in with plenty of comments, and their tone was not favorable to Chet.

"Trapped yourself, didn't you?"

"Golly, it's about time!"

"Not feeling too arrogant now, are you, Chetster?"

"Whoa, here, this is something I thought would never happen."

"You and me both."

"Unbelievable. Looks like Bob's going places from now on."

Baldwin sat steaming, his countenance growing more and more angry with each new unwelcome remark from the group that he felt now considered him to be someone less than a demi-god predestined by divine edict for a guaranteed seat of honor in the sacred pantheon of International Grand Masters.

Billy smiled. It was the kind of smile of satisfaction that comes only too rarely if ever in an ordinary person's life, and he wanted to savor the moment.

Then a red-headed boy broke the pent-up dam inside Baldwin by observing with a laugh that,

"Oh, hey, Chetster, like you always tell me after you beat me every time, too... nobody's perfect!"

"Goddamn you, Beaudet!" Baldwin exploded, rising with a vengeance from his chair. "God-fucking-damn you! If you'd kept your dip-shit mouth shut, this - - I'm going to... "

"You'll do nothing except keep your seat, Mr. Baldwin!"

Mr. Kline had thankfully materialized from the hallway and placed a firm restraining hand on the lividly angry boy's shoulder, forcing him back down heavily into the chair and stating in no uncertain tone, moving so as to look Chet eye to eye directly and closely,

"I do not care one iota how adept a player you either are or think you are, or how long you have been on this team, you will not speak using such gutter rat vocabulary and low-brow manner in here to anyone, not while I am this club's advisor! Young sir, you have most effectively and permanently earned for yourself your walking papers from this extracurricular activity!"

As Kline finished speaking, Billy pivoted on his heels, unwilling to show appreciation for how the chess club members near him were praising him and beginning to tell Kline how brilliant Billy's advice to Bob had been. One short little freshman asked Billy,

"Wait, wait, how'd you see that move to check so quickly? You'd had no time to study the board! No time at all!"

"Maybe some other time, huh? I got to go catch the bus."

"Care to join the team, Bill?"

Billy swiveled at the waist to face the man who had made the offer. Never in anyone's memory had Mr. Kline called any student by his or her given name. Never. The kids all around them, even the bitterly fuming Baldwin, caught the importance of the moment. All ears keyed in on Billy's response, the crowd certain it would be eager acceptance.

"Can't right now, sir," came Billy's words with the effect of someone having successfully skipped a hundred pound stone over a calm lake surface. Billy swallowed hard and, summoning up additional courage, added, "Anyway, you said I need to learn the rules first. Remember you telling me that?"

Mr. Kline's eyebrows reflexively elevated in shock and offense at this bold refusal. As he sped away from the scene of sudden confusion and toward the safety of the waiting yellow leviathan beyond, an ecstatic Billy Beaudet whispered to his beloved companion,

"We got them all, Rém', we got them all better than anyone ever has, you reckon?"

Good job, Billy.

"No, it's you who did it, Rém', not me. It's you who made me look good. Dang, I feel like I'm ten feet tall and walking on air! I've never felt like this before, Rém'!"

Billy slid through one of the building's many blue exit doors and looked with second nature for the same bus number he had for nearly every school day afternoon since elementary school. The dispersing crowd of students were fanning out to their individual diesel-powered transports and Billy shifted his filled book bag to a more comfortable carrying position, feeling Rémy's words as he did so,

Rémy always help Billy... always...never leave Billy... love you... Billy.

■　■　■

Rémy had no doubt that he was looking up at folded money. The miniature legionnaire wondered for a moment how best to get up to the top of the lamp stand so he could grab the bills.

Except for the dull moonlight, the house was dark and its furnace was turned on. The dull hum helped to mask his and Rubberbuster's footsteps. Still, although he could sense no human brain activity other than that of a single person sleeping soundly on the other side of the place, there was something unhumanly aware of them and it was close by. It was not the same type of entity as had been the creature at the house he had burned down, but it did seem to be a hunter. Plus, this unknown entity might actually be stalking them.

Rémy noticed the lamp cord. He could hoist Rubberbuster up to the socket connection and direct him to crawl up. Once there, he would push the bills off.

Billy will be pleased.

Rubberbuster followed Rémy, who was now clutching his three inch barbed spear tightly. Yes, he did sense a presence, and it was indeed a dangerous one. The pair halted under the plug-in.

Rémy could feel raw cunning and power, but how much he could not discern. Whatever was sharing the room with them was some type of active predator. He and Rubberbuster would do best to take whatever quantity of cash that lay up there and leave without further exploration.

The buff soldier kneeled, set his weapon beside him, and cupped his molded hands. Rubberbuster stepped into the interlaced styrene fingers and Rémy prepared to hoist his unthinking companion to the lamp cord.

There was a muffled rush of padded feet and Rémy and Rubberbuster flew backward in a sprawl under a spacious upholstered living room chair. As Rubberbuster lay inanimate, Rémy jumped to his feet and found himself face to face with a big Manx cat. Its face was wide and although its expression seemed dispassionate in the moonlight, Rémy knew better. This thing was plainly a chewing machine and Rémy had no intention of losing Rubberbuster as he had Louie.

Between the beast's front paws lay the spear. Rémy rushed forward but again was knocked aside several feet. He feigned death and watched.

The Manx, curious as to what this strange prey might be, cautiously prodded Rémy, who could tell the creature was absolutely dumbfounded. It knew the intruders to be not of flesh and blood, but was not yet willing to walk away and leave them alone.

Rubberbuster rose and Rémy guided him around the cat to where the spear lay. Taking up the weapon, Rubberbuster gingerly came to a position just under the cat's belly as it slightly crouched, still concentrating on Rémy's unmoving form. Rubberbuster became fixed into place and Rémy commanded,

Now!

The olive green automaton sprang straight up, shoving the steel tip into soft feline flesh, but not so deeply as to hook the barb. The thick Manx fur protected its owner just enough.

The wounded animal screamed and hopped vertically, slapping Rubberbuster as it did so. The small javelin bounced toward Rémy who was already on his feet again. He caught it in midair and rushed at the surprised and confused cat which was spitting and hissing, unable to decide what to do about this unexpected counterattack.

Rémy aimed at the cat's eyes but instead the barb found and stuck inside its right nostril. There was another horrendous feline shriek as it backed around in circles, slapping at as it dragged its former intended victim who clung steadfast to the spear handle.

Rémy jerked his lance backward and meat tore away freely from the hook's embrace. Blood sprayed onto the hardwood floor and the legionnaire once more found his footing and braced for another and hopefully more effective jab.

The cat, though, had had enough of this combat. It shot down the central corridor, leaving a bloody trail as it did so.

The room flooded with harsh yellow light and Rémy heard an elderly female voice ask, "Muffin, what is your problem?"

The awakened woman looked down the dark hallway the cat had fled into and noticed the blood drops. "Oh, my, did you hurt yourself?"

Rémy stood still, staring up at her. She was chubby, white-haired with a bit of purple dye showing, and clad in an ankle-length plaid flannel nightgown. She fumbled with her glasses, secured around her neck by a short silver chain. As she put them on, she watched in disbelief as Rubberbuster strode up beside Rémy.

"What is this?" she asked aloud. "Wind-up toys? Who brought these in here? Who's in my house? Who hurt my cat?" she demanded into the obviously otherwise vacant room. "I'm going to call the police!"

Rémy took ten steps toward her and flashed his eyes, purposefully locking his gaze into hers. *Fuck you, old lady!*

"Oh, no, you're evil things! Oh, Lord, help me! Please..." Her face quivered as she stumbled back in shock. She tried to grasp an archway that separated the living from the dining rooms, but her aged fingers were unable to hold on. She collapsed heavily and the back of her head struck her solid oak coffee table. Her fragile neck snapped with a sickening crack, and all became silent once more.

Rémy cocked his head for a long moment, listening with his entire psyche for any more trouble. Satisfied that they would have no more opposition, he and his mindless servant returned to the socket with its plug in and cord that led to the money.

■　■　■

"I don't know. Franco just didn't want to go to school today. He says he's done quit. He said he was gonna ride his bike up to the college this morning and hang out there watching the big girls." With a forefinger Donald Campbell thumped a Squeed twin's ear. She stared back angrily, her ear stinging with pain.

"You stop that right now, Donald Campbell!"

"Shoot her the bird, Rémy." Donald opened his coat slightly, exposing the top half of Rémy's body. The third grader watched, wide-eyed, while Rémy elevated his middle finger in mocking salute.

"Pammy!" Marilyn Squeed complained, "He's got that little man with him and he's making nasty signs again!"

Billy nudged Donald, and the boys chuckled. Pammy, coming to the rescue of the small girl she sat with, ordered,

"Quit bothering Marilyn, Donald! I swear, you're as big a pest as your brother!"

"Is that why you don't give him none no more? 'Cause he's a pest? Or have you done turned into one of them, uh, them lez-buns?"

"Doo-nell! Hush up about that!" Billy admonished, unable to repress his laughter.

"You stop lying! I'll whip your little ass!"

"Why don't you try it, then? Shit on you!" Donald barked in defiance. "If I'm lying, then you done growed a dick on your nose! Shoot her a double bird, Rémy!"

"Doo-nell," Billy began, concern creasing his brow, "I wouldn't show any - - "

Rémy rematerialized and with each middle finger repeated his gesture of a moment earlier, only to vanish again into the warmth of Donald's clothing. Pammy was surprised long enough to blink.

"Real good, Donald. Where did you find that thing? Or is that Franco's? It looks like something Franco would buy. It's a nasty toy."

"It's not a toy, you stupid girl! He's alive, and he's Billy's!"

"Sure, Donald!" she cynically taunted.

"He is alive! Billy, tell her!"

Billy opened his big algebra book and held it over Donald's belly, shifting the book to his lap as Rémy moved underneath it. He raised the tome to conceal Rémy's movement into Billy's jacket pocket.

"Aw, no! Come on, Billy, show her!"

"She's not ready for Rémy, Doo-nell."

"Aw!" the younger Campbell whined. "I want to scare the dookey out of her! She's a dookey girl that drinks dookey juice from both holes in her dookey nose!"

The bus groaned to a laborious halt. Air brakes hissed like a gigantic waking primordial leviathan as the Squeed twins arose in tandem from their seat. Billy trailed after them, offering Donald a compromise over his shoulder,

"We'll let Rémy show her something next week. Okay?"

"Aw!" Donald wheezed, unconsoled.

■ ■ ■

As Billy entered the carport the kitchen phone stopped ringing. Before he could close the screen door his mother handed him the receiver.

"It's Franco Campbell," she said, spitting out the name like it was sour milk. "Didn't he go to school today?"

"I don't know," Billy lied, moving past her, preferring the privacy of his stepfather's bedroom phone. He set his books on the meal table and extracted a history test from one of them, hoping to please his mother. "Take a look at this, Momma."

Mrs. Capler slowly accepted the folded paper and Billy grasped the telephone. *Ah, hell*, he figured, *I'd better get it here. At least she won't be listening in on the other line like she always does if she's in front of me.*

"Mnnn!" Mrs. Capler grunted approvingly. "A hundred! Well, William, you're finally starting to live up to your potential!" She drifted to the sink where the patchwork sunlight reflected off the automatic dishwasher's enameled surface, leaving a trail of boiling tobacco smoke in her wake as always.

"Yeah," Billy spoke guardedly into the receiver.

"Bro'!" Franco hurriedly said. "I, I got, I got arrested yesterday!"

"Where are you at?" Billy studied his mother's face, trying to determine if she had noticed the question. She halfway smiled, reading Billy's essay section.

"I'm at Daddy's office. Me and Eddy Mundy tried to rob the gas station." Franco whispered the last sentence. "Can you say sheet, or is your moo-ther listening?"

"Afraid so."

"Oh, hey, man, we foqued eet up. Eddy couldn't find his fake gun so we used a knife, but what got us caught was, old man Hoffman shot at us. Man, I thought we was dead for sure, and, see, we was going to use Eddy's daddy's car to get away in, but he didn't ask to use it 'cause he ain't got no license, and his daddy, ah, hey-ull, you don't want to hear all that sheet! We didn't get half a day-um mile before the cops had us pulled over! They even put handcuffs on us and all that sheet. Man, I was scared!"

"Are you okay, bro'?"

"Naw, sheet, naw." There was a long pause. "They give me some kind of truth serum."

"What for?"

"To make me talk."

"About what?"

"I can't say on the phone. The cops might have it tapped."

"So when can you be at the pipe?" Billy asked rapidly, hoping that with speed of delivery the question would somehow slide past his mother's ears.

"I can't."

"Why not?"

"Listen, I got to hang up before Daddy gets back. He got me out of jail and he's mad as hey-ull at me. But I had to tell you, they give me that truth serum. It made me talk about all kinds of sheet. I don't even remember but they said I talked about Rémy."

"What'd you say about him?" Billy fought to keep the pitch of his voice even. His mother was still engrossed in the essay.

"I, I, Billy, I didn't tell them nothing about nothing that we've done! Just that Rémy's real!"

"They didn't believe it?"

"No, I don't think so. They thought I was crazy as hey-ull. Bee-ly, I wouldn't have said nothing at all if it hadn't been for that truth serum they made me drink! They held me down and made me drink it, I swear to... I... don't be mad! Okay? Pal?"

"I thought you said you didn't remember."

"What I said - - I mean - - "

Billy heard the heightening terror in Franco's voice. He wanted to ask him if the police had mentioned his name, but he knew he'd have to delay it. His mother had finished reading the test paper and was setting it on the table.

"I'll call you later." Billy hung up without saying good-bye. "Momma," he said.

"Well! I told you, you could do it, son. You're doing real good now, so keep it up!"

"Thanks, Momma. Momma, is there such a thing as a truth serum?"

"Truth serum? No. That's just a lot of fantasy on TV and in the funny books. Why? That's… an odd thing to ask."

"Just wondered," Billy came back evasively. "I've got to go on upstairs, study some, maybe work a few chess scenarios through. I showed them a thing or two at the chess club today, Momma. Mr. Kline even asked me to join, but I said I needed to go home and study instead."

"William, I don't have any inkling about what it is that's caused you to buckle down, but I'm proud of you, son. I think your father would be proud right now, too. I like your new attitude."

Thanks, Momma. And, you know, Momma, you've been right all along about Franco. Franco's… I like Franco, I always will, but he's… well, he's a dummy. There's no other way to say it, and I don't want to be a dummy, too."

"There you go! Glad to hear it!" Mrs. Capler almost shouted, clapping her bony hands together with a hallelujah sort of motion.

For the first time within memory, Billy had obtained his mother's approval. He was angry with Franco, not for telling the police about Rémy, but for lying to him, making up that truth serum garbage. Billy wondered what else Franco might have said under pressure… and most of all, he was extremely worried about what he might have to do about it.

Above all else, Billy knew he would never let anyone or anything separate him… ever… from his tiny guardian angel he kept so dearly pressed against his heart.

■ ■ ■

"William, it's such a beautiful day. I'm going to the hospital to see Mrs. Mills for a little while. Would you like to come?"

Billy eyed the small backpack he had laid out on his bed. *Two sandwiches, a box of raisins, a coke, and a can opener should be enough,* he figured. *And Rémy, of course, with his spear. He might need the spear to nail Chubby the cat if he comes after him. He's a spoiled little calico turd, but still, a good kitty…*

"William, did you hear me?"

"What, Momma?"

"Do you want to come?"

"Where?"

"To visit Mrs. Mills for a few minutes. Don't you think you should? She's been awful good to you. And she's so miserable, not being able to move. She may never move again."

"I'd really like to, Momma, but I've got to be somewhere else today."

"William, I don't want you going over to the durn Campbells! Mrs. Squeed told me Franco got arrested the other night for armed robbery. He's bad news! So you just steer clear of him!"

To his mother's delight, Billy complied with,

"I will, Momma. I promise."

"What are your plans?"

"Something good. You'll see."

"You should find the time to come with me to see Mrs. Mills first. She'd be grateful you thought enough of her to come see her."

"Please, Momma! I - - am - -trying - -to - -do - - right! One thing at a time!"

"Make sure you lock the durn door behind you! Don't forget to put the key behind the loose brick in the carport!" Mrs. Capler commanded huffily prior to hurrying downstairs, not wishing to undo the improvement she had seen growing in her son.

Billy listened, waiting for the carport door to slam. When it did, he picked up his backpack and said,

"Let's go fix those sandwiches, Rém'. Hey, don't forget your spear."

Rémy had it already. He held it to his side while he jogged through the soft woolen hair of the hallway carpet. Rémy hopped down the three steps connecting the split with the ground level of the house and rushed into the kitchen. Billy knew his friend was there as soon as he heard the clackety-clack of plastic feet on linoleum tiles. He nearly called for him to slow down, but a flash of white beyond the front curtains told him his mother already had her little Rambler in the street.

"I wish you could eat, Rém," Billy said as he followed. "Good food is good not just because it tastes good. It feels good, too. It feels good going down and it feels good coming out. You've seen me smile when I take a shit. I wish you could take a dump... then you'd know."

Billy took the loaf of bread and peanut butter from the cabinet and concord jelly from the refrigerator. He fixed his sandwiches and, after wrapping them in wax paper, stuffed them in his pack, sticking a heavy bottle of cola and a church key in after them. All the while, Rémy stood patiently by.

"Let's go, little bro.' We're going to have a good time today. I promise." Billy, infused with enthusiasm at the thought of the approval his surprise would earn for him, hefted his backpack over his left arm and opened the side door.

Rémy was again ahead of him, jumping off the single step to the carport's rough concrete floor.

"Hold it," Billy unexpectedly commanded. Rémy stopped and looked back curiously at him, cocking his head slightly. The boy stared in disgust at the rear of his Deltawasp and muttered,

"Shit. It's always one thing or another. Come on back in a minute with me, Rém."

Rémy did as he was told. Billy took the telephone from its wall-mounted receiver hook and dialed a familiar number.

One ring... two... three... more... after the tenth, the boy, seething with frustration, angrily spat,

"Nobody answers! Damn it!" Billy slammed the receiver on its base. "Goddamn bike tire's flat as a fucking pancake, Franco's got my damn bike pump and nobody answers! Shit on this!"

Walk bike, Billy, Rémy, standing beside the oven, recommended.

"Reckon we'll have to. Want to ride in the pack like a papoose, Rém'? You can look around. Just don't fall out!"

Rémy's styrene right fist shook once.

■   ■   ■

"It don't look right, Rém'. All of them are gone, I reckon. Franco's momma's usually here every Saturday morning. Wonder where all of them went? It's already about ten, ten-thirty or so. I want to get on over to Grammaw's…"

Billy rapped once more on the door of the screened-in porch.

"I don't see the rocking seat or the coffee table. Only things I see are those three fifty pound sacks of concrete mix in the corner."

Not here?

"No, I don't think anybody but us is here. Let's see if… Rém', can you reach in and unhook it?" Billy positioned Rémy at the door's thin brass handle. Rémy's small right arm extended over it, intruded into the crack and knocked the simple screen hook up and out of the eyehole. Billy, still carrying Rémy, walked onto the porch. The boy strained to see through the opaque white door drapes blocking the view of the interior.

"I don't understand this. Hey, I know how we can get in through the back way. Come on."

People not here.

I know, I know." Billy pushed his crippled Deltawasp to the rear patio. "Rém', you can get in through that busted plank beside the door. Go over to the sliding glass door and take the round stick out of the groove at the bottom so I can get in, too."

Take things?

"No, bro', we won't steal anything from here!" Billy laughed out loud, not concerned about any neighbors spotting them. "Hey, if anyone sees me, I'll just tell the truth. We'll find my tire pump, use it, and go. Mr. C. won't care."

Keep pump, Rémy advised, leaping from Billy's shoulder and landing like a tiny khaki panther.

"Good thinking. We'll find something to tie it to the handlebars with. In case my tire goes flat on us again, we'll have it."

Rémy wedged himself into the void between the door and the rotted portion of wood. Billy met him at the sliding glass door ten seconds later. Rémy again informed him,

People not here.

"I know…" Billy entered to see the dowel which had braced the door shut rolling unobstructed on the floor. The basement bed, the cabinets, G. C. Campbell's prized Spanish gun rack and the Persian rugs were all gone. A solitary rusted wheelbarrow lay on its side in the center of the room, a lonely, out of place relic.

"Oh, shit," Billy breathed. He raced up the short flight of steps to the main floor, expecting to see the clock on the wall. Only a vacant, pale circular pattern on the living room wall paneling was there. All of the furniture was missing. The beige carpet which Mrs. Campbell was so proud of remained, its numerous stains and indentations providing mute reminders of past human presence.

People not coming back.

Billy turned, sat on the top step, and shook his head. Rémy was at the base of the stairs. The laundry room door behind him was open, revealing an empty area. At least a score of dust balls swept into a pile occupied the space where the Campbells' dryer had set for a decade. On the pale pink wall two feet or so up from the dust balls were the penciled words in Franco's semiliterate scrawl:

Beet yur Meet.

FeaL GooD.

Shoot Loats of Sprem.

"They sure as shit won't. They've moved!"

18

Billy picked up the orange extension cord and tossed it over the little red electric lawn mower. *This must have been the three hundredth time this day I've done this*, he estimated. *Thank God this is the last row of leaves to chop up!* Out of the corner of an eye the boy saw a big, stealthily crawling calico cat.

"Uh-oh," the teenager muttered. "Chubby, this time you're about to bite off more than you can chew."

Billy squeezed the handle lever. The soft whine of the machine's electric motor was soothing, but he was too excited by the prospect of Chubby meeting his match to appreciate it. He kept the overweight calico in sight, pretending not to notice him.

"Where are you, Rém'?" Billy wondered aloud, slowly mulching the few remaining leaves. He saw his tiny friend twenty feet away, following an ebony wood beetle. "Heads up, little bro'. The cat's coming!"

Rémy stood and waited, facing Chubby as the cat came to a halt six inches from him. The legionnaire held his spear in the ready position. Chubby crept nearer and crouched, his bright yellow eyes wide as if asking, "What are you?"

Billy spotted several small fish hooks threaded into a loop of angler's line slung across Rémy's shoulder. Chubby's right arm reached curiously in an attempt to prod this odd new creature.

"Don't mess with him, Chubby," Billy advised. He's got more than you want."

Unable to elicit any response, Chubby reached toward Rémy a second time. Rémy's spear flashed to the left and slightly cut a pad of Chubby's extended paw. The cat squealed and ran like a bolt of landbound lightning toward the driveway. Rémy chased him to the base of the ten foot high plum tree in which Chubby sought refuge.

Billy laughed so hard that his cheeks glistened with tears. Rémy angrily shook his spear at the bewildered feline, then dropped it and unfastened his new apparatus. He took a hook in each hand and mounted the plum tree's trunk.

"Damn, Rém'! You never stop surprising me! You climb that plum like a dadgum expert linesman! Whoo!"

Billy completed his last row of leaves and casually walked to Chubby's rescue. Rémy was five feet up and standing on the lowest limb when Billy offered his cupped hands. Three feet higher, out of space and dangling precariously, a dumbfounded Chubby mewed feebly for help.

"Come on, little bro'. He's learned his lesson Come on, Rém', I know you're mad at him but he can't help it. He does what he has to, Rém'... come on! He's just a cat!"

For the briefest fraction of a second, Rémy's eyes shone a brilliant green. Chubby began to shake.

Kill thing!

"Rém'! No! He just does what nature tells him to! You done got him good already! Why do you hate him like that?"

Reluctantly and without answering, Rémy fell backwards into Billy's hands. As Billy turned, the seething Rémy continued to watch the terrified creature.

■　　■　　■

"I can't believe how easy it was getting here, Rém'. Some old man in a pickup says, 'Hop in', and it turns out he knows Grammaw... and he went out of his way to get us here. We got here lots faster than we would have if we'd rode the bike. Don't reckon there's any problem with leaving the bike in Franco's basement. What do you think?" Billy swallowed his final draught of cola and shoved the empty bottle into his backpack. The waxed paper which had protected the peanut butter and jelly sandwiches crunched under the glass cylinder.

Rémy hate thing in tree.

"I know, Rém'. I know." The pair sat between the two great pines at the street's edge. Billy's friend was to the left of him, his spear traversing his lap. "I'm glad you put those hooks in our pack. Hey, don't accidentally stick me, okay?"

Love you, Billy.

"Rém', are you all right? You seem a little uptight today."

Rémy watched the traffic move along for a long moment. The teenager sensed the message, not particularly directed at him.

Billy not ready yet.

"Ready for what, little bro'?"

Love you, Billy.

"Whatever it is bothering you, Rém', we can whip it together. We're a team. Damon and Pythias, you know? I'll read it to you, Rém'. Grammaw's got a book in there, see, these two guys a long time ago, they were best buddies..."

Long time, Billy. Rémy here so very, very long.

"I do hate it about Al getting killed, though."

Boy stupid. Talk too much.

"That's a fact! Ah, fuck him. He was a loudmouth. Only thing is, I kind of worry about what Grammaw would think if she knew about all this shit. Well, she'll be happy about what we've done here today. Stepdad will be glad, too, I'll bet you. I sure hope he says something good to me about it. That would be nice. Real nice.

"You know, Rém', I'm glad God sent you to me to help me out, but... it seems to me that the older I get, the more confused I get about all kinds of shit. My dad, my real dad, gave his life for this country. I've always looked forward to being a Marine one day, myself. But I don't know why anymore. See, what good did it do him? What good did it do Momma? And me? The kids at school, most of them, think I'm fucked up for being patriotic. Fuck them, I don't care."

Billy still not ready.

"Whatever you mean by that, Rém', will you help me get ready? Whatever you want me to do... you let me know."

Kill Franco?

"No, Rém', definitely no. I know he lied to us, but he was scared. They had to have bullied it out of him or tricked him. And I'm sure he won't say anything else that he absolutely doesn't have to. He's still our friend, Rém'. Okay?"

Franco stupid like Al.

"That's right. He is. But we won't hurt him. We won't! He's still a Little Boy and always will be. Okay?"

Not hurt Franco.

"Oh, man, am I happy to hear you say that! Hey, little bro', listen! You know who's coming?"

The scrape and clatter of metal wheels on asphalt greeted their ears. Billy explained,

"I love this guy. His name's J. D. Davis. He's all right, Rém'. I bet you not even one in a million grown-ups are as cool as he is."

The elderly black man's head swayed from side to side as he hummed an old spiritual. He wore the blue wool sweater which Grammaw Capler had given him. As he pushed his can-laden grocery cart, he conveyed an ease gained from long years of experience in the trials of life. Upon recognizing Billy, he smiled broadly, his ruined remnants of teeth displaying uneven shades of dingy ochre. He passed by and Billy waved, warmly querying,

"How are you doing today, Mr. Davis?"

"Hey there, Mister Billy! And hello to you, too, there, little fellow!"

Absently, Billy glanced to his left to see Rémy waving to Mr. Davis. Billy held his breath and watched as the man trudged on down the street, nodding and smiling to motorists and stopping at a driveway across the street to speak to an old woman who was devotedly watering her bushes.

"Why can't everybody be like him, Rém'?" the teenager asked at length. "He's smarter than any other grown-up I know. No wonder Grammaw likes him. He's the only person I ever saw, besides Grammaw, who knows what the Golden Rule really means. Mr. Davis accepts you the way you are. You could see that, couldn't you, Rém'?"

That man good.

"Accepts you the way you are. Like Grammaw says Jesus does. Not the way people think you ought to be or for what they think you can do for them." Billy let out an empty sigh and added,

"I suppose I really don't like most people much, Rém'. Not any more, I guess. This world needs its ass kicked."

Billy almost ready.

"Hmm? Yeah, Rém', I'm ready to go. Jump in the bag, bro'! I'll hold it open for you!"

Rémy tossed his spear in and dived headfirst after it into the backpack. Billy stepped into the street, extended a thumb, and felt the thrill of success when the first oncoming car slowed down.

■ ■ ■

"That's a real nice surprise. Mulching your grandmother's yard. That's a really sweet thing to do. What's your name?"

"Billy... Billy, uh, Baker," came the abrupt falsehood. Billy didn't feel comfortable. The middle-aged, sophisticated-looking gentleman in the gray suit reminded Billy of someone, but who? He seemed familiar, and despite his air of congeniality, disturbingly so.

"Which way are you wanting to go, Billy Baker?"

"Garden Pines subdivision, sir," Billy responded readily, quickly formulating a plan to be let off at Franco's house. He smiled at his cleverness, deciding to walk his bike back home.

"We could pick up Faron Road from this direction, but I know a shortcut. Yes," the man, suddenly strangely light-voiced, continued, speeding up his green sedan, "I certainly do know where that subdivision is."

"Are you a teacher or something, sir?"

"Ha! I love to hear boys ask me that! It flatters me! No, I used to be one, though, at Central years ago. But you live over at Garden Pines, so you probably go to Gilmore. Right?"

"Yes sir," Billy replied, sensing that something was, contrary to the question, not right.

"You don't have to call me 'sir'. Call me Bobby." The sedan stopped at a red light. "Did you know a boy named Stanley Marx?"

Oh, shit! Billy remembered with alarm. *The queer! That goddamn queer! How could I be so stupid not to know right away who this was? Rémy! What am I going to do?*

"Did you, Billy?"

"What?" Billy's legs tightened. His knuckles became white as he squeezed the straps of the pack in his lap. He wondered if or when he could risk jumping out.

"Did you know Stanley? Stanley Marx?"

"Yes sir - - ma'am - - Bobby," Billy gulped as an unwelcome hand touched and rubbed his knee. The boy knew they were now past the last stoplight for quite some distance. He attempted to contact Rémy, thinking hard: *What the hell am I going to do, Rémy? Rémy? Damn it, Rém'! Are you asleep? I need some help here!*

"We'll go this way. Oh, I miss Stanley so much."

"He was a sweet boy. Really nice," Billy blurted, not knowing exactly why. The cold sweat of fear began to form on his forehead.

"Yes," the man agreed. "You remind me so much of him. I need to talk to someone about him. I've been so lonesome since he... he killed himself. It was so horrible. He needed me, and, well, you know... I feel so guilty." The last word choked in his throat.

"Oh, yeah," Billy stated, doing his best to conceal his revulsion as the man kept caressing Billy's left leg and arm. Swallowing hard, looking for a chance to escape, he dared ask,

"Why don't we pull over somewhere and you can show me what you and Stanley used to do?"

"Reeeeally?" The man was enthused by the suggestion, all pretense of grieving gone. "You won't try to run away, will you? I can still outrun any young boy I know. They've tried before."

"No. I mean it." *Rémy! Rémy!* Billy concentrated as hard as he could. *Goddamn it, Rémy, answer me! Answer me! This fucker's maybe going to butt fuck and then kill me!*

Bobby swerved his sedan off of the blacktop and onto a nameless dirt road. Billy considered jumping but hesitated, preferring to keep trying to contact his oddly silent friend. While the man talked about his favorite sixty-nine position being side by side in bed with a barely teen partner and timing their orgasms simultaneously, a hot jet of vomit shot up into Billy's esophagus. It thankfully came to a halt at the base of his tongue and bubbled back down, leaving a harsh, hot, and sickening taste in its wake.

The road had become little more than a cow trail and the car was moving at a bumpy crawl. They were at an illegal dump, an eyesore in a slice of forest littered with bald tires, rusted appliances, and other sundry trash items.

"Here we are. Want to go for a walk?" Bobby asked, turning off the ignition.

"Sure." Billy opened his door and exited. His legs were weak and rubbery. He knew he was too frightened to run. He recalled how he had seen Bobby and Stanley wander off into the woods. "Rémy!" Billy hissed. "What am I gonna do?"

Kill man!

"How can I? He's too big and I ain't got no weapon! "

"Come on, Billy!" The man grasped Billy's free hand. "Down this trail! Not many people know about this creek down here! It's really romantic!"

Numb with indecision, Billy allowed Bobby to lead him into a clearing. All around were strewn all types of used household and business items.

Get stick! Hit man! Hit hard!

Billy saw Rémy's arm protruding from the pack, pointing to a defoliated red maple tree. Against the tree was a mop handle. Only the rusted metal clamp remained attached to it.

"Put down your purse, little boy," Bobby ordered, his voice completely feminized. "We'll have us some fun! You're going to looove this! I'm going to make you feel soooo good!" the man added, wagging his dripping tongue almost too quickly to see. "My balls are on fire, Billy Baker... on fire for you!"

Not wait! Must hit fast! Get stick!

Bobby's eyes rolled back and he fumbled with his belt buckle, his fingers clumsy with passionate anticipation. Billy set down his backpack and sidled to the right enough to put the mop handle within arm's reach.

141

"Little boy? Rém', he said - - "

"What the hell is this? Oww! It's stinging me!"

Rémy shoved his spear's barb deeply into the adult's right leg an inch above the ankle. Bobby jerked away, stepping back with the lancet still stuck in his leg and calling loudly,

"You little bastard! You hurt me! Billy, what is this thing? Grab it!"

"Fuck you, faggot!" Billy screamed, seizing the mop handle.

Bobby attempted vainly to kick Rémy. The man's trousers fell around his ankles, leaving him an open standing target.

Billy brought the metal-layered end across the bridge of Bobby's nose with every bit of strength he had in his adrenaline-flooded body. The aluminum bent and the stick broke in a rain of splinters as the man's nasal bones and cartilage separated, opening a hideous, mutilating wound which spurted blood profusely. Billy kept up his attack, using the shattered three feet of handle to stab Bobby's stomach beneath his reddening pastel blue shirt. The would-be molester fell to his knees. Billy plunged his sharp fragment a second, third, and fourth time. Bobby tried to beg for mercy, gurgling frothy plasma which splattered Billy's denim-covered legs. Rémy shook his fists in synchrony with each new killing thrust.

Again! Again! Billy! Again! Good! Again! Kill!

Bobby collapsed to one side. The heel of Billy's right shoe smashed into the pitiful pulp of what had been a face, then into a shoulder, knocking the fatally wounded homosexual onto his back. Billy cursed him as he renewed stabbing him viciously. A minute later, the exhausted boy's arms fell limply to his sides. The corpse of Bobby lay amid the garbage, staring with unseeing eyes into the clear, cold sky above the trees. Billy hurled his weapon into the tangled mass of a kudzu patch, its bloody tip displayed diagonally like a banner of victory over the dark leaves.

Billy Beaudet stumbled, exhausted, to the edge of the clearing and sat heavily. Rémy caught up with him and began urgently tugging at his jeans.

Up! Up! Move car!

Dreamily, Billy watched Rémy return to the body and rustle about in the corpse's bunched trousers. When he emerged, he was dragging a dozen folded bills and a set of car keys.

"Holy shit, Rém'..." Billy, still in a state of semi-shock, said, counting the money, "There's two hundred and forty bucks here!"

Up! Not wait! Move car! Billy! Up!

Furtively double-checking every bird and squirrel's movement in the woods, Billy and Rémy went to the sedan. Billy started the vehicle, asking,

"Rém', you sure we ought to move it?"

Hide car in woods. Deep as we can go.

"Okay," he wheezed, slipping the drive lever into "D" and cautiously maneuvering the machine between the pines. "This is the first time I've ever done this. Stepdad won't teach me nothing about driving, and Momma uses every excuse not to, too. Am I doing this right? Dang, this is scary!"

Go!

"How far?"

Go! Go!

"Down the hill? Really?"

Down here, Billy! Must hide car down here!

"I see the creek he was talking about, Rém'. Pretty little waterfall there, ain't it?" The vehicle slipped sideways as its traction failed. A concerned Billy turned off the ignition. They kept sliding, almost going into the creek. Rémy found a paisley handkerchief in the rear seat and began to wipe the inside front door handles.

"Good thinking, Rém'. We'll clean it off anywhere I might have touched."

Keys! Rémy demanded, offering the handkerchief in trade.

Billy did as Rémy wished and proceeded to wipe off the steering wheel, gear lever, and outside door handles.

"Rém', do you reckon we should torch the car? Rém'? You think we should?"

No! Must not!

A dripping Rémy was across the creek, standing on a mossy bank. He released the keys and they fell into a backwash pool beneath him. Rémy dislodged several fist-sized mudbound stones which he pushed to fall atop the keys, effectively covering them.

As Rémy strode back through the babbling water, Billy reasoned,

"Burning the car would attract attention. Right?"

Get pack.

Billy lifted his friend from the musty soil and confessed,

"Yeah, hell, we can't forget that! My damn name's on it! You know, it felt good killing that queer. I know it was wrong, but - - but what would Grammaw say if she knew? Ah, hell, Rém'," Billy decided as he retrieved his backpack, "she doesn't even know about shit like this. She probably doesn't even know what a queer is. Everything's church to her. She doesn't have to deal with this fucked up world."

Billy feel okay?

"Guess so," Billy answered, trying to orient himself to the unknown territory. "I'll feel a lot better when we get home, I'll tell you that. Where the hell are we, anyway?"

19

NOVEMBER 19

BILLY'S MOTHER LAUGHED into the telephone receiver. It wasn't the fake put-on, holier-than-thou laugh reserved for official functions and politically obligatory conversations, nor was it the hesitant, patently forced eruption which she used whenever she was unsure of herself or didn't understand something. This sound was genuine. Billy sat in his stepfather's chair at the end of the kitchen table and soaked in the praise.

"William, Grammaw says 'Thank you very much' for the job you did yesterday. Uh, no, Mom. Oh, all right, I'll ask him. William, she wants to know if you want a couple of dollars." The friendliness in her face departed. Betty's lips formed an unspoken "No!" accentuated by her suddenly stern eyes. It was an expression which could melt cold steel.

"No way. My treat." Billy smiled, placating his mother.

"What's that? No, Mom, we won't be coming over today."

"Nuts," Billy murmured. He'd been looking forward to reading *Greek Tales* to Rémy, in particular the story about the friends Damon and Pythias.

"Jack called me last night," Betty continued. "I'm afraid he won't be back until Saturday now, after Thanksgiving. He's really building on a lot of old acquaintances. Oh, I'm so excited! We're invited to the... Governor's... mansion... in March! The spring coming-out! You know Jack's friend Marty Bowman, the lawyer from Richmond? Next summer we're going on a cruise on his... yacht."

Billy's smile grew wider. His mother's air du temps had returned, and it was stinking. *She sure knows how to lay on the bullshit,* he mused.

"Ah, she's just practicing for the real dog show," he hushedly mumbled to Rémy, hiding inside his shirt. "Can't wait to hear this when she blabs about it to all the neighbors, as if they give a shit."

"His yacht, Mom. Yacht. Yes, like in big boat. Marty's got a yacht on the James and we're sailing up to the Potomac River and cruising on into Washington next summer!"

Billy imagined Grammaw's unimpressed reaction matching her "Oh, well, as long as she's happy" ever-tolerant demeanor.

His mother's tone of voice changed. She was suddenly too serious.

"I'm keeping the .38 in my - - our - - top drawer now." Mrs. Capler momentarily switched her attention to her son, slightly pulling her face away from the telephone. "William, have you seen or heard anything about a strange car parked off the side of our street... over the spillway?"

"No, ma'am." *Spillway?* Billy silently wondered before realizing, *She means the pipe!* "Reckon I ought to go check it out?"

Ignoring her son's offer, Mrs. Capler explained to her mother-in-law,

"Somebody's been parked there for an hour or two every night lately. Naw, Mom, ain't no law I know of, says you can't just pull over and sit. Why report it, then? I wonder if it's someone who's involved in these break-ins we've been having all over the subdivision? Do you know... Mrs. Wilkins over on Maple Lane had her three thousand dollar pearl-studded necklace stolen last week? I'm keeping the .38 loaded. If William can hold him long enough for me to take aim, I'll drop him deader than a doornail."

She paused to smile at her son. Billy could picture his grandmother's dismay at the prospect of his mother shooting anyone, even a burglar. "Yeah, I'm right proud of him, Mom. He seems to finally be growing up."

■　　■　　■

"I'll make you another spear to replace the one you left sticking in that damn queer's leg. You need more than those two fish hooks to protect yourself with." Billy waited for Rémy to squeeze between the large nails blocking the six inches of terra cotta pipe protruding from underneath the basement door. "Stepdad put those nails in the ground there to keep out wharf rats. It's a better way for you to come and go than by using the window. Come on, little bro," Billy beckoned, expertly negotiating the slight drop at the Mills' driveway and crossing it. "Let's go to the pipe." Rémy trailed behind, his fish hooks dangling from their translucent wire. "Whoa," Billy said unexpectedly.

He gazed at the Mills' house, its red brick sides partially obscured by the score of slender Virginia pines populating the large back yard.

No one there.

"Looks lonesome, don't it? Sure wish I could have stuck it to Janet at least one more time before... oh, fuck her! The bitch deserved what she got. But I do wish she could walk again. I guess it would be awful, being paralyzed."

Billy want Rémy to heal nerves in woman's neck?

"Yeah! Yeah!" Billy's countenance softened slightly. "When they send her home... would you do that, Rém'? You healed my astigmatism... could you... ?"

Rémy shook his right fist once.

"Like... I don't hate Janet... I... hey, bro', reckon Sharee would, naw, I tell you the one I want to get my hands on! That tall girl, Debbie, that hangs out with Sharee. Man," the boy added, following the well-worn path on the marshy ground blanketed with grasses hiding tangled masses of biting thorn branches. "I bet she'd be a lot of fun in the bed. I'd sure like her long legs around me squeezing the shit out of my guts! What do you think, Rém'?"

Not know.

"Reckon not. Sorry, Rém'. Hey, here we are. I love this place. Guess it's all ours now. Can you get in by yourself, or would you rather I set you inside?" Billy sat on the big oak root and extended a foot into the pipe's interior.

Billy! Pull root!

"Want me to make a bridge for you out of the root? Hey, man, isn't it great to see Momma happy like she was when she was talking with Grammaw back at the house? And how about those trips they're going to be taking? I know I won't be able to tag along, what with me being what Stepdad calls a 'inconvenience', but, hey, you and me will be able to stay at Grammaw Capler's. Sheee... wonder when the cops will find that dead queer? I still feel really good about killing him, Rém'. I know I'm supposed to feel bad, so why don't I feel bad? What I feel is: Shit on him!"

Billy! Pull out root!

"Why?"

Must pull, then dig! Dig, Billy!

Billy grabbed the root with both hands and jerked so hard that a rotted chunk of it came out. He lost his balance, stepping backward into the creek.

"Damn, Rém', this is fucked up. Why?"

Billy know soon! Dig!

"Let me get something to dig with, little bro." Billy snapped off a two foot length of limb from a close-by Chinese privet bush, and after stripping off the leaves, began gouging the earth around the root. Billy scraped and plowed away with his hands and cut again, unable to rest because of Rémy's impatient urging,

Not quit now, Billy! So close! Not quit!

"I got to take a break, bro," Billy pleaded after five minutes more of furious digging. Rémy was now standing above him on the bank. He appeared to be shaking as if violently ill, his gaze transfixed at the hole Billy had opened up.

"Rém'! What's wrong? You're all uptight."

Not talk! Must make hole bigger! Reach in! Pull dirt out!

Billy blinked. "What the hell is this?" he questioned. "Right here under where the root was..." Billy rubbed an exposed piece of dull red surface. "What is this damn thing, Rém'? Is it some kind of metal? Is it an old car?"

Dig below it! Dig more, Billy! Must free!

"Free what?" Mystified, Billy obeyed, attacking the dirt a yard under the object and wearing out both the stick and his arms in the process.

"I got to get a new stick, Rém', or go get a shovel. This is tough work, Rém'. I can't dig a whole damn car out of here. How did you know about it?"

A large mass of dirt separated from the object's underside. The creek yellowed with the influx of earth and Billy leaned into the crevice he had unwittingly caused to form.

"Sheeee... this thing is like a flat circle... is it a wheel?" Billy's fingers scraped at what looked like a small dark knot in the middle of a mud-encrusted hatchway. "Can't see it too good, Rém," Billy, on his stomach, informed his friend. "Dang, man, what is this thing?" The boy did half a pushup and spotted the legionnaire sliding down the bank. Rémy held a toothpick-sized lance which he had been busily sharpening on the rough pebbles up at the roadway.

"If this is the center, right here..." Billy touched the knot, deducing aloud, "... then the whole ball of wax must be about, I guess, four or five feet across. Rém'!" Billy's eyes blazed with sudden insight. *That dream I had awhile back.... That dream!*

While visions of sugar plums danced in his head...

"Damn! If this is what I think it is, then you... no, no, you can't be! You're..." Billy's body filled with an irresistible drowsiness. Every cell in his body seemed to be begging for sleep. "You can't be. You're a gift for me... from... from..."

Love you, Billy. Sleep. Time for you to know it all now...

"God gave you... to me... me. This is... can't... I..."

Billy sleep. Billy learn. Billy... ready.

Rémy's hands softly brushed Billy's cheeks and chin. The familiar glow of love and warmth accompanied by the beautiful symphony from his dreams acted like a narcotic. The teen's tousled blond head, gently guided by Rémy's strong little arms, touched the clods of semi-dry bank side dirt. A cool wind swept along the watercourse, causing the remaining leaves on the surrounding shrubbery to vibrationally meld with the alien symphony. In his mind's eye Billy saw once more the descending scarlet saucers. The comforting message he had heard so many times came once more, mixing with the tonal esthetics from a faraway civilization and the reassuring unspoken words of his guardian angel...

Love you... Billy... Rémy never, never leave you!

■　■　■

The saucers and their haunting music were gone. In their place was an odd blue-purple sky full of unhappy dark clouds. Billy's consciousness drifted aimlessly in the miasma until a faraway whine called his attention to a tiny silver pinhead within the distant cloud banks. The whine grew into a fierce scream and the pinhead became a gigantic onrushing warplane of a type Billy had never before seen either in pictures or on television.

Billy found himself inside the craft, watching the crewmen. They were clad in navy blue uniforms fringed with pink, but Billy knew,

"You're not human!"

Some of the crew scurried about. Some sat at their stations, intent on accomplishing their duties, their bug eyes reading sensors and their long pale green fingers, six per hand, constantly making instrument adjustments. A heavy-set creature projecting an overbearing air of authority peered above the shoulders of several of the crew, then walked to the fore end of the gigantic sky ship. He sat behind and between two men Billy understood to be the pilots. The overweight man snapped an order to them, causing their rosy nape hairs to stiffen.

"Fash!" he barked. "Koufa lan!"

"What is going on here?" Billy demanded. "Are you the captain or something? What?" *Hey!* The boy realized. "You don't see me! So am I really here, or are you just another crazy-ass dream?"

The clouds ignited. The sky parted and went white. Billy floated miles above the site of an atomic assault. He watched without pain as the blinding light level quickly dropped to reveal a city burned to a crisp, its millions of inhabitants incinerated. The odor of roasted flesh was unbearable. Billy remembered that smell all too well.

"What have you assholes done?" Billy, back on the flight deck, screamed. The portly chief officer rose from his seat, bellowing hearty congratulations. The pilots grinned at each other. Billy angrily tried to grasp the leader but his fingers melted uselessly into the big man's body. The captain returned to the crew duty area and proudly announced,

"Kay-ma! Lou-lanka mesor! Whoom!" His crimson-gloved hands swept up in imitation of the city's destruction. The crew clapped. Some whistled.

"Piss on all y'all! What's so great about killing a bunch of helpless people that can't even defend themselves?"

The Kind...

"What?"

The Kind... repeated an unseen presence.

Billy stood on an icy mountaintop, not uncomfortable even in the cold. The war was over, Billy somehow sensed, due to the intercession of some other type of people, beings from very far away.

"But who? How?" Billy asked, able to see the green victims rebuilding their obliterated city. With them in the valley worked others, small entities with stout, strong frames and waving tentacles. Each had a single shining slit for an eye.

The Kind...

"Will these folks be okay?"

No more war!

"You got to be kidding me. There'll always be war, man. War's just a fact of life."

■　■　■

It wasn't much of a house. The sole candle in the small cabin was nearly out of wick. A woman sitting at a bare and cracked table was crying. In a corner, on a thin blanket spread on the dusty floor, a baby also cried, its belly bloated with hunger. The woman swept her long, shiny, straight blue hair aside and the door creaked open. Billy watched the entering man drop his ragged coat, his multi-faceted golden eyes full of pain.

"Naffa. Ko tak. Mishwat," he said under his breath.

"How come I know you said that everybody at your factory just lost their jobs?" Billy tried to wake himself, but the compelling scene seemed so real...

"Sayla woo?" the woman wondered.

"Nika tot," the man responded flatly.

"Ah, hell, there's got to be jobs some damn where!" Billy attempted to pull a chair out from under the table. Once again his fingers were unable to contact anything solid. He studied the miserable family and told their unhearing ears,

"Hey, y'all, I'm going outside. I can't handle this!" Billy melted through the door and saw a line of people, all wearing torn, dull colored clothing, trudging through the muddy lane a few yards away. In the background, starkly set against a gray, somber skyline of strip-mined grey hills, rose an idle smokestack.

The Kind...

Billy blinked and knew he'd jumped several years forward. It was about noon and the double suns directly overhead shone brightly in the mauve heavens. From the smokestack there spurted a welcome white rush of steam, accompanied by a shrill whistle.

Billy heard the door of the freshly painted cabin open. The golden-eyed man emerged, smiling and carrying a fishing pole on his shoulder. He held hands with his eager young son, now no longer hungry and old enough to be walking. In the boy's other hand was a tentacle of an oblong-eyed, very stout creature. The wife, her face beaming happily, called after the trio,

"Ya kow na palay mox!"

"Be home before sundown, both suns down," Billy somehow translated while the man, his son, and their small, strange friend walked up the lane paved with shimmering burgundy tiles.

No more want!

■   ■   ■

The fire raged out of control. Dozens of bald, squealing blue people with large feet and webbed hands bravely fought the ravenous flames with brooms and buckets, but the village's staple crop of lop was doomed. Without the precious lop, all of the families would face a brutal and perhaps fatal winter.

"Hang on!" Billy commanded, towering over the six inch high, straw-hatted, panicked villagers. "I'm a friend! I'll stomp out the fire for you!" To his dismay, Billy's feet had no effect on the burning lop.

"I can't even dig a damn ditch around the fire!" he discovered, his hands sinking ethereally into the dirt. "Damn this shit!"

Night brought no relief. The lop burned until morning. Several thousand people forlornly eyed the smoldering ruin of a field. Many cried. Some groped about in the hot ashes, searching on their hands and knees for any surviving seeds.

"Damn... what can they do about this?"

The Kind...

"Right. The Kind. So how are you going to fix this big mess, Mister Kind, whoever you are?" Billy went to the river, wanting to wash his face, hoping the coldness of the water would wake him, only to find,

"Ah, crap. I can't even get my hands wet!"

Billy visually revisited the rural town. On the village common sat two scarlet saucers. The oblong-eyed people were busy helping the azure people dig an irrigation ditch. Behind teams of men leading pairs of yoked dragon-like animals plowing new furrows came women, each holding up her apron with one hand and tossing out lop seeds with the other.

No more hunger!

"Reckon so," Billy had to agree.

■　■　■

"Genanna! Hak!"

Both men were scaly, reptilian. The helmeted larger of the two shook the kneeling smaller one mercilessly. As a court audience gleefully watched, the judge waited impatiently at his elevated bench, a powdered white wig perched unevenly atop his scute-coated head.

"Genanna! Hak!" the guard demanded anew.

"Confess to what? What has this man done?"

"Makka vit!" The judge declared the man guilty by reason of refusal, smashing his bone gavel to his desk simultaneously with the guard's blow to his prisoner's head. The convicted man fell and was dragged unceremoniously in irons to a windowless, filthy cell.

"This is bullshit, your honor." Billy spoke boldly, secure in his physical aloofness from the drama. "How would you like it if it was you who - - "

The Kind...

Now it was the judge kneeling before the bench. The prisoner who had been beaten was his accuser. The former magistrate squinted, seeing the angry man raising a threatening fist.

"Smack the living shit out of him!" Billy shouted righteously. "If anybody's got it coming to him, it's him!"

A tentacle whipped upward, holding fast the ex-prisoner's hand and preventing him from striking the prior master of the court.

The Kind.

"You can't possibly want to help that shit head."

The remainder of the trial sped by in a type of fast forward mode. Though convicted, the ex-judge was humanely escorted, unfettered, to a clean, cheerfully lit cell. Billy noticed that the former guard was already there, sitting on a padded bench and sucking on a pink cigar which smelled of cinnamon.

"Meet your new roommate," Billy quipped.

No more oppression!

■　■　■

Two knobby-skinned yellow youths loitered at a street corner. Their narrow eyes strained to identify the coming figure. One chuckled and the pair ducked behind a building corner to wait.

"What are you fuckers up to?" Billy saw an elderly gentleman approaching, carrying a sack of groceries. He was white-haired and had orange skin even knobbier than that of the yellow teens.

The ambushers laughed.

"I know what you've got in mind, you little bastards. You ain't going to get away with it!" Billy dashed to the old man, screaming, "Stop! Go the other way! Damn it, I can't even touch you! Listen to me! Why can't you hear me? They're right there! They're aiming to rob you, or worse! Stop, right now!"

The boys sprang from their cover and beat the old gentleman to the sidewalk. The grocery bag ripped and the contents were scattered. Several yellow adults across the street were not amused but were afraid to intervene. A three-wheeled vehicle slowed down and its ochre-skinned driver said something, only to drive away in a hurry.

Billy aimed a fist squarely at the larger boy's bulbous nose. It swept through his head with no effect.

The Kind.

"Where? Where are you, Kind? Help this old guy! They're going to kill him!"

Billy saw the old gentleman, unhurt, approaching again from his original spot. The ambushers were nowhere to be seen. Now and then a small scarlet disc dipped into the canyons between city buildings and drifted for a carefree while, to soon lazily rise again.

"Where are those two assholes?" asked Billy.

The old man arrived at the street corner. A young yellow girl, looking perhaps ten years old, smiled, took his arm, and helped him cross. Trailing them came a pair of the small, stout, tentacled people.

"So what else do you do?" Billy absently questioned the pair, shocked when they both responded by addressing him personally with the overwhelmingly powerful thought,

No more hate!

■   ■   ■

The little bristly-skinned girl was dying. She coughed and coughed, unable to ward off her pain. Her parents emitted a low trill, a prayer for her to die, for release from the horrid bone ailment which killed so slowly and cruelly.

A doctor, Billy presumed, came in and felt the girl's fuzzy head with his own down-covered hand. He backed away and the mother's huge eyes watered the floor.

The Kind...

"Aw, man, this completely sucks!" Billy walked out, expecting to see a hallway. "How in the hell did I get here? What kind of a ball field is this? Where did the hospital go to?"

He was in a bleacher seat, watching a strange game in which a cube was batted about on outstretched feathery arms. Or were they wings?

"I know you! You're the kid's parents!" Billy recognized the adults beside him, but accepted the fact that they could neither see nor hear him.

Their well, strong little daughter half ran, half flew, to the metal goal posts and waved to her parents who clapped their approval of her efforts. The father, without warning, whistled loudly, causing Billy to almost fall from his bleacher seat.

Billy noticed a red saucer at a corner of the bleachers. The disk was parked innocuously at the edge of some tall grass. A tiny tentacled vendor wearing a white garrison-style cap and carrying a frontally mounted box of packaged seeds and nuts walked from the vehicle to the spectator stands, his oblong eye surveying the crowd for customers. He stopped and studied a surprised Billy, who felt him thinking the words:

No more disease!

Billy floated above the bleachers and, as the tentacled man made a sale to the little girl's father, reality or what passed for it seemed to close inward.

In a whirlpool he saw intermittent images of a single multi-limbed pilot, a violent saucer crash in a blinding rainstorm, and the seasons repeating without end around an aging oak. He saw the starlit face of a screaming Indian, and still more seasons coming and going, a young woman falling forward to die in a burning house, more seasons... and a window sill... the window sill outside his own room.

Home... home... finally... home.

■　　■　　■

Billy groggily raised his head, pleased by the sweet-scented aroma of the creek mud.

Love you... Billy...

"Rém'... what's wrong?"

Billy's friend lay on his back, his left hand draped across his stomach, his right hand clasping the Chinese privet branch now worn to a nubbin.

"Rém'! Come on, man! Get up! Please, Rém'!"

Billy! Here! Look over here!

A willowy shadow danced across Rémy's prostrate form. Billy rolled to his back. A stout little figure stood poised on the saucer rim, its twin tentacles whipping nervously under its arms. An oblong eye flashed from side to side in its oval head.

"That was... you..." Billy shot a glance at the now scoured out topsy-turvy hatchway under which lay a small heap of dirt. "That bump I felt was... your head. Who the - - what the - - hell are you? What have you done to Rémy?"

Billy still not know?

The Being hopped from the rim and sat to the right of the stilled form Billy knew as Rémy. Green gas jetted from the oblong eye and enveloped the plastic legionnaire. The Being slumped forward and became still. Reanimated, Rémy rose in his usual single motion. Billy could feel a powerful need, almost a pleading.

Love you, Billy...

"Damon and Pythias. You and me, little bro'...you and me forever." Billy added, eyeing the tiny, multi-limbed body collapsed in the dirt, "Wow. What do we do now, Rém'?"

20

NOVEMBER 20

"I LOVE THIS stuff, babe." Billy used his fork to scrape Sharee Post's meat loaf from her pressed tray to his own. "Thanks. I need to eat. I'll be real busy for the next few days. Need to stay strong."

"Strong? Strong for what? You're strong as it is already, Billy."

"I've got a lot of work to do over Thanksgiving break later this week… and I've got some great news!"

Sharee's nose wrinkled, signaling her worry. She reached across the student dining table and touched Billy's hand. The boy stopped eating. It was overly warm in the cafeteria, but Sharee's fingers were cold, clammy.

"Billy, you're not going to get in some kind of trouble, are you?"

"Why do you say that?" He passingly thought of the man he had killed. He had told no one. "What do you mean?"

"Billy… "

"Whatever it is, Sharee, tell me!"

"I gotta get on over to the gym, Billy-Bo!" John Marston winked at his friend and nudged him playfully with an elbow. John rose from his seat and followed Arty Johnson to the disposal line.

"Billy… Mother's been asking about the, the stuff, you've been giving me. She's concerned about where, or from who you've been getting it."

"Your mom's a fine lady, Shar'. Tell her it's taken care of."

"Billy… it's not stolen, is it?"

"I did not steal it, Sharee."

"I didn't ask you that." Sharee's eyes burned holes in Billy. He started to blush, admitting, "My friend gets it."

"Your grownup friend?"

"Shar'!" Unexpectedly, Billy squeezed both of Sharee's hands tightly, so tightly that they hurt. "Shar'!"

"Billy? What is it?" Surprised, she involuntarily recoiled at the boy's unforeseen burst of fiery enthusiasm.

"He's… he's…" Billy's expression became distant. "He's so much, so much more than I ever would've believed! You wouldn't believe the people and places I've seen! Shar'! Listen to me now! Soon, very soon, you will understand. Everybody will. It will all be crystal clear. Just wait a few more days, or weeks at most."

"You're not going to quit school and go to work somewhere?"

"No!" Billy laughed in three short, rapid volleys. "No way! As a matter of fact, I'd like to offer you your choice."

"Choice? Of what?" Sharee's face gave away her amusement mixed with relief when Billy released her hands.

"Anything in this world you want. Anything at all. You're going to be a princess of this planet Earth. I swear it!"

"Princess? Billy, you're not making any sense. This isn't like you."

"I know it's hard to understand now. But all I'm asking is that you trust me. My friend Rémy is the man with the plan!"

"Rémy? Is that your friend who - - " Sharee rubbed her pearl necklace. "You know Mother doesn't think I should wear this."

"Just trust me, Shar'. A new age is about to begin. The old days… the war, the race hate, the crime, all of that is about to get shot to blazes… all to hell and it's never coming back!"

"I still - - Billy, I still don't get it. I'm sorry."

"No, don't ever say you're sorry! Never again! To anyone! I can't wait to see how all these stuck-up kids will try to play up to you when - - you can tell them all to go to hell!"

"Billy, I've never heard you say as much as 'darn.'"

"History records the years as either B.C. or A.D. It won't be long before we'll be in P.K."

"P.K." Sharee smiled weakly.

"Pax Kindorum… Year One! Sharee, Rémy is so much more than I thought. He's - - he's from - - "

"Is Rémy the one who engraved my bracelet?"

"Yeah, that was easy for him. Nothing at all! Sharee, you just wait! That's all I can say about it for now! Hey, walk you to the library after school?"

"Sure," Sharee answered. "I have to go now."

"I feel better telling you about Rémy, even just this little bit." The boy resumed eating the extra meat loaf.

Sharee's troubled thoughts dogged her all the way to the walkway connecting the cafeteria to the academic building. A tall, leggy brunette waited for her, asking,

"Did you tell him?"

"I couldn't, Debbie. He's so sweet. But I'm really afraid this friend of his is going to get him in serious trouble. And he sounded, well… crazy."

"His friend? I thought Franco was gone."

"No, this is some grown-up named Rémy," she revealed as the pair made their way to their next class. The bell rang and Sharee added with a note of resignation, "Just when things were really looking good. I'm going to have to let someone know. This is serious. It might even be really, really bad."

■   ■   ■

"We're not that big a department, Mrs. Post," the younger investigator said with a smile. "Sergeant Wayman and I check up on a lot of different types of situations."

"Robbery, drug sales and trafficking, even a murder now and then." Rick Wayman added sourly, "Sometimes more now than then."

"I guess y'all have been busy, what with all this I've done saw in the paper lately. And poor Mr. Broward!" Mrs. Post, a thin ebony-haired lady showing more years than she had credit to, set a bulging brown grocery bag on the low table and seated herself between the policemen. Her fingers shook a bit as she rolled the bag's top down to expose its contents

"Here it all is. I know I should've called you all a lot sooner. I thought at first they was gifts decently bought. But there's so much of it! And - - " She picked up a yellow brooch, adding, "This one here is pure gold, or so it looks to be."

"Yeah," Ross agreed, inspecting the underbelly of the shiny cast grasshopper. "Twenty-four carat, it says on the back." "Um-hmm." Wayman found the item on the second page of his clipboard-bound list. "Mrs. Coleman... on Bell Drive."

"Two streets west of Garden Pines."

"Right, Paul. This could be hers. What else do you have there, Mrs. Post?"

"Here's one that's real purty." Mrs. Post lifted a bracelet. This one's silver, looks to be."

"Sure seems like it," Wayman quipped in agreement, gently taking the shining piece from her fingers.

The door opened and Sharee came in to the small green living room. Her expression conveyed a depth of realization.

"Mother... you called."

"I had to, honey. It just wasn't right not to."

"Come talk to us, Sharee. I'm Rick." Wayman stood respectfully. "Rick Wayman. This is Paul Ross. We're here to talk to you and your mother about who you got this stuff from."

"It is... stolen... isn't it?"

"I'm afraid it probably is, honey." Wayman had seen on the list an item which could have been the necklace Sharee had on. Where was it? Where? He sat and impatiently searched the list.

"Right there on top, Sarge. Mrs. Wilkins," Ross helpfully stated.

"Maple Lane, right smack dab in the middle of Garden Pines," Wayman acknowledged, looking to Sharee again.

"Is it stolen?" the girl demanded, now wanting a definitive answer.

"Sure looks like it," was as much as Wayman could comfortably tell her.

"Honey, come on over here and sit," Mrs. Post told her. Sharee did as she was directed, asking Wayman,

"Am I going to jail?"

"I don't believe so, dear. Your mother says these were gifts. From your boyfriend, right?"

Mrs. Post nodded to Sharee, silently urging her to tell the men everything she knew. Sharee looked at a painting on velvet, hanging between cracks in the wall, of Jesus staring heavenward. Her head turned and she rested her gaze on Wayman.

"Do I have to? He said he didn't steal it."

"Who is 'he'?" Ross asked.

"Will he go to jail?"

"We'll have to interview him. Whether or not we actually take him in depends on a lot of things, Sharee," Wayman said, accepting the necklace the girl offered.

"He swore he didn't steal it. I kept asking him who did. At lunch today he told me it was his friend that was getting the things."

"Who told you? And who did he say stole it?" Ross pressed.

"He didn't say the guy stole it. Just that he got it and not to worry about it. Here, you might as well take this bracelet, too, before I forget. I especially hate giving this up. It's engraved. See?"

Wayman perused the inside surface. "'To SP from WB.'" Opposite the engraving was a series of nine digits. "Look, Paul. Positive ID. Social security number without the dashes."

"Here's the same number on the sheet. Wouldn't you know it?"

"And from Garden Pines. And would you look at these initials! Just like on the gold wrist cuff. Sharee, I've got a feeling that I know already, but I have to ask you this, sweetheart. You're the 'SP'…"

"Right."

"Who is 'WB'?"

"Aw… Mother!"

"Honey, you tell the man. You've got to. I raised you to tell the truth, even when it ain't to your favor. Do the right thing, baby."

Sharee's lips trembled and she, almost inaudibly, said,

"Billy Beaudet."

Wayman's eyes met those of Ross. *That's all I need*, the older man's expression seemed to say. *That's enough to pick his little thieving ass up, and Sheriff Gibbons be damned!*

"But it was his friend!" Sharee's pleading voice spoke up. "It was his grown-up friend who did the stealing! It was Rémy! Some guy named Rémy! Don't put Billy in jail! Please!"

"I can't promise you anything, Sharee. But you did do the right thing in telling us. You did." Wayman patted the sobbing girl on her shoulders, trying to comfort her. "I can tell you that Billy needs help. If you hadn't told us, you wouldn't have been helping him."

■   ■   ■

"Not a bad day, eh, Sarge?"

Wayman gave the Post home, a tiny one-story wood frame badly needing a new roof, a fresh coat of paint, and real gutters, a long farewell look before starting the car engine.

"Nah, not bad. We'll pick him up at school tomorrow morning."

"I'm going to watch his house one more night."

"What the hell for? Enjoy the moment, Paul!" Wayman stated. "This is not something you have happen every day. We're like the eagle who's about to snatch the fish out of the bear's paw. He doesn't even see us coming."

"Still, I still think this kid's one smart cat burglar. How does he leave no trace at all that he's been there?"

"That really beats the hell out of me. You know, he's manipulative, too. This 'Rémy' stuff is probably a big red herring." He brought the unmarked Pontiac onto the main road. "Even if there is some punk named Rémy involved, we've got young Mr. Beaudet on quite a few counts of theft by receiving if not taking."

■　■　■

"Shee, you were right, Sarge," a lone Paul Ross conceded, checking his wristwatch for the last time. "Eleven-thirty. If the kid comes out tonight, I won't catch him." Ross got out of his Buick and walked across the darkened street, telling himself,

"Gotta pee. Damn fast food soft drinks always make me pee a lot." Ross urinated on the road bank, listening to the creek's hollow resonance as its water entered the spillway pipe. A glint of reflected moonlight caught his attention.

"Wheelbarrow down there," he mumbled. "Couple of bags of something else over in the bushes. Concrete? Sand?" Ross finished voiding his bladder and smelled in the cold night air the odor of his own urine mixed with dirt. He extended one foot down the bank and saw a small semicircle protruding from the greenery near the pipe's inflow.

"Well, well, well... What's that? A barrel? Is that what you keep your stash in, Mr. Beaudet? Ah - - shit!" Ross blurted loudly, slipping and landing hard on his buttocks. He returned to his car chiding himself for his carelessness. "Stupid son of a bitch, you'd never have made it through that year in 'Nam if you'd have been this clumsy!"

A memory resurfaced. Paul Ross had nearly forgotten the sensation, an eerie, uneasy feeling he had learned to healthily heed half a world away.

"Shit," he breathed. "I swear somebody's watching me!"

Ross carefully closed the car door and found his binoculars in the hamburger wrappings littering the passenger seat.

"Better drop this trash off somewhere," he mumbled, surveying the Capler residence. "We'll get your little ass soon enough, kid. We can check out your stash, too, if that's what it is."

■　■　■

Ross didn't mind the detour one bit. The dumpster behind the girls' college would be a good place to get rid of the fast food bag and wrappers. He wheeled slowly behind the girl's dormitory, unable to resist the urge to scan the windows.

"Hasn't been that long," he reminded himself. "Just a few years. Hell, I can still appreciate beauty. I'm still a young man as long as I can appreciate beauty."

Ross could have driven by and pitched the garbage into the container, but he elected to stop instead. He took the binoculars as well as the trash with him and stood beside the dumpster.

"In you go." He tossed the crushed bag into the open top, where it bounced around noisily. Ross opined aloud, "Shit, I shouldn't do this. I can see Sarge's face if I show up in the line up instead of the muster line in the morning."

A lithe blonde girl on the third floor came into view. She was laughing and swinging her pink lace pillow at a chunky but very attractive redhead wearing unbearably crimson lipstick. Ross raised his binoculars.

"Nah, shit, I'd better not. Ah, fuck it, one look won't hurt." He studied the girls for a fantasy-filled moment before reluctantly and with a twitch of guilt retracing his steps. As he sat, he felt strangely uneasy again. His fingers hesitated on the car keys. "What in the hell is wrong with me tonight?"

From the corner of his right eye he glimpsed a movement atop the headrest. Something sharp punctured Ross's neck. He turned, raising one hand to ward off his attacker, and with the other hand opened his door.

The interior light came on and revealed a small blue figurine almost touching his face and holding a syringe. A larger buff-colored doll pushed the plunger end, pumping air into Ross's carotid artery.

"Oh! Oh, fuck!" Ross ripped himself away and dashed backwards, hitting the dumpster so hard that he stunned himself and slid to the pebbly ground. The air bolus entered his heart and Ross sat helpless on the grimy asphalt, watching in disbelief as Rémy and Blue boy leaped from the headrest to the seat and, still carrying the syringe, to the street.

"Aaahhh!" The pain was excruciating, so much so that Ross was unable to call for help. His violated heart fibrillated and the pain was more intense than Ross could ever have imagined.

"Catch the little bastards, Sarge," he gasped, watching a moonlit Rémy discard the killing device into the gutter. *Oh shit,* came Ross's final thought, *my wife is gonna be mad as hell at my dumb ass...*

■　　■　　■

Wayman shivered in the brisk pink light of the Tuesday dawn and studied the chalked outline on the dumpster and street for the fifth, or was it the sixth? time. How unnatural it had been, Paul Ross's body in that grotesque sitting position, his legs drawn up and his forearms elevated as if the man had been reaching for someone or something... but Paul's yellowed face had been the worst part of it. The mouth was agape, a stalactite of saliva frozen and hanging from the chin. Ross's eyes squinted in agony. Wayman thought bitterly, *What the hell am I going to tell your wife, Paul?*

"The EMTs are saying it's a probable heart attack," one of four uniformed officers present informed the sergeant. "Campus security, some old guy named Willie, found him right before six o'clock. He was already stiff as a board. Want to talk to him? He gets off at eight, so I better go ahead and go find him again."

"Later." Wayman entered the ambulance through the rear access doors. The body, covered by a sheet, sat upright on a stretcher. An amused young attendant smiled and stated,

"I ain't never had one sitting up like this. And look at his face! Whatcha think? Ain't this a squeal?"

"Be quiet, you dickhead," Wayman ordered calmly, pulling the sheet up and forward to expose Ross's rock-hard face. The attendant, taken aback, responded,

"Yes sir," and left the ambulance.

"I'm sorry, Paul. I wish I'd been here to help. You never know when it's your turn to…" Wayman noticed a tiny dot, a hole, like that caused by a bee sting, directly over Ross's carotid. A miniscule droplet of coagulated blood flanked the protein-plugged spot. "Uh-oh…"

Without replacing the sheet, Wayman exited the way he had entered and began to search the curbside and the ground around the dumpster. Many curious, cream-covered coed faces above watched silently.

"Jerry," Wayman called to the officer he'd spoken with a moment earlier. "Look for an ice pick, or… "

"Ice pick? Are you saying this is a murder?"

"…a syringe." Wayman's face lit up at the sight of the object in the gutter and twisted in tortured satisfaction. "Yeah, that's it… a syringe. Would you also please get my tweezers and a baggie from the kit under my front seat?"

"Sure." Jerry hurried to comply.

"'J. M.,' it says on the plunger end. 'J.M.!' Who in the hell could 'J. M.' be?"

"Here's your stuff."

"Thanks." Wayman gingerly used the tweezers to drop the syringe into the small bag.

"Think somebody might have injected him with something? Doesn't seem to be any sign of a struggle here or in the car."

"Seen any indication that anybody else was with him?" the investigator queried, heading for Ross's Buick, its door still open.

"No, uh, well, just a couple of fish hooks near the top of the headrest. Stuck in."

"Fish hooks? Paul never mentioned fishing that I can recall in more than six months of working together."

"There they are. See them? They're connected by a couple inches of fishing line."

"Yeah. Man, that is weird. Shit, are they nasty looking!"

"Rusty, aren't they?"

"Good Goddamighty! There's a trail of holes leading up from the bottom, here, at the bottom of the back of the seat."

"You got to be shitting me, Sarge. Shit, you're right."

"It's like a miniature mountaineer's been climbing around in here. Ah, that's crazy as hell. I have no earthly idea what happened here last night, but I'm putting everything else on hold until I find out. Would you call the forensic techs for me, Jerry? I'd say we've got a possible homicide, all right, and where's that old campus security guy?"

21

"I KNOW IT ain't much, Rém', but I figured it's at least a little something I could do for you. You've done so much for me." Billy observed his friend, for the moment in his original body, crouched in the saucer hatchway. The two had pulled the craft from its centuries-old prison and set it right side up underneath some bushes on the other side of the creek. "Anyway, it's the thought that counts. Right?"

Billy good boy.

"I'll mix all this powder shit together in the wheelbarrow this afternoon. The Campbells will never miss it nor all that powdered concrete they left on the porch. I do wish I could talk to Franco and Donald, but hey, if I'm going to get to rule Henry County, too, everything will work out fine. Hey, little bro', just think. When the concrete dries, you'll have your own personal landing pad right here by the creek. I'll even scratch your name in it. Want me to?"

Love you, Billy, came the thought as the alien continued his repair work.

Billy saw the legionnaire's prostrate body under the saucer's stubby port wing. He couldn't keep from saying anxiously,

"You know, Rém', it's okay with me no matter what body you use, but I guess I've gotten used to, you know, you as Rémy. You wouldn't mind being in that body at least sometimes... would you?"

Not mind, Billy.

The Being came out of the cockpit, holding a glasslike rod, its interior displaying five violet spheres set apart in a line.

"What you got, little bro'?"

Signal component.

"Is it broke?"

Test. Must test.

"How?"

Billy fight.

"Fight? I can't fight worth a shit!" Billy laughed.

Rémy help. Billy not worry.

"Who do you want me to fight? Anybody special?"

Big, stupid Pinson boy.

"Big Red? Rém', he'd kill me!"

No! Billy must have faith! People never follow Billy if Billy has no courage! The alien's mind waves emanated fiercely outward. His tantrum caused the hair on Billy's arms to bend and the leaves on the overhead privet hedges to rattle. Billy choked out the question,

"You'll help me?"

Rémy always, always help Billy! Not have fear!

"Never seen you this mad, Rém'. Don't be mad at me. Okay?"

Not mad at Billy, the Being replied, calming considerably and adding, *Billy... have faith.*

"I do. I reckon if I'm going be the king of two or three counties, I'm going to have to show I got guts. But you will help me? I need you, Rém'. I can't do nothing and don't want to do nothing without you."

Rémy need Billy too. Rémy help. The invader laid the device beside the legionnaire's form and revisited his gaze on the boy. *Billy need fear nobody. Ever. Billy believe Rémy?*

"I'd die for you, Rém."

■　　■　　■

Billy broke his recollection of the previous afternoon's proceedings. The words hung like lead weights on his soul:

"I'd die for you, Rém," he involuntarily mumbled.

Several girls giggled. Coach Hale's eyes darted up from his desk and briefly scanned the young faces. His curiosity about who had spoken ebbed rapidly, and he resumed reading his newspaper's sports section.

Billy was, like the rest of the class, supposed to be studying. He was more than healthily worried about what was due to happen very soon. He was, in a word, terrified. "I'd die for you, Rém," he'd sworn. *Maybe,* he achingly thought, *that's what I'm about to do! How can Rémy, hidden in that thick bush at the Glade, with that component thing, that signal gizmo, save my ass?* Billy remembered how, before first period, Big Red had offered to let his verbal transgression slide.

■　　■　　■

"Get outta here, Billy. You're just a little punk. You ain't nothing!" Big Red Pinson growled, his omnipresent retinue of semiliterates grinning like hungry buzzards.

"So listen to this, Red. Look, I wore my stepdad's heavy shoes today."

"So what? Go on to your homeroom, you little fart, before I get pissed off."

"Whoop him, Red!" several of the sycophants urged.

"See, Red, these wingtips, they're my shit kickers. I put them on to kick your stupid redneck ass with." *Oh, shit! Billy knew, this is the point of no return!*

"Hey, kid..." Big Red got up from the hallway monitor's desk that doubled as his morning roost. "You done fucked up now, Billy!"

"Whoop him, Red!"

"Whoop his ay-ass!"

"Lunchtime, chump," Billy taunted, sidling away, barely able to resist fleeing in terror, his heart thumping in triple time cadence. "At The Glade. Don't chicken out on me, you big, ugly chicken shit!"

"You just make sure you call the funeral parlor in advance, punk! Make your reservation now!"

The lunch bell rang. The class rose in unison, all eyes fixed on Billy. The remarks began to fly immediately.

"Good day to die, Billy."

"Nice knowing you, Billy."

"'Bye, Billy."

In a daze, Billy drifted into the hall. A familiar voice pleaded,

"Hey, Billy, don't do this. You ain't got a chance, man." John Marston pressed his point. "Come on, brother, you ain't got nothing to prove!"

"It'll be okay, John. I can't die but once."

"Aw, man, why? That mother fucker's one big, bad, and stupid dude! What you want to do this for? Why?" John melded into the crowd, his eyes on the floor. "Hey, I tried. I tried, my man."

Sharee Post was thirty feet away, her troubled eyes searching Billy's face. Behind her, tall Debbie pushed her along into the flow.

"Well, you'll see, too, babe," he said knowing she couldn't hear him. From a different time Billy remembered Franco's answer to Pammy concerning his reason for fighting Lou. "Maybe I can salvage something out of this."

"You sure were a good kid... when you were alive, Billy," a ninth grader said, patting the small of Billy's back before laughing.

"We'll visit you at the hospital!"

"Or the cemetery!"

Numb with indecision, Billy shuffled to the same double doors which Stanley Marx had hit so hard. Two boys Billy had known since second grade opened the doors for him, one stating,

"Glade's waiting, Billy!"

"Got to hand it to you, Billy," the second respectfully commented, "You got more lots more guts than anybody I know."

Rémy, Rémy, Rémy, please still be there! Billy mutely begged, a rush of chilly late November wind blowing away none of the boy's fear.

"'More guts than anybody I know'", he whispered, thinking, *so... even if I get the living shit stomped out of me, nobody will want to fuck with me anymore. They'll think I'm too crazy to fuck with. At least that'll be something.*

"I knew it. I knew I should have taken the rest of the damn day off." Wayman grunted out the words to whatever spirits might hear them and pulled his unbearably lonely unmarked vehicle behind the three squad cars lined up like waddling ducks on the hilltop country lane. A big-eared policeman with sparse brown hair and wearing an open coat as thin as his frame allowed met the investigator as Wayman got out and stepped onto the muddy earth.

"Hey, Rick. Got anything about Paul yet? "

"Uh-uh," Wayman shot back prematurely. "Not yet, anyway. What's happening here?"

"Guy hunting rabbits found a body. White male. Somebody sure butchered the bastard."

"Um-humm." Wayman slowly approached the gas-swollen corpse, remarking,

"Looks to me like he's been here a couple days or so. Maybe a week. 'Possums and rats have been having one hell of a feast on his face and hands."

"Messy one, isn't it?"

"Know who he was?"

"Guy named Robert Jackson. He's got a rap sheet for child molestation. Boys. Turns out, he used to teach over at Central. They fired him for making advances on his male students. His wallet was on the ground, cleaned out, of course. Funny thing, the ID was still in it. They're dusting the car for any prints now."

"Car? Where?"

"Down there." The thin man pointed. "Down in the woods. Almost in the creek. Rear wheels are sunk up in mud."

"What was he killed with?"

"Busted broom handle. Got both pieces of it in my trunk. Handle was in the kudzu, off to the right of us, there."

"Somebody popped him hard."

"Didn't they, though?"

"Anybody touch the body?"

"Nah. We waited for you to get here first. We already got pictures. Cartwright had his thirty-five millimeter. Hee hee, he said his eight year old's been pestering him to take some police photos to show the other kids."

Wayman grinned wryly and bent down for a closer examination. A small sliver of bamboo protruded from under the disheveled pants bunched up around the body's ankles. Wayman gripped it between a thumb and forefinger and was surprised when it resisted his pull.

Wayman lifted the trousers to expose the three inch long shaft. He twisted it a bit and the tip slipped out of the rotting flesh effortlessly.

"Barbed."

"Some kind of dart?" the thin man asked.

"Don't know. Could be."

"Can you beat this? We've got some kind of weirdo on the loose. The dart killer. What do you think, Rick?"

"Like a little mountaineer," Wayman dreamily replied, staring into the forest's thick depths.

"Rémy! Rémy! Dammit, Rémy, where are you?" Billy hissed, his back to the thick Chinese privet hedge bush he'd placed his friend in four and a half hours earlier.

The Glade was crowded for the big event, much more so than usual for a fight. Billy recognized with alarm that,

"Rém', in case you're interested, wherever you are, I don't have any friends here. At least, none of them that want to see me stay in one piece." Billy viewed the grinning faces with disgust. "Shit, Rém', they're mostly a damn bunch of eighth and ninth graders. There's even some girls here. Oh, no..."

Up the trail, surrounded by his in-group, Big Red Pinson sauntered towards the anticipating mob. A smirk of confidence was slashed across his square-jawed countenance.

"Is it too late, I reckon, to pray? Well, I ain't going run, Rém'. I ain't running!"

The group arrived amid guffaws and boorish laughter, and a young man wearing a shirt as greasy as his hair handed Big Red two white cotton gloves. Big Red leered at Billy as he donned them, saying,

"I tried to let you slide out of this, punk. You're a goner now. Take a good look at these here gloves, boy. They're gonna be my personal present to you!"

A low moan rose from the crowd. Another member of the retinue, a tow-headed boy known as Key Chain, swaggered over to the trembling Billy, sneering as he explained through a wad of tobacco as big as a golf ball,

"See here, boy, a'ter he whoops the shit outta yore ay-ass, he gives ya them there gloves as a souv'nir. Only they're dyed. Red." Key Chain grinned widely at Pinson, then to Billy he added, "He might still take it easy on you, boy. He said you weren't worth much sweat. But then, who can say what Big Red will ever do?"

Billy timidly followed Key Chain to within five feet of Pinson, who was preparing for the kill, flexing his shoulders and popping his knuckles.

"Go ahead, Red," Billy heard himself hollowly plead. "Get this over with, okay?"

"Nah, Billy. You asked for it and I'm not gonna disappoint you." Big Red held back his mace of a right fist, ready to let fly the first bone-crushing blow.

Billy's adrenaline volume doubled. A voice within him said to run, but an overriding command came:

Billy! Now! Hit now!

Big Red inexplicably froze, staying immobile for a full two seconds. Billy gasped.

Billy! Watch him!

Pinson shook his head, and at the impatient urging of his blood-hungry companions and the other students alike, pulled back his beefy arm for a second effort.

Now!

Billy half-heartedly swung his own right fist. It bounced off of Big Red's chin, but it was a second or so before the larger boy acknowledged it.

"Man," Pinson said with a tone of respect. "You're pretty fast, Billy. But not fast enough."

Duck!

Big Red's entire frame seemed lethargic, as if operating in slow motion. His fist passed harmlessly well over Billy's strawberry blond head.

Now! Hit now!

This time, with much more vigor, Billy brought a right jab into Big Red's stomach and was surprised at the softness his hand sank into. Big Red grunted.

Again! Billy not wait! Quick!

Billy swung wildly but managed to land another right, this one bouncing off Red's neck. For half a moment, the school bully seemed to regain his speed and sense of timing, warning,

"You little fucker! You've had it now! I'm gonna kill you!"

The audience released another unified "Whooo!" Several of the bolder ninth graders were even daring to cheer for Billy.

Big Red blinked. This time, just before his foe froze, Billy noticed a violet reflection in Pinson's eyes. *So that was it! he realized. Rémy's using that signal thing as some kind of stun gun!*

Not waiting for his unseen friend's cue, Billy gathered every bit of strength he had and let fly a right cross aimed at the redhead's temple.

Big Red's two hundred and fifty pound mass collapsed in a fleshy heap, his head snapping brutally to the right from the force of the perfect blow. Billy recoiled in pain, shaking his hand and yelling, to the crowd's glee,

"Goddamn! That hurt!"

"Beautiful shot!" someone cried.

"Damn!" Key Chain let his displeasure be known. Others piped in,

"I can't believe this!"

"Man, this is history!"

"Sleep tight, big boy!"

Billy blinked, unable to immediately accept the results but in no way disappointed. He could merely mutter,

"I, I did it. It's over. So fast, it's over."

Get gloves!

"Why, Rém'?"

Get gloves! Quick!

None of the retinue protested as Billy removed the unconscious Pinson's white gloves. None of the straphangers knew what to say, much less do, about this unprecedented and unimaginable alteration in the student body's pecking order. Most of the remainder of the kids clapped, cheered, and a few whistled as Billy waved the gloves high in triumph.

"Listen, y'all! These gloves are going to stay white! No more bully boy bullshit!" Billy shoved the gauntlets into his trousers and ordered,

"Key Chain! You and the rest of your dummy buddies get Red out of here!"

"A'right," came the weak reply. Pinson's stooge spit out his slimy wad of chewing tobacco and backhandedly motioned for the other thugs to join him. They hustled the semiconscious Red rather roughly up the pathway they had come.

The plaudits of the dissipating crowd waned thin. Lunchtime was drawing to a close. The last group of excited kids wound their way back to school property amid continuing "damn good fight" and "best fight I ever done seen" remarks.

Rémy came out from beneath the privet hedge bush, patting his violet-studded component. Billy grinned widely.

"I'm so sorry I doubted you, little bro."

Ready to signal.

"Is it time, Rém? I want to enjoy this feeling for a while first."

Come, Billy. Must make subspace signal.

"Pax Kindorum?"

Rémy shook his fist, telepathing,

Soon, very soon... Fleet come. Signal required first.

"Wonder how many of these dumb asses will realize we're saving mankind from itself?"

Not many... at first.

A lean male figure dashed from under the cover of a low-branched mimosa tree. Billy recognized him.

"Jay Lucca! Stop!"

The boy halted. He shook his collar-length mass of black curls backwards, his large brown eyes unable to break away from Rémy. Jay Lucca sputtered, unsuccessfully trying to smile.

"Billy! What the - - who the - - he can't be real, you know, like, alive, can he?"

"You fucked up, Jay bird. You've done seen him now."

"I won't, I won't tell nobody! Swear to God, Billy!"

"Oh, I know that, Jay. I know that." Billy neared the boy and grasped his shirt collar tightly with both hands.

"Billy, please don't bust me up like you done Big Red! Please! I ain't never done you no wrong!"

"Yeah, that's true." Billy's expression softened slightly. "Okay, I won't, Jay, if..." Billy grinned foxily at Rémy, who was watching the captured boy intently.

"Swear to God I won't say shit!" Jay repeated, desperation lacing his entreaty.

"This here, Jay bird, is the Devil's helper!"

"Devil's - - the Devil's helper?"

"Yep. You say one word, one little word about my friend there, and I'll curse your mother blind and crippled. Understand? This stays right here with us!"

"Yes sir! Yes sir, Billy!"

"Run, Jay, run! Run and don't you dare stop!" Billy commanded, releasing the boy who wasted no time in loitering. "Don't you stop or your mother will go to hell!"

Young Lucca's lanky legs stretched like oversized rubber bands, propelling him at world competition speed toward Gilmore High's high brick walls.

Rémy cocked his head and wondered,
Why Billy do that to boy?
"Don't know, don't know..." Billy confessed. "I guess I just felt like fucking with him." He laughed. It was a strange high-pitched laugh. He felt very different than he ever had in his life.
Go to pipe now. Time has come.
"Let's do it! Pee Kay One!"

22

"Nora... did you hear..." Betty Capler took in a deep drag from her menthol cigarette and continued, "...they found Inez Hayes dead on the floor in her house this morning?"

Mrs. Capler smiled with wicked satisfaction. She knew by the short audible breath at the other end of the line that her acquaintance on the far west side of Garden Pines was reacting exactly as she had anticipated. Betty ignored the woman's barrage of questions as she waited for the right moment to say what she was determined would be a coup de grâce. It made her feel important to pass on information, especially if she could do so in a way that gave the impression of her being in the know, privy to details that most people did not have the privilege of access to. Besides, Nora Wolfe was gullible and always one of the last to find out anything.

"Well, her daughter found her. She'd gotten worried after her mother wouldn't answer her phone." Mrs. Capler sprayed the surface of the kitchen table she sat at with tobacco smoke and idly waved a bony hand through it. "They think she might have had a stroke or heart attack and fell and hit her head on the coffee table."

Betty began to quiver with anticipation. The time had come for the real shocker, the punch line she would take such sadistic delight in delivering. She had even practiced how she would exactly say the words before she had called Nora.

"She'd been laying there dead for at least a week, they reckon. But she wasn't recognizable... because her goddurn cat had completely eaten off her face."

Nora gasped in horror. Betty was so keenly focused on her reaction that she did not notice the loud, rapid footfalls approaching through the carport outside.

The screen door snapped open and the inrushing teenager told his mother,

"Be right back!"

Distracted, Betty Capler could not plainly hear, much less remember her neighbor's next question. She sat open-mouthed, holding the telephone receiver loosely, equally unable to accept the fact of Billy's appearance. With her son's footsteps receding into the upper hallway, Betty, her menthol cigarette dangling from her lips, finally managed to state flatly,

"I'll call you back, Nora. William's home... three hours early."

Billy was busy lacing up his sneakers and concentrating on the task ahead of him when his mother, leaning against a side of Jack Capler's bedroom entrance, demanded,

"William, what are you doing here? It's not even a quarter after one o'clock."

"Oh, yeah, Momma. I thumbed a ride home. Ah," Billy nodded at the dusty wingtips on the floor. "I wore them to school today."

"What on earth for?"

"I'll clean them off and even shine them up later."

"I didn't notice you were wearing them this morning."

"I thought I might have needed heavy shoes today." Billy smiled.

Mrs. Capler's thin face reflected puzzlement. Behind her, in a line, Rémy and behind him, all of the Little Boys, quietly sped toward their closet crack means of egress. Billy's smile widened at Rémy's boldness.

"Why'd you think you needed heavy shoes?"

"Big Red Pinson, Momma. Remember how he gave me such a hard time in elementary school? Me and all the other boys? How he used to pound on us 'til we'd cry?"

"What about him?" Mrs. Capler's eyes searched for an ashtray. Billy took one from the top of his stepfather's desk, dumped out the dozen or so pencils it contained, and handed it to his mother, exclaiming proudly,

"I whipped him! Whipped him good! At The Glade!" Billy extracted the white gloves from his pocket.

"Whaaat?" She extinguished her cigarette and wanted to know, "Whose big idea was that?"

"I don't get it, Momma," Billy complained, throwing the gloves to his stepfather's bed, resentment in his words.

"Get what? You'll get in trouble, probably, for fighting! And skipping classes!"

"No! You listen to me for once, Momma! Big Red was going to turn these gloves here red with my blood! My blood! Your only son's blood! And you don't care! You're always telling me to take up for myself! So finally... finally I do it! Now all you can do is gripe about it like you gripe about everything!"

"William, that's ridiculous! Don't get so... dramatic! You're headed for a sad lot of trouble!"

"I won't get in trouble, Momma. He's had it coming for a long time. Too long." Billy eased past her. She followed him into the kitchen, continuing,

"You'll be sorry you did it. You should have... ignored him."

"That's not what you used to tell me, Momma. You used to say, 'Get mad!' at him. You did! You know you did! So finally I do something good about it and all you can do is torment me like you always do! I swear nothing here is ever going to change!"

"You hush up right there, William! You wait now just a goddurn minute!"

Billy halted and allowed his hand to fall from the screen door latch, thinking, *Maybe, if the Kind hasn't arrived by next week, I can get Stepdad to take up for me.*

"I don't want to hear it, Momma!"

"Well, now, you're going to have to hear it!"

"Stepdad will be proud of me! You wait and see!"

"Your real father would turn over in his grave! I'm glad he can't hear you talking like you are! You sound like... white trash."

"My... father..." Billy growled, "was a United States Marine. He knew how to fight. He'd have understood. He'd have loved to have seen me clobber Big Red today."

"He would not approve," Mrs. Capler tossed back lamely, realizing herself that Billy was correct on that point at least.

"Ah, bull fucking shit." Billy opened the screen door. He heard a loud crack and felt numbness spread across his back. His mother's shrill words bit into him:

"What did you say?"

"Is that the best you can do... Mother?" he queried, becoming aware of the incredibly sharp pain washing over his shoulders. Through the fog of hurt that he with all the effort he could muster refused to acknowledge, he saw his mother holding the lower half of a shattered broomstick.

He could still hear her loud crying as he cut diagonally across his front yard and visually probed the downhill swamp grass for any swaying which would reveal the Little Boys' location. Almost imperceptibly to himself, he whispered,

"It'll be all right, Momma. I'll make it all up to you. You won't have to hurt any more about anything at all... ever. You'll see. You'll see."

■   ■   ■

"Platoon formed. Right, Rém'?"

Right.

While Billy used his stepfather's shovel to noisily mix the water and cement powder in the Campbells' wheelbarrow, the Being and Rémy's body crowded together in the saucer's interior, making final adjustments. Beside the craft, two immobile squads of Little Boys stood at attention, their green stone-sharpened brushwood spears held rigidly across their chests. Rubberbuster, an inch in front of the group, held a smaller piece of wood in his hand, emulating a swordsman's stance.

"We got them lined up like in my dad's old photo. He was a platoon leader, like Rubberbuster there in front of the first row. Damn, Rém', I need a little more water in this shit." Billy scooped up several shovelfuls of creek water, putting it in the wheelbarrow-bound mélange. "But I don't want to get it too juicy."

Billy's eagerness was making him clumsy. A glob of cement slipped off of the spade's working end and landed on a saucer side fin. The clod fell heavily, leaving a gray mud mark on the ship.

"Sorry, Rém."

The Being's oval head emerged. He perused the stain, only to quickly resume his work, telepathing to Billy,

No damage.

"I been thinking about a lot of stuff we need to do to make our part of the world a lot better. You know, we can't allow all the Big Reds and their flunkies to push other kids around. That sucks."

The Being's head extruded again. The verdant oblong eye flashed at Billy, who preempted the thought by confessing,

"You're right, Rém'. Jay Lucca. I was a real asshole, I admit. I shouldn't have treated him like I did. I don't know what came over me. I acted like those stupid rednecks I hate. I'll make it all right with him soon. You'll help me stay straight, won't you, little bro'?"

Rémy help Billy. Rémy always help Billy. Billy not forget!

"I can't get the wheelbarrow much fuller. How close are you to signaling? After you do, we'll have us a Little Boys ceremony with the platoon there. Then we'll pour the concrete for the pad."

Few minutes now, Billy.

"Aw, man, I'm getting excited! How long before the Kind fleet arrives?"

Week. Month. Maybe up to six months.

"Ah, shit! That long?"

Not certain. Signal always required first.

"That's what you told me. The signal has to come first. No signal, no show. Never."

Rémy here so long alone... so very long...

"You'll never be alone again, Rém'. Man, you said you've counted over three hundred years by the change of seasons. That's a hell of a long time."

"Hold it, Billy! Don't move!"

Billy's heart leaped into his throat. Out of a tunnel in the underbrush a man came, his slacks cut by thorns and his sports jacket dotted with sticky flecks of leafy matter.

"Who are you?" Billy asked, his voice cracking.

"You don't remember me, Billy? I'm Rick Wayman."

"Oh, shit. Rém', it's the cop."

"'Oh, shit' is right, son. How do you explain that bag of stolen goodies I just found in the brush?"

"I didn't steal none of it."

"Come with me, son. We can do this the easy way or we can do it the hard way. It's your choice."

"Easy way, I guess." Billy was regaining his composure. Surely Rémy wouldn't allow him to be arrested.

"Good thinking. What's all this you've got here?"

"This is my gang. The Little Boys."

"These? These are the Little Boys I've heard so much about? I thought the Little Boys were real guys, not something like this. I don't get it. Not even your buddy Franco is dumb enough to be scared of toy soldiers."

The detective cocked his ears, listening for any movement not that of the flitting, chirping thrushes in the brush around them. Franco might be there somewhere, might have a weapon, and might be scared enough to try something really, really stupid. Wayman asked another question,

"Billy, are you alone here? I heard you talking."

"Just to Rémy. He's in the saucer."

Wayman eyed the scarlet craft, thinking, *This kid has a problem! Keep him calm, Rick!*

"Billy, that's a fine-looking model. Make it all by yourself?"

"No sir. And it's real, not a model. It's Rémy's space ship."

"Billy..." Wayman reached for his handcuffs in their belt pouch at the small of his back. "Put down the shovel, son. It'll be okay. Come with me. I'll make sure nobody will hurt you. Come on, you said you'd take the easy way."

"Yes sir. I will." Billy lowered the shovel but did not drop it. "I ain't going with you, though. I can't. Rémy needs me."

Wayman's patience was rapidly wearing thin. He forced his irritation aside, knowing from experience how best to humor a suspect with a mental disorder.

"I'll talk it over with Rémy, Billy. You know, your friend Franco's scared of Rémy. He must be a real mean guy."

"I know, sir. But Rémy won't hurt him. We talked about it. And I can not go anywhere with you or anybody else right now."

"Son, you are coming with me and coming now. I promise, no one will hurt you."

"No sir. I told you I can't."

"Okay, son." Wayman swung the handcuffs forward. "You made your choice."

"It was your choice, sir. Now I'll have to show you. It's going to be your own fault, whatever happens to you now." Billy's gaze dropped to the awakening platoon, then rose to meet Wayman's shocked face. "Mister Wayman, meet the Little Boys!"

23

WAYMAN DARED NOT blink. The Little Boys were forming a semicircle ten feet to his front. He recognized that this had become a different game, but what? This was something terrifingly beyond the realm of the possible. He watched the ten figurines move, drandishing their wooden weapons at him, unable to believe the evidence before him. An eleventh, the legionnaire, took his post atop the saucer. Wayman fleetingly noticed inside the damaged saucer the bobbing head of the feverishly working Being.

"What in the living hell is this?" the detective demanded, startled again when the tiny troops in unison in response to an invisible command assumed the stance of at-the-ready.

"Now you see why I can't come with you, Mister Wayman. Even if I wanted to, and I don't, I have to help Rémy there."

"What in the name of God is all this, Billy? What kind of trick are you trying to pull? Who is Rémy and where can I find him?"

"Ain't no trick to it, Mr. Wayman, there never has been any trick. Rémy's a scout. He's a scout from another world. And he's right there in front of you. Right there." Billy pointed to the saucer with pride and a measure of self-assurance which crossed the line defining arrogance.

"Scout?"

"The Kind sends out scouts."

"The Kind?"

"That's what they call themselves. The Kind. Like I was saying, they find inhabited planets that are in trouble. You know, places with wars going on, plagues, places that ain't going to last much longer without help. And the Kind saves them."

" 'Saves them'? Saves who from what?"

"The people they help. See, they've got this need. They have to, I guess you could say, be loved by the people they save. It's some kind of trade-off for having evolved out of physical bodies. Rémy told me all about it. See, Rémy could have, if he'd have wanted to, come into that body there," Billy further explained, pointing again to the plastic legionnaire, its arms swaying as if it were ready to jump, "and dug out his original body there in the saucer. But he needed me. Me, Mr. Wayman, me. Billy Beaudet. He chose me."

Holy shit! Wayman thought with rapidly mounting alarm. *These aren't just a bunch of battery-operated toys, and that little bastard in the saucer is for real!*

"Chose you for what?" the sergeant asked, a part of him still not believing what was happening there in the swamp.

"To be his friend."

"Friend? Is that what he tells you? I thought you were patriotic, Billy. Now I see you playing the kapo, and you're about to sell your whole planet down the drain! You know what a kapo is, Billy? A traitor! Someone who turns on his own! What the hell would your father now say if he knew what you were doing with this, this invader?"

"He'd understand. What did he die for in Korea? Tell me why, Mr. Wayman. I'd really like to know. What did he throw his life away for?"

"Ah, hell, son, I can't tell you why. Nobody can. But I do know that this... this Kind outfit, they won't be saviors. They'll be conquerors!"

"They just want to save us from ourselves!"

"Billy... you can't let somebody else solve your problems for you. I'll admit to you, sure, we haven't done a very good job of it on this Earth. But it is our Earth and it has to stay our Earth! It doesn't belong to, well, to them and we can't let that happen, no matter what kind of bullshit they tell us they can do for us!"

"No... no, a new age is about to begin... Real peace. No more hate or hunger..."

"Billy, don't you get it? It won't work because they'll use their solutions, not ours! Hell, I know all about other people's solutions! I fought a bunch of bastards like that before you were born! What if this Kind decides it can best take care of only a few of us and kills off the rest? Huh? Or ..." Wayman's furious thoughts coalesced into a mental image of rusted fish hooks. "...or like a little mountaineer. How many people has he killed already, Billy?"

"I didn't want him to, Mr. Wayman. He was protecting me."

"Your little bastard of a buddy killed my partner last night... my partner and my friend. How many more are going to have to die, son?" Wayman's voice was rising with his anger. "What price are all of us going to have to pay for this great new peace?"

"I'm sorry about your partner. Rémy was protecting me. He didn't know who the guy was."

"Tell that to his widow. Worst part about it, Billy, is... you don't even think for yourself any more." Wayman was gingerly easing his fingers under his jacket to his holstered .38. "And you don't want to, either. It's all up to me. I've got to stop him, son."

"You can't! Hurry, Rém'! Signal the fleet!"

Kill man!

The Little Boys closed in, lunging with their lances. Wayman kicked three away, but they hopped to their feet and returned to aid their frenziedly jabbing comrades. Several found their target, punching their spears through the investigator's socks and into his ankles.

Wayman fired a shot which blew away a soldier's head. The body bounced high off of the ground with a bizarre tumbler's kip and fell, coming to a twitching rest amid the tangles of seemingly endless thorn vines.

"So you little fuckers can be stopped!" Wayman booted a jousting Blue boy a few feet to his front and took aim. "You little shit, your toothpick broke off in my goddamn foot!"

Before he could fire a second shot, Billy's shovel scraped violently down the left side of Wayman's face, ripping his ear open and stunning him. He fell to the dirt, narrowly averting being blinded by the slashing wooden sword of Rubberbuster who with a downward stroke opened a two inch gash under the detective's right eye.

"Dirty sons of bitches!" the officer screamed, sitting and preparing to ward off Billy's next blow. The shovel missed Wayman's left arm and hit his right hand, sending the blue-black revolver spinning handle over barrel into the dense bushes.

"I ain't going to let you stop him! Hurry, Rémy! Hurry!"

Seconds...

"Bullshit I won't!" Wayman was up and he crashed into the teen, shoving him hard all the way into and across the creek. He landed heavily, pressing the boy into the embankment. He snapped Billy around, intending to throw him into the charging platoon which was still targeting the detective. Instead, Billy tripped backward. His head and right shoulder hit the cement-laden wheelbarrow and toppled it onto the saucer.

No! No! Billy!

The attackers' momentum slowed. They kept advancing, but very awkwardly. The legionnaire had fallen from the craft and appeared unable to stand, its limbs vibrating as if from a form of epilepsy.

"So that's it! Rémy's the one inside the saucer!"

"Rém'! Signal! Now!" Billy screamed, stumbling from the creekside, his face grimacing and his head gushing blood from its impact with the wheelbarrow.

Wayman's hands hurriedly scooped more cement onto the saucer hatchway. The Being moved underneath but couldn't quite get out. A tentacle clasping a violet-studded rod snapped upward out of the muck, only to be crushed down by a desperate Wayman.

"I won't let you ruin everything!" Billy grabbed Wayman by the waist and pulled hard, yelling, "Rémy! Don't worry about me! Get the Little Boys to dig you out!"

The front line of troopers veered, ever so slowly, toward the saucer. Blue boy, his stub of a lance gone, fell on his face and flailed his arms uselessly. The khaki legionnaire nearby wobbled onto his hands and knees, still quivering but unable to stand.

"It's over, Billy!"

The battling pair fell backward. Wayman rolled over onto the boy. He gripped Billy's collar, ripping the boy's shirt as he jerked him halfway up, only to find himself looking into the chromed double barrels of his own .32 caliber derringer backup weapon.

"Hold it right there!" Billy commanded, cocking the hammer. "I swear to God, I'll kill you right here and now if I have to!"

"I know you will, son," Wayman panted, his nose inches from the double barrels of the shiny little pistol. "I know you will. You've killed before, haven't you? Tell me... did it feel good killing Mr. Jackson?"

"Who? I don't know nobody named that."

"The man at the garbage dump. Remember him? You did a real pro job on him."

"Oh, him, yeah. Didn't make me feel bad. He deserved it, anyway. Damn queer."

"How about me, Billy? I'm not like he was but tell me... do I deserve killing, too, Billy?"

"No, but... I can't let you interfere. You don't understand. This has just got to happen. It just has to."

Wayman's sense of urgency rose as he watched the crimson Max clamber over the legionnaire's back, mount the saucer deck and begin to scrape away the wet cement encapsulating the struggling Being.

"Billy! If there's any little piece of the old you left at all... listen to me! This is not the way!"

"I'm sorry, sir. I really am."

Billy squeezed the trigger and the hammer dropped... on the safety block.

Wayman's right fist smashed into Billy's rib cage. The boy crumpled like yesterday's newspaper, the wind knocked out of him, sideways into the creek. The detective pocketed his dropped derringer and jerked Billy's upper body out of the water, noticing the frothy blood spray the boy was coughing out of his mouth and nostrils.

"Busted your ribs, huh? I got no more sympathy. No more for you, son."

Wayman slapped Max, sending him flying a full fifteen feet. The tiny figure ceased moving. On the saucer, protruding from the thick gray goo, an unmoving tentacle lay motionless, bleached to a pale tan like a drowned earthworm.

"No, you don't. Not today." Wayman upended the wheelbarrow to a fully vertical position. The loosely adhering cement cascaded viscously over the spacecraft's top deck. "Not any day... hell, no."

Wayman used the shovel to gather each Little Boy with an accompanying pound or so of dirt. He piled them all one by one by the saucer, mashing each down into the swamp floor with his bleeding feet which he felt beginning to ache.

A man clutching a fishing rod appeared forty feet away on the earthen dam dividing the lake from the swamp. He demanded to know,

"What the hell's going on down there? What are you doing?"

Billy's eyes widened in recognition of the voice, but the wounded teen was unable to speak or even wave for help. He lay helplessly gripped by pain throughout his young, battered body, fighting for breath, his matted locks settling begrudgingly into the moist clod-covered ground where the embankment married the rushing coldness of the creek.

"Ambulance! We need an ambulance!" Wayman called loudly.

"I'm going to have the law on you, mister! Don't you dare hurt that boy!" Dwight Mills ordered, dropping his rod and rushing toward his house.

"You do that," Wayman muttered. "You do that." He continued piling dirt higher and higher on top of the saucer.

"I can't see it at all now." The shovel slipped from his fingers' grasp and with a lot of effort his abused body lay down on its back beside his entombed foes. Wayman was beyond exhaustion, longing for the sound of wailing sirens and thankful that above the foul-smelling swamp and the tortured gasping of Billy Beaudet, he could see only lazy, cottony clouds sliding across a beautifully pure azure sky.

24

December 2

THE MIDDLE-AGED MAN wearing frayed jeans, a plaid flannel shirt, and muddy cowboy boots paused to gently rub the harshly ragged scab under his right eye.

"I wish I could scratch this. Ii itches like a son of a bitch. I can't rip it open, but at least I can let it get air. My feet aren't that lucky. You really put a lot of holes in them, you little asshole. The damn gauze wrappings around the holes are irritating me to death, and giving me a rash, too."

Rick Wayman knelt and with the shovel which had almost two weeks earlier been used to batter him, patted the new layer of cement covering the out of place yard high earthen mound. He let out a frosty breath into the yellow light of the almost-winter-in-southern-Virginia early evening.

"Hey, mister?" came an inquisitive question from the roadway above.

"Yeah, honey. What is it?" Wayman replied to the teenaged girl leading her obviously blind brother. Her right arm interlaced with his left as she protected him from any traffic that might approach from their rear. Wayman noticed that the boy's glasses were unusually large and dark, as if obscuring some injury or deformation.

"Is it true they're going to fill in the lake soon?"

"Sure is."

"It will sure look weird around here when they do that. We've always had that lake and swamp here, as long as we've lived here, anyway. Come on, Jimmy. Are you ready to go home?"

Jimmy Cass silently nodded and the siblings turned around and walked away. Wayman smiled inwardly, not intending the girl to hear,

"Not half as weird as it almost was." After a long moment he added, this time to his unseen enemy,

"I hope you caught all that, Rémy. More accurately," Wayman elaborated, discarding the shovel with a high toss over the brush, "rerouted. See, I talked to the owner of this prime piece of property, a guy named G. C. Campbell. Sound familiar? He graciously listened to my idea that he could fill in the lake as it is now and flood all this behind the dam. Of course, he'll have to put two or three houses up there and make an access on the other bank of the lake. He's got to make a buck or two in the deal, and it's a good deal for everybody except you, Billy, and your Kind.

"So you see, even if Billy gets released in a few years, and he might because I don't know how his sanity's going to be judged, you'll still be stuck here. Even with all this cement and dirt on top of you, well, maybe he could break you out. But you'll also be under anywhere from twelve to fifteen feet of water. Eventually, a lot of silt will settle on top of you, too. You're stuck here forever and I don't feel one bit bad about it."

Wayman felt a sudden unannounced chill, the kind that cuts to the bone. Initially he tried to pass it off as a natural consequence of doing hard work in cool weather, but he knew there was more to it... much more. "Billy's told a lot to me in private. Off the record, just him to me. You sure put a snow job on the little fucker. I feel sorry for him, despite what he's done. How could he resist your bullshit line about helping mankind? He really did believe he was going to be saving the planet. You slick little piece of shit!

"I feel the temptation, too. I admit I do. I feel the temptation to dig you up, maybe make a deal with your... Kind... to help us out. Just a little. I don't hear you, though, in my head the way Billy did. Are you quiet because you know I'm curious to assure myself that you didn't at the very last second manage to, like Billy says, 'gas off'? Maybe you want me to uncover all this so you can escape? No way, pal! I'm not going to take even the least chance on that happening!

"We've got a war escalating in Southeast Asia, a hell of a lot of confused kids here at home who are asking why, hell, we've got race problems there don't seem to be answers to, riots in the streets, more and worse crime, crooked politicians that can bullshit even better than you can... humanity does need help. If anyone in this universe needs help, it's us.

"But it wouldn't be 'just a little' help, would it, Rémy? It would be total domination... on your terms. Well, that's it... and I'll take your secret with me to my grave. It's a damn shame that you can't suffocate in there. That's my only regret... that I can't kill you and be done with it."

Rick Wayman turned and clawed his way up the well worn embankment. Before he entered his waiting light blue '60 Galaxy parked in the spot Ross had put his car on the night he died, something fifty feet away from him caught his eye.

It was a round white object very much out of place amid the innumerable chunks of iron-browned stones and tan, musty dirt clods. Wayman was intrigued by and oddly drawn to it.

"Ah, the heck with it," the investigator offhandedly spat, deciding to leave without having a closer look. "Maybe the damn alien stole a cue ball." Wayman sat, hard-faced, and fired up his car's ignition. He gave the frowning lip of the embankment a final regretful minute's worth of stare and murmured,

"I am so sorry, Paul."

The powerful engine roared to life and the detective purposely spun his tires in the crusty earth before they met the blacktop with an angry squeal. The whirling dust cloud they had churned settled rapidly onto the road, the trees and bushes, the embankment, and the odd white object lying upon it, liberally dusting its ancient, pitted, hand-carved porcelain face. Above the broken nose of the doll's head, two chipped agate eyes flashed, for the briefest portion of a second, a bright fluorescent green.

The chilly north wind increased its velocity as twilight descended on the Old Dominion. All over Garden Pines, newly placed Christmas trees blinked their message of hope for mankind as mothers finishing their supper meal preparations called in their children from their Saturday evening games, leaving a darkened, deceptively tranquil landscape with only its own shadows remaining to revel in celebration of the night.